WHAT HAPPENED ON MY SPACE VACATION

Also by Ethan A. Cooper

Horripilations Unearthed (with Benjamin Cooper)

What Happened On My Space Vacation

A Novel

by

Ethan A. Cooper

Illustrations by Benjamin Cooper

This book is dedicated to you, Dad.

You came up with all the good ideas for this story.
Thanks for letting me write it for you.

"Ships and sails proper for the heavenly air should be fashioned. Then there will also be people, who do not shrink from the dreary vastness of space."
— **Johannes Kepler, letter to Galileo Galilei, 1609**

"In spite of the opinions of certain narrow-minded people, who would shut up the human race upon this globe, as within some magic circle which it must never outstep, we shall one day travel to the moon, the planets, and the stars, with the same facility, rapidity and certainty as we now make the ocean voyage from Liverpool to New York!"
— **Jules Verne, *From the Earth to the Moon,* 1865**

"Are we there yet?"
— **Any child**

[CHAPTER ONE]

WHAT HAPPENED AT THE SUPER ULTRA MEGA MARKET

"So, when is your baby due?"

The question took Sabatha Storm by surprise, almost causing her to drop the box of meal tablets in her hand. She'd been about to hand it to the young, female clerk standing behind the safety barrier. Sabatha paused. She wasn't sure what sort of question she'd expected. Something more along the lines of "Do you want all this express-tubed to your home?" or "Were you aware that there's no money on your credit cube?" perhaps—certainly nothing as personal and as potentially embarrassing as what she'd actually been asked. She quickly came to the conclusion that she hadn't expected any questions at all, since the clerks usually express-tubed the purchases right to your home unless you asked them not to.

"Do you know if it's a boy or a girl?" the clerk asked as she took the box of meal tablets and dropped them into the processing chute. Sabatha's lack of response to the first question wasn't enough to deter the follow-up.

Sabatha looked over her shoulder to see if the girl was talking to somebody behind her, but the only person standing there was a red-haired, dwarfish man. The Dwarf—as Sabatha's mind dubbed him—was carrying an armload of boxes so garishly pink and yellow that she had to avert her eyes. She knew exactly what was in those boxes since Holiday had more than a few of them at home. Yeah, there was no mistaking Quantum Girl!!'s trademark colors. Under one arm, the Dwarf was carrying at least ten Quantum Girl!! dolls, each in a different outfit. Under the other was a single, bigger box that had Quantum Girl!!'s spaceship, the *Quark Pony!!*.

The Dwarf didn't look like he was capable of being pregnant, or at least he wasn't showing if he was, so Sabatha turned back to the clerk, reached into the hovering basket that contained the rest of her purchases, pulled out another box of meal tablets, and slid it across the counter, fully expecting a third question—perhaps something along the lines of "How many more children are you planning on having?"

"Are you saying you think I'm fat?" Sabatha asked. She looked at her belly. She worked out three times a week, and her stomach was flat. She could do a hundred sit-ups.

"You're not fat," the girl said without looking at Sabatha. "You're pregnant."

"I'm not pregnant," Sabatha said, hoping that would bring the issue to closure.

The clerk—whose name was flashing in red neon letters on the front of her tight head covering: SHALA—looked at Sabatha with eyes the color of Martian sand. "You're not pregnant." It hadn't been a question. She'd said it in the same tone that one might use on a person who had just denied that water was wet.

"No, I'm not," Sabatha said, pulling more items out of the basket and sending them toward Shala. She couldn't be, but Little Miss Pregnancy-Obsessed Shala didn't know that.

"Are you sure?" Shala asked.

"Yes."

"Really sure?"

"Really."

"That's funny. I always know."

Actually, what was funny was that Shala *thought* she would always know. Sabatha wondered if the Super Ultra Mega Market knew that one of their employees was so talented. Or at least *thought* she was.

Sabatha took the last item out of the basket—a handheld star map datapad for Holiday—and handed it to Shala. Since it was empty, the basket floated away, searching for another customer to serve. "That's okay, you can't be right all the time."

"Never been wrong. You wanted this all express-tubed, right?"

"Tubed would be great." Sabatha handed her a credit cube. "Why do you think I'm pregnant? If you don't mind me asking." As soon as she said it, she felt silly. Did she actually care?

Shala looked around, pressed a button on the black watch she wore, then stated, "You were thinking about being pregnant."

"Sooo…you read my mind?" Sabatha didn't really believe such a thing was possible, but she liked to keep an open mind. And besides, deep down she was attracted to the idea of a world where such things were possible.

Shala looked around, but didn't look scared about having done anything wrong. "It's not mindreading. You sent me your thoughts."

"I did?"

"Yeah. And it's not my fault I picked them up."

"Sure. Of course."

"We can keep this between us, right?" Shala asked, looking around a second time.

Sabatha wasn't pregnant, but she was tired and wanted to get back home. Tomorrow was a big day, and there was still much to do. "Well, just us and the Dwarf."

"Who?"

Sabatha jerked her head backward.

"Oh," Shala said, leaning her head to the side and giving a smile and wave to the Dwarf, who was small enough to be completely hidden behind Sabatha's slender form.

"He's deaf," Shala said.

"Of course he is," Sabatha said.

"He didn't hear a thing. So, just between us right?"

Sabatha wondered what Shala would do if she responded in the negative, but didn't find out because she made herself respond with, "Absolutely. Just between us. I promise."

Shala looked around one final time, pressed another button on her watch, waved her hand in front of her console and said, "Your items will arrive at your home before you do. Thanks for visiting us at Super Ultra Mega Market. Have a nice day!"

Sabatha made her way toward the exit, signaling her car for pickup. Her thoughts, however, refused to leave the store. Even as she left the Super Ultra Mega Market property, entered the hyperway, and sped toward home, her thoughts remained on Shala's questions. She fought to clear her mind and focus on the evening ahead. What disturbed her most, Sabatha realized in the end, was that even though she wasn't pregnant, she *had been* thinking about it.

Specifically, how Super Ultra Mega Bad it would be to be pregnant the day before you strapped yourself into a rocket that weighed one million tons and produced over three million tons of thrust, launching you and your family toward the moon on your very first space vacation.

[CHAPTER TWO]

WHAT HAPPENED WHEN MAXIMILLION ASKED FOR ONE LAST KISS

The fact of the matter, straight up and out, was that Maximillion Storm wanted to go on his family's much-hyped vacation through the cosmos about as much as he wanted to amputate his drawing hand and cook it for lunch.

If only Nika understood that.

But Nika didn't understand. Either that, or she was just being pouty. Whichever it was, Max found there was little he could say to pacify her.

Nika's full first name was Veronika, but anybody foolish enough to call her that got a face-melting glare. Max had used her full name once in a moment of breathless passion. It was their second make-out session, both of them sitting on a tree stump in the park, the wind whipping her hair against his cheeks, and it had ended rather abruptly the moment her name slid from his lips to hers. Too bad really, it had been quite nice up until that point.

"I just don't see why you let your parents push you around like this," Nika said. "You're old enough to make your own decisions. You don't have to go if you don't want to. Just tell them you're staying here."

Max sighed. "They won't go for that. They want us to do this as a family. With my final year of high school coming up, they're treating this like our last vacation ever."

Nika reached back and tugged on one of her pig-tails—a sure sign that Max was in big trouble. "I had my parents sign me up for Wilderness Camp because you said we were going together. Now you're backing out. I hope you know how that makes me feel, Max."

The thing was, she was right, and Max felt pretty bad about reneging on the deal. Still, she could be more understanding, right? "I know. I'm sorry. I want to go to Wilderness Camp more than anything, but…"

"But you're not going to."

"I can't."

Nika shook her head, eyes furious in a way that made Max weak at the knees. "No, Max, talk straight to me. It's about *won't*, not *can't*. What it comes down to is that it's your choice. Your parents would respect your decision to stay and follow through on your commitment to me."

"Maybe…"

"They would, and you know it."

"Maybe, but Holiday wouldn't understand."

Max knew he'd said something especially wrong that time; she was tugging on both pig-tails. "Wonderful. Now you're trying to dodge me by making it your little sister's fault. Simply brilliant." At that, she threw her hands out and turned her back on him. The skirt she was wearing flared nicely around her hips. Max wasn't distracted enough to not notice the bare skin at her thighs. Her socks came up over her knees. Her shoes sparkled with obsidian and ruby, matching her hair ties. Her shirt, which was too tight and left her arms and neck bare, proudly proclaimed in color-shifting letters that she was a BATTLE ANGEL. Her hair, black against the pale of her skin, glittered like a sky full of stars. The outfit was one of his favorites, and he couldn't resist pig-tails. She'd done it all on purpose of course. She didn't play fair.

"No, that's not what I meant," Max said, wondering if he should move closer to her, maybe around to where he could look her in the eyes. It only took a few milliseconds to decide against that.

"Then say what you mean, sweetie."

When she said things in that tone of voice, it was all Max could do to not fall to the ground and grovel at her cute little feet.

Nika interrupted him before he could speak. "This is it, isn't it? You're breaking up with me!"

Max ignored the loud warning klaxons and the red flashing lights in his brain, stepped closer to Nika, grabbed her shoulders and turned her to face him. She didn't resist. "No," he said, his face inches from hers, "I'm not breaking up with you. I'm just going on vacation."

"In space, Max. On vacation *in space!* This isn't like you're just driving south to Neo Mexico. You're actually *leaving the planet!*"

Was that what this was all about? She was worried about his safety? Worried that he might not come back? "Nothing bad is going to happen," Max said.

"Accidents happen."

"Yeah they do, but not this time."

She put a hand on his chest. Max could feel his heart beating against her palm. Her eyes were brown, heartbreakingly liquid. "You're still backing out on me, and I sorta hate you right now for that."

"I'm sor—"

Nika put her other hand over his mouth. "Just shut up, Max. You can't apologize for something you're about to do on purpose to me. I think I love you more than just a little, but right now I'm not sure if I should slap you and leave or if I should be kissing you with everything I've got because tomorrow you're leaving my universe for a month."

Max wasn't sure either. It was possible, in Nika's current emotional state, that either would be painful.

"One last kiss," Max said, "would be really ni—*OW!*"

She'd slapped him. Hard too. She was strong. Max's cheek was numb, well, except for the tingling.

"You come back to me, Maximillion Storm," Nika said, leaning into him. "I'll be very upset with you if you don't. And upset is not a state you want me in, sweetie."

In the minutes that followed, Max learned that when Nika put everything she had into a kiss, there was both pleasure and pain, and they were deliciously intertwined.

[CHAPTER THREE]

WHAT HAPPENED ON EPISODE 297 OF *QUANTUM GIRL!!*

"You'll never get away with this, Klarg!" Quantum Girl!! screamed.

"Did you hear something, Lieutenant Flegg?" Commander Klarg asked.

Lieutenant Flegg shook his scaly, reptilian head. Flegg didn't talk much because Quantum Girl!! had shot his tongue off several weeks earlier.

Commander Klarg laughed, his tri-forked tongue slithering out between lips the color of swamp rot. "I thought I heard the pitiful squeaks of an animal caught in a trap."

"Let me go!" Quantum Girl!! yelled, her fingers white as they gripped the bars of her hanging prison. The cage was suspended over a volcano-shaped crater that boiled with blue, alien goo. The goo popped, fizzled, and gurgled like an empty stomach. The cage, held in place by an ancient, rusted chain, swayed and jerked, lurching precariously over the goo.

"What's the matter, princess, don't like your accommodations?" Commander Klarg asked. "So very sorry, it was the best I could do without warning. If you're going to invade my secret lair and try to thwart my plans to destroy moon base Luna One, then you're going to have to give me more advanced notice."

Quantum Girl!!'s faithful companion, a spunky cat/dog named Quasar!!, let out a threatening meow-bark, his feline teeth extended, hair bristling. If the gaps between the bars had been bigger, Quasar!! would have leaped through and attempted to snatch the cage control module from Commander Klarg. Quasar!! was that fearless and that smart.

"No, boy," Quantum Girl!! said, placing her hand on Quasar!!'s head, right between those spotted, floppy ears of his, "Don't do anything rash. We'll get out of this." She adjusted her yellow tunic and her pink skirt and sighed at the black scuff marks on her knee-high boots. She ran fingers through her silver and gold hair, smoothing a few strays back into the fold. Underground caverns were so damp, and the excess moisture played havoc with her epidermis. Cosmic rays helped her maintain her flawless skin tone. A timely escape was imperative. "Bad guys always get what's coming to them."

Commander Klarg roared in laughter at that. "You came to me, princess. That means I get you! You're mine!"

"Stop calling me that, you big ugly lizard!"

"Not a chance. Your boyfriend isn't going to save you this time. I made sure your beloved Captain Xeode has troubles of his own. He'll be occupied for quite some time, my pretty princess."

"I'm not your princess. I'm not anybody's princess!"

"That's not what you told me on our last date, babe!" came a surprise voice from behind Lieutenant Flegg.

"Oh, Jack!" Quantum Girl!! said, clapping her hands. Quasar!! meow-barked his agreement.

Commander Klarg roared, going down on all fours, his segmented tail slashing through the air. He held the cage control module close to his armored body, one scarred finger resting on the big red button that would release the cage. "Not a step closer, Xeode, or your girlfriend gets an acid bath!"

Captain Jack Xeode stopped in his tracks. Lieutenant Flegg had his ray gun out and was pointing it right at Captain Xeode's head. "I'm sure we can work out some sort of deal. How about you put me in the cage and let her go?"

"Oh, Jack!" Quantum Girl!! swooned. "That's so sweet!"

"Ah ink ah gon ee ick," Lieutenant Flegg spat. *I think I'm gonna be sick.*

"You can dip me in the acid instead of her. There's a shortage of perfectly-shaped bodies in the universe, and it'd be a cosmic shame to melt hers down. So, what do you say, Klarg, old buddy of mine, do we have a deal?"

"Nope," Commander Klarg said and pressed the cage release button.

Quantum Girl!! screamed, *"JAAAAAACKKK!!!"* as she and Quasar!! fell.

Captain Xeode dove forward, yelling, *"BETTTTHHHH!!!"*

Lieutenant Flegg pulled the trigger on his ray gun. A beam of energy lanced toward Captain Xeode's head.

Then everything went black, except for:

To be continued...

Holiday Storm blew out a breath and let her upper body fall back onto the bed. The holo dome unit on the wall flared briefly, then went dark when she said, "Holo off." Her voice was calm, though her heart was racing. *Quantum Girl!!* episodes always did this to her. She held up a hand and found that it was shaking. She concentrated but couldn't force it to hold still. This sort of reaction was the precise reason why her mother tried to limit her holo viewings of *Quantum Girl!!*. Of course, that didn't stop Holiday from sneaking in an extra episode or seven on a daily basis.

She'd just watched episode 297 for the sixth time. It was fresh from that morning's holo feeds, and it had been one of the best ones *ever!*

Of that she had no doubt. She replayed the episode in her mind—something that came quite easily since she had flawless recall. Her long-term memory was extraordinary, but her short-term memory was otherworldly. With her recall ability, when she closed her eyes, her advanced visualization allowed her to view any episode in its entirety just by imagining the backs of her eyelids as holo screens. She technically hadn't needed to watch the episode six times, but she preferred the real thing to the copy in her head.

She smiled and laughed as she reviewed the events of the episode, though it all filled her with a certain sense of dread. Episode 297 meant that episode 300 was only a few weeks away, and episode 300 was bad news indeed, since it was going to be the final episode of *Quantum Girl!!.*

Holiday didn't like to think about it.

The holographic masterpiece that was *Quantum Girl!!* was drawing to a close, and that was a tragedy. An epic tragedy.

The holo dome unit winked to life. Holiday raised her head and opened her eyes.

A transparent female face peered into the room. "Honey, were you watching that show again?"

It was a rhetorical question, and Holiday knew it. Her mother had a log of her holo access.

"Yes, Sabatha," Holiday replied.

"Holi…"

"I mean *mom.* Yes, I was watching it."

"How many times?"

"Six so far."

"That's enough for today then. No more *Quantum Girl!!.* In fact, no more holo at all."

"But Mom, it was the best episode ever!"

"They all are, honey. Anyway, you have things you need to do for

24

tomorrow."

"I'm ready. Everything's packed."

"Really?"

"Of course, mom, you know me."

Sabatha smiled. Her hair was straight, at her chin, and black with red streaks in it. She could've had her eyesight corrected, but she'd resisted. Instead, she wore glasses with thick, black frames. She looked younger than her forty-two years because she took care of herself and ate right six out of seven days. She pushed her glasses up. "You'd like to think so, wouldn't you?"

Holiday wrinkled her nose at her mom's silliness. She'd been packed and ready for over a week. Her mom must've forgot—she did look a little preoccupied.

"Sorry, honey," Sabatha said. "I'm thinking about a thousand things. I'm almost home. I ordered dinner. It'll be there in fifteen minutes. You hungry?"

"Yeah," Holiday said.

"See you in a few minutes. Bye."

Sabatha's face faded and disappeared.

Holiday briefly considered watching episode 297 again. Maybe her mom wouldn't get mad if she only watched the last five minutes…

She got up from the bed and moved over to the sink, deftly dodging her luggage. The luggage was pink, and unmistakably Holiday's due to the extensive custom artwork she'd commissioned Max to etch across every available surface. Max had crazy artistic talent running through his veins, and she'd caught him at a weak moment. Truth told, he had a soft spot for his younger sister and didn't mind feeding her addiction to a certain holo show and its associated merchandising. His crowning achievement was a full-color Quantum Girl!! in a complete set of battle gear. She was trademark-infringingly accurate, from the shooting star tattoo on her left cheek to her antigravity wristbands and her short, pleated skirt. She was winking and aiming her ray gun right at whoever happened to be looking at her. It was the most cosmic thing ever. Holiday had given her brother a big wet kiss on the cheek when she'd first seen it. He'd recoiled appropriately, but he'd been grinning.

Holiday waved her hand under the faucet and started the flow of water into the sink. She grabbed a ribbon from the shelf above the sink and tied her hair into a ponytail. She splashed water in her face, letting the cool liquid wash away the desire to turn the holo back on. It failed, big time, but that wasn't a surprise.

She looked in the oval mirror above the sink. The face that stared back at her was a younger version of her mother. They had the same hair—shadow and tar—though Holiday's lacked the red streaks and was longer, down to the middle of her back. While Sabatha let hers hang free to frame her face, Holiday usually pulled hers back. Holiday didn't need glasses either, and even if she had, she didn't have her mother's aversion to lasers aimed at her eyes. Holiday blinked water away, drops flinging from her eyelashes. She thought that maybe, just maybe, her eyes—so dark brown they were almost black—were the best thing about her face. She thought they made her look mysterious, and if she couldn't have excitingly-green eyes like Quantum Girl!! then she'd settle for mysterious.

Mysterious was good. Definitely.

Holiday moved back to the bed and let her whole body fall backward onto it this time. The skin on her face tingled as it dried.

Finally banishing episode 297 from her mind, Holiday was able to concentrate on more important things. Like what they were having for dinner. And tomorrow's launch. Her thoughts strayed to wondering what space would be like.

[It'll be okay. There's no danger. At least not to them.]

Holiday sat up.

Okay, who said that?

It had sounded like the person—a man—was in the room. Holiday looked over at the holo dome unit on the wall. It was off. Gooseflesh ran up her arms. She held her breath and listened, but she heard nothing more.

Who said that?

When she closed her eyes, she tried to bring the voice back, to recall it just like she did with *Quantum Girl!!* episodes. It wasn't there though. It was as if the recording had been deleted or overwritten. She could remember what the voice had said, but the audio wasn't coming with it. Had the voice sounded familiar? She wasn't sure. Maybe.

Too much holo, she thought finally, *that's all it was.*

Holiday waited, silent and listening, but she didn't hear anything else. By the time her mother called her for dinner, her thoughts had drifted back to episode 297's cliffhanger ending and how exactly her heroine could possibly survive till the finale.

[Chapter Four]

What Happened In Rian Storm's Office

Not even Sabatha knew that Rian Storm, her beloved, her first, her one and only, her husband of seventeen years, was bringing unregistered weapons with him on their vacation to the moon.

The weapons all rested on a table in his office. Holiday was home, so the office door was locked. She had a minor distaste for real-life weapons, even though that holo show she watched all the time was filled with staggering quantities of ray gun violence.

There were two Remington Pyros, which fired magnesium-tipped shells that made all sorts of pretty colors when they went off as long as they didn't do so inside a person. Next to the two Pyros was the Glom and Dom Mark Seven Neural Disrupter. That one didn't use a projectile of any sort, but if you pressed the tip of it against somebody, perhaps in the soft flesh of their stomach, they went down fast, and without bowel control. There was a small, ovoid container that contained restraining wire. A button on the side of the container allowed the wire to be coated with a numbing agent as the wire was pulled out. Rian had found this to be particularly useful in the past, and he never went anywhere without it. A person who did what he did and dealt with what he dealt with had to have the proper tools. The final item on the table was his favorite. It was the oldest item of the bunch, but it was as effective now as it was the day seventeen years ago when he'd brought it home for the first time, its surface still gleaming from the oil they coated it with during manufacturing. Rian paused, staring down at the gun that didn't look like anything special—yet that's exactly what it was. It was a Reaper, and it lay waiting to be used. The Reaper was all curves; there were no flat faces anywhere on its surfaces. It was coated in light-absorbing paint, so it looked more like the black, shadowy outline of a gun than an actual weapon. The Reaper was a simple weapon. Simple in that if you got shot with it, you died. Period. No second chances.

Rian's Reaper had never been fired.

That's the way he wanted it, and precisely why it was his favorite. The knowledge that pulling that particular trigger meant that somebody's life was ending wasn't something he dwelt on. It might be necessary someday, and if it came to that, he'd deal with it in his own way, as he had before.

There were two gray cases on the table as well. Rian put the Reaper in one and the rest of the weapons in the other. The ammo, which had been neatly ordered on the table as well, he divided appropriately between the two cases. He double-checked both the weapons and the ammo, then loaded the final two objects—one in each case. The two objects—flat, business card shaped pieces of plastic—were necessary to make sure that the cases would pass through security checks without interference. He'd used them before, and they'd worked well enough. He preferred to avoid carrying weapons on public transportation, but the logistics of this particular operation hadn't afforded him time to make other arrangements. This was a family vacation, so every piece of luggage was going to have to survive standard security procedures.

Rian didn't like combining work and vacation. Even if it would be mostly vacation from the launch till they arrived on Luna, once they landed it was likely going to be all work. He didn't know what he was going to tell Sabatha and the kids. He already felt guilty every time he looked at his wife and lied to her about what he'd done at work that day. He'd tell her someday. She could keep a secret.

Rian gritted his teeth, putting his fists down hard on the solid table surface, wondering if throwing a punch at something would help. He blew out a long breath and reminded himself that everything he did was ultimately to protect his family. Somebody had to verify and secure the target before it fell into the wrong hands, but he couldn't shake the notion that abandoning your family on their first space vacation was a terrible thing. Unfortunately, there were surprisingly few operatives they could trust with this particular assignment. The target was in a precarious position. They still believed it was secure, which merely meant that nobody else had discovered it yet.

The call had come in last night, and Rian hadn't fully hid the disappointment in his face when he'd returned to the dinner table after receiving his orders. Sabatha, though she didn't know what he really did—not many people did, least of all his family—sensed that something was wrong right away. Rian was afraid Holiday had too. Max had been too preoccupied, sketching something on his napkin. The Storm women were scary perceptive. Holiday especially. Rian had made up something about work pressuring him to cancel his vacation because of some crisis, which wasn't a total lie he supposed. Though telling his family that vacation was a go and that work wasn't going to interfere *was*. He promised himself that he'd make it up to them afterward.

Rian locked the cases, then spoke the password that would have to be repeated to unlock them. There was a series of small hisses as the cases expelled all air, venting through small valves. The vacuum was a safety precaution for the special ammo that the Pyros and the Reaper used. Explosions in space other than those used for propulsion were generally bad. Rian wanted to avoid all bad things until his family was safe on Luna.

Glancing at the timekeeper on the wall, Rian saw that Sabatha would be home soon. He rubbed his eyes, feeling suddenly tired. He wondered if he was doing the right thing. He could cancel the vacation. He could take the trip to Luna himself, and they could take the trip as a family another time.

No.

No. No. No. That wasn't an option. This was Holiday's only break from school for at least six months. Max had given up Wilderness Camp for this trip. Sabatha had done a ton of planning to make this all happen, and she was excited about doing it as a family. They didn't do enough of these sorts of activities. Cancelling it would be worse. Much worse. Nobody would understand why, since he couldn't tell them the real reason. They'd blame him. Besides, it wasn't like they were in any danger. The trip itself was completely safe, and as long as they were inside Luna One, he didn't have to worry about them while he took care of the moon's little problem.

Rian left the sealed weapon cases resting on the table, unlocked the exit door with a single word, and stepped from the room, reassuring himself by thinking, *It'll be okay. There's no danger. At least not to them.*

[CHAPTER FIVE]

WHAT HAPPENED AT THE DINNER TABLE THE NIGHT BEFORE

Max was the first to the table. He took his usual chair—the one facing the kitchen—and waited for everybody else to arrive. He was a little breathless from Nika's attentions, his blood still racing for its life, hands shaking. He'd brought a pen and a palm-sized drawing pad to the table in a feeble attempt to focus, get his muscles back under control, but it wasn't happening fast enough. He continued to sketch, but when he discovered that he was drawing an all-too-realistic image of Nika, he stopped, ripped that page out, folded it, and put it in his back pocket.

His mind informed him he'd finish that sketch later.

"Where's mom?" Holiday asked when she came in, then not waiting for an answer: "You wore that to see your girlfriend? She must really like you. Either that or she's losing her sight. I know Veronika has good fashion sense, so she must be going blind."

"Very funny," Max grunted. "Don't ever call her that to her face. I'd hate to lose you, Sis. And besides, what's wrong with what I'm wearing?"

Holiday sniffed, her eyes traversing him from head to toe as if he were a distasteful area of the city she had to walk through. "Have you looked at yourself in the mirror today? Tonight was the last time you'll get to see her for at least a month, and you didn't even put on a nice shirt. You really want her to remember you like this when she's lying in bed dreaming about you? Don't you like her?"

"I like her." Max looked at himself. Okay, so maybe he could've done better. His pants were clean at least, though the knees were starting to wear. His shirt was red with a black lightning bolt in the center. His brown hair was longer than his dad's, so it could actually get messy. And so it was. He ran his hand through it, but it had its normal reaction and went all over the place. Nika seemed to like it well enough, so he figured it didn't look too bad.

"You're funny," Holiday said. "Funny looking."

"Who's funny looking?" Rian asked as he entered the room. "I know it's not me."

Holiday giggled. Her dad was over six feet tall, and with his hair cut close and arms banded with ropes of muscle, he could be just a teensy bit scary at times. The tattoos helped that image. Though he was wearing a gray, button-up shirt that covered them, he had the Space Command emblem on his left shoulder, and a skull and crossbones on his left forearm. When she was younger, Holiday had imagined that the skull was laughing at her when her father flexed. Come to think of it, she still thought that. Rian was forty-seven, and only had a few gray hairs in among all that brown. Sabatha sometimes teased him by lying next to him in bed and searching for new ones. Rian had really intense eyes. They were as brown as his hair, and Sabatha got lost in them on a daily basis. Rian liked that he could have that effect on her with just a glance. Sabatha complained that it was just this side of hypnosis. Not that she complained all that loudly.

"No, Dad," Holiday said. "It's not you."

"All packed?" Rian asked.

"Since last week."

"What about you, Max?"

"Not yet. I don't have that much stuff though." Max couldn't keep all the frustration out of his voice. He didn't really want to get into a rehash of how, despite how cosmically awesome space was, he'd much rather be spending the next month out at Wilderness Camp with his girlfriend and his friends than confined to a rocket and a moon base with his family.

"The earlier you do it, the less likely it is that you'll forget something," Rian said, sitting down.

"Yes, sir," Max said, keeping his head down, his eyes on his drawing pad. The tip of his pen was stationary, and the paper was sucking the ink downward, a dark splotch spreading like a cancer across the page. Maybe he should've told his dad he was staying. Seemed a little late for that though…

The front door opened, and Sabatha came in. "Hi, family of mine. Is dinner here yet?"

"I think Dad forgot to check," Holiday said.

Rian stood, but tapped Holiday on the shoulder as he passed her. "You're not an invalid, young lady. You could've checked."

"And was everybody waiting for me to get home so I could set the table too?" Sabatha asked, kicking off her shoes. "Honestly, sometimes I think you'd all starve if I didn't make it home in a timely manner. And that includes you, dear." She stood on her tiptoes to give Rian a kiss. An arm at her waist, he pulled her body to his. She gave a little squeak, and then a sigh, melting a little. Holiday rolled her eyes. Max thought of Nika.

"I'm on it, Mom," Max said, pushing his chair back.

Max had the table set in no time, and Rian had dinner from the delivery chute to the table a minute later.

"Ready for some space travel?" Rian asked when they were all seated and eating.

"I hope the food's okay," Sabatha said. "It's from that new place down the street. *Neon Tina's.*"

"That why the food's glowing?" Max mumbled.

"It's not radioactive or anything," Holiday said. "It's just been energized."

"So, about space," Rian said. "Anybody looking forward to tomorrow?"

Both Holiday and Sabatha raised their hands. Max made sure his hands were busy shoving pieces of blue meat in his mouth. Whatever it was, it tasted like chicken.

"What are you looking forward to most?" Rian asked, twirling some phosphorescent noodles around his fork. "You first, Holi."

That one was easy. Though it was a distant second to *Quantum Girl!!,* Holiday did have a second obsession: gymnastics. "The Low-G Gymnastics Exhibition Sponsored by Energistix!" she proclaimed.

"Do you always have to add in the 'sponsored by' part?" Max asked.

"Yes," Holiday sniffed, turning her nose up at her brother. "Because that's what it's called."

"It's a little weird to have the primary sponsor of an athletic competition be a drug company, don't you think?" Max asked.

"It's not a competition—it's an exhibition, and besides, everything they sell is legal and safe."

"That's what the holo ads say at least. And we know they'd never lie to us through advertising."

Sabatha shot a warning look at Max. "Leave your sister alone." Then, to Holiday, "We'll have fun at the exhibition, even if your brother doesn't, okay?"

Holiday stuck her tongue out at her brother. Max couldn't help but laugh.

Rian wiped his hand on his napkin and took Sabatha's hand. "What are you looking forward to, my fair wife?"

"That's easy. Moon shopping."

"Naturally," Rian said, leaning over to kiss her cheek.

Max and Holiday looked at each other, each performing their ritual brother-sister gagging noises.

Sabatha had a wicked gleam in her eye. "I've been saving up. Be prepared for a spending spree the likes of which you have never seen on this planet. We're going to need a second rocket to carry it all back to—"

A melody interrupted whatever she was going to say next. Sabatha leaned back and extracted a phone from the pocket of her pants. She looked at the caller. "Oh, it's Dana. I'll only be a minute." She disappeared down the hall into the master bedroom.

"What about you, Dad, what are you looking forward to the most?" Holiday asked after a minute or two of everybody eating in silence.

"Spending time with my family, of course," he said with a slow smile.

"Dad, you get to do that every day," Max said.

"Not in space, and not on the moon. This isn't just a vacation; it's an adventure. It'll be exciting and fun—more than you realize right now."

"We'll see," Max said, wishing he hadn't, because his dad's eyes looked a little hurt. The next second, the hurt look was gone, but Max knew better.

Sabatha came back. Max noticed that her makeup was streaked a little at the corner of her eyes. Had she been crying?

"Everything okay, Mom?" Holiday, as perceptive as ever, asked.

"Sure is, kiddo, pass me some of that pudding. I think I'm ready for dessert."

"You want green or purple?"

"Both, young lady, now hand them over."

Holiday sighed. "So dramatic, Mom."

"I was in theater in high school, you know." Sabatha batted her eyelashes.

"Max, is there *anything* you're looking forward to about this vacation?" Holiday asked, filling her mouth with green pudding that tasted like chocolate and left her whole mouth glowing green, as if she had some alien life form nesting under her tongue.

Coming home, Max thought, but managed to keep from saying it out loud. He didn't want to feel worse than he already did. "Uh, seeing Earth from space, I guess."

"It's one of the best sights you'll ever see, Max," Rian said. He'd seen a lot during his time in the Space Command. He'd even been stationed on the moon for six months.

"Hey, we can see if kissing by earthlight is better than by moonlight," Sabatha said, leaning her shoulder into Rian.

Rian smiled a smile he only ever gave Sabatha, then leaned over and whispered something into her ear. Max caught something about *low gravity*, but he couldn't stop thinking about Nika. He pushed his chair back and walked over to the sliding door that led to the balcony.

"Not without your glasses," Sabatha called from behind him.

"Don't worry, Mom," Max said. There were hooks on the wall next to the sliding glass door where the family's viewing glasses hung. Max picked his from its hook, waved a hand across the small sensor, and opened the door.

The door itself was some fusion of glass and plastic, only it had an opacity control, allowing the door to go from crystal clear to completely opaque. All the windows—there were only four of them—were made from the same material. They compensated automatically depending on the intensity of light from outside. With the sun so low, the door and the windows were all darkened.

Holiday followed Max out onto the balcony, which was big enough for about four people and was ringed with a solid concrete rim. Sabatha didn't let them keep anything on the balcony because she was afraid it would get knocked off, or blown off, or something like that.

Max put his glasses on. Holiday did the same. The balcony was seventy floors up, and it gave them a good view of San Diego Two. The city stretched out below them, stopping only at the jagged line of blue and gray that was the Pacific Ocean. The coastline didn't look like it used to. Then again, not much did. The Quake had seen to that. Built from the ruins of its predecessor, San Diego Two was a mixture of wreckage and rebirth. The new skyscrapers, metallic and reflective, mirrored the cityscape below, neon against impending night. The newer buildings rose right from the rubble of the old ones. Humanity defying its history, defying its mistakes, doomed to revisit the past. It was only a matter of time.

The sun was attempting to hide beneath the sea. Max's glasses darkened to compensate. They said you could go blind in ten seconds if you looked at the setting or the rising sun without protection. With the glasses on you could look at it directly, stare it down as it dropped, prove yourself a man or woman, that sort of thing.

Max stared at it now, with his sister at his side. It was such a dangerous thing, but utterly beautiful. Would it be the same in space? Without Earth's atmospheric protection—a barrier that grew weaker and less effective with each passing year—the sun was much brighter, much more deadly. Would it be as beautiful, unfiltered and raw?

In that moment, with the memory of Nika's kisses, her touch, and her pretty face running on endless repeat through his mind, Max found that he really didn't care.

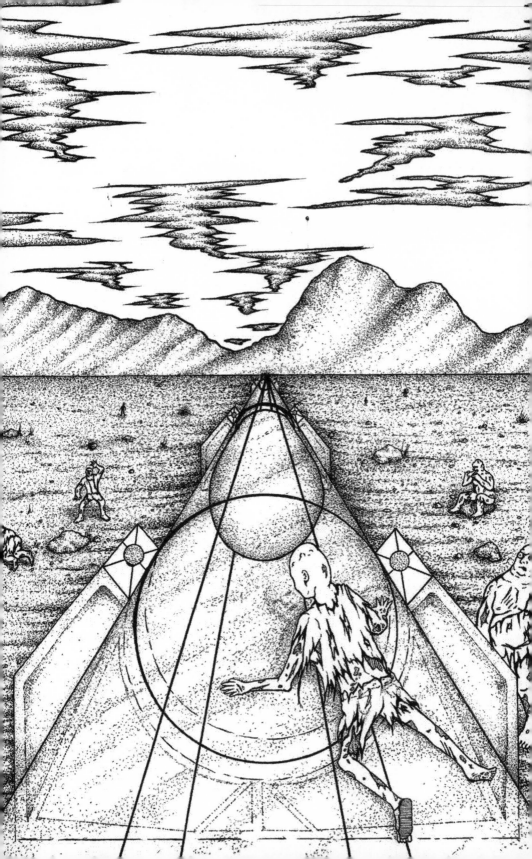

[CHAPTER SIX]

WHAT HAPPENED IN THE CIRCUITSTREAM

Max was amazed at how little a family had to bring with them to take a trip into space. In many ways, it was as uncomplicated as a camping trip to the nearest federal forest preserve. Max had one suitcase, as did Holiday and Sabatha. Rian had the smallest suitcase, but he was also carrying two other small cases. Anything else they needed for the trip had been sent on ahead and would be loaded prior to launch.

The whole family was wearing everyday clothes. Space travel was common and targeted at the consumer, but the Storm family had somehow made the whole process look mundane.

The four of them were standing on the queuing platform at the San Diego Two node of the Interstate Transport System. There were ITS nodes in all major cities throughout North America. It wasn't cheap, but it was the fastest way across the continent. Rian and Sabatha had decided that if they were splurging on the moon vacation thing, then it wouldn't do to skimp on the trip there. Of the four, only Rian had traveled using ITS.

ITS consisted of a series of nodes and tubes that made use of cylindrical passenger pods to ferry people between nodes. The system had been in use for five years, and had been in the building phase for the previous fifty. The system had its detractors. They claimed it was inefficient, expensive, and a drain on resources. They were right, but there was little they could do since the system was practically complete.

And it worked. At least, there hadn't been any major incidents yet.

They called the tube network the circuitstream.

Even though he was trying to hold onto his anger, a night's sleep had drained much of his resolve. Anger had turned to resignation, which was gradually giving way to wonder. Max gaped a little. He had never been this close to any part of ITS. A good portion of the tubes were underground for great distances. Only one of the San Diego Two tubes went above ground, and it was built that way for reasons not as much practical as they were profitable—the exposed section was etched with the Fuzz Cola logo.

San Diego Two's node would have been a dead end, except for the fact that it was one of only two gateways into Neo Mexico, with the other being the Texas city of El Paso. Because of this, the San Diego Two node served more than a dozen separate tubes.

Max watched the switching station at work. It was an enormous thing, shining glossy gold in the early morning light. The switcher consisted of a central shaft, from which sprouted six pod carriers. The switcher rotated, transitioning pods from one tube to another. A pod came in from a tube, and the switcher accepted it into one of its carriers. The switcher raised or lowered a carrier till it was mated to the destination tube, and the pod was sent on its way. Pods with San Diego Two as their final destination were sent into an arrival queue.

Max could see that all the tubes actually consisted of four smaller tubes. This way, the pathways between nodes were able to accommodate multiple pods and bi-directional traffic.

Each pod had four rails on its outer shell. These served to keep the pods oriented properly, as well as provided the method of propulsion. The rails were energized, making use of magnetic levitation to move a pod through the tubes.

It was a gigantic dance. Pods came whooshing in, and were just as quickly shot down another tube. The switcher spun and whirled, efficient and precise; it never seemed to stop moving, even when pods transitioned from tube to pod carrier. The movements of the switcher were entirely computer controlled. Constant communication with the pods moving through the system was necessary to ensure that the intricate ballet was performed without flaw.

"What happens if a pod gets stuck in one of the tubes?" Holiday asked.

"That's never happened, honey," Sabatha said. Morning sun beamed down through the curved glass ceiling that housed the queuing platform. The light lit up the red streaks in her hair, making them look like tongues of woven fire. She was wearing her red-framed glasses. They were her "fun time" glasses, which she only wore when she was out of the apartment. She thought they made her look younger and vibrant. Max didn't know if that was true, but she did appear to be happier when wearing them. Just then though, she looked distracted, her mind elsewhere.

"But it could happen," Holiday said. Not a question.

"I suppose so," Sabatha said.

Rian put his hand on Holiday's head. "They have safety measures in place for that sort of thing. There's no need to worry."

"I'm not worried."

"Good."

"I'm just scaring Max."

"I love you too, Sis," Max said. He did have a slight problem with enclosed spaces, but he had told himself that the pod wasn't going to be a problem. They'd only be in it for three hours. As for the trip to the moon, he'd make it through that somehow. From launch to landing, the trip was scheduled to take just under three days. Plus, the ship was bigger than the pod. If it got bad, he planned on putting on some holo goggles and losing himself in some wilderness sims.

Rian shifted his weight, but didn't release either of the two cases he was carrying. His suitcase rested at his feet. He looked like a tourist. That is, a tourist who wore black slacks, a button-down shirt, and a thin, black tie. His shoes were also black, freshly polished. Max thought he looked like an accountant. Well, perhaps an accountant that had done some time in Deep Locker Six. His Space Command tattoo peeked out from beneath his short sleeve, and the skull and crossbones was clear and shiny in the morning light. Yeah, definitely an accountant. Well, or an assassin. Max briefly imagined that his dad had guns in the cases.

But that image only made him laugh.

Sure, he was all buff, and he'd been in the Space Command, and he knew how to fly, but the image of his dad using a gun didn't hold water—not if you knew how regular he really was. Max liked guns way more than his father did. He would've been able to hold and use some entirely awesome weaponry at Wilderness Camp. The thought of shooting guns with Nika made Max a little queasy. He was equally intrigued and scared at the thought of her with a deadly weapon cradled in her hands.

"A few more minutes," Rian said. The queuing platform was a flat area where travelers lined up while they waited for their turn to enter a pod. Empty pods were placed on a track beside the platform. When the pod was full, it was moved forward, where it was loaded into a pod holder that was capable of rotating to mate up with the switcher. The whole setup resembled the line to a thrill ride at an amusement park. Parents wrangled luggage and children. Solo riders were lost in their handheld datapads or the IIUs—Internet Interface Units—strapped to their heads or built into their sunglasses. There was talk of imbedding IIUs into people's bodies. Max shivered when he thought about it. It was a concept straight out of the movies, but that didn't stop them from thinking that it just might work if only they could figure out how to do it without killing the lab animals they used to test the procedure. Paralysis was a big risk when you were talking about interfacing directly with a person's brain stem. Infection and brain damage were in there too. Happy thoughts.

Then it was their turn. A pod slid to a halt in front of them. Max smiled, fought to keep a laugh in, because now that the pod was so close, he couldn't stop himself from thinking that they were about to be riding inside an oversized, mutant pill. It was cylindrical, but the ends were tapered, more for aesthetic reasons than aerodynamics—for most of the length of any particular tube, the pods were moving through a vacuum. Near the ends of a tube, as pods were decelerating, they passed through an airlock of sorts. Each airlock was several miles long due to the speeds at which the pods traveled.

Max was holding his breath. He blew it out slowly when he realized what he was doing. Holiday was striding confidently toward the pod as a seam appeared in the side of it, then expanded, creating a doorway.

An attendant that Max hadn't noticed before stepped forward. She was dressed in white, was wearing something on her ear that extended a small microphone against her cheek, and had a red nametag that scrolled YUKI SAN followed by DRINK FUZZ COLA. "Storm family?" she asked. "Right this way." She gestured toward the doorway into the pod.

"Cosmic!" Holiday said, practically leaping through the doorway.

Sabatha entered, then Rian. Max paused, taking a deep breath. He thought of Nika and imagined how embarrassed he'd be if she was watching him hesitate. That got one foot forward, his body through the door, and his rear in a seat.

The interior of the pod was scattered with calming shades of light brown and dark, rich reds. There were eight cushioned seats arranged in two rows directly in the center of the pod. Each was mounted on a rotating base to allow for reorientation as the pod changed directions after passing through a switching station. At the side of each seat there was a flat screen that permitted the person sitting there to fend off boredom as they travelled. Off to the right were compartments for storing luggage, as well as a single restroom. To the left, there was a small counter; underneath it were drawers and cabinets. They were labeled with signs indicating FOOD and BEVERAGES and DISPOSAL. Above the counter was a wall-mounted holo dome. The floor was carpeted and soft, a little springy, displaying the bold, silvery ITS logo. Light was provided via ceiling-mounted fixtures. A trail of safety lights was embedded in the floor where the carpet met the walls. Ringing the walls near the ceiling was a single strip of black.

"Place your luggage in the storage containers," Yuki San said, standing just inside the door. "Then please take your seat. For your safety, you will need to remain seated for all accelerations and decelerations. At all other times, you may stand if you need to stretch or use the restroom. Your food selections have already been loaded and are available for you at any time during your trip. There is a variety of reading materials, music, and holo feeds available at your individual consoles. Internet access is also available, as well as an interface connection port compatible with all known systems except for Takiyoma's Digital Demoness models. Please do not attempt to use one of these devices, as they will result in harm to the pod, as well as permanent damage to your eyesight. If you need any assistance with your luggage or seating, please let me know now. Are there any questions before we send you on your way?"

"After we get going, how can we see outside?" Holiday asked. "Or do we have to stare at blank walls the whole trip?"

Max looked around. The walls of the pod were anything but blank. Instead, they were filled with disclaimers and warnings about what could and couldn't be touched, how ITS, Inc. couldn't be held liable for anything, beginning at dissatisfaction with the quality of the service, all the way up to and including the deaths of the pod's passengers.

Nothing was their fault. The lawyers had done their job.

Yuki San gave Holiday a girlish giggle, but her eyes betrayed her real feelings. Her smile, instead of being friendly, said something more along the lines of: *Thanks for asking a question, you naïve, prepubescent lover of stupid holo shows for little girls. I only have four minutes to say my lines and get this pod moving. Nobody needs help with their luggage, and nobody asks any questions. Thanks for ruining my day!* Instead of a tirade, Yuki San said, "The pod is equipped with external cameras and all the interior walls have been painted with digital paint. You can project the outside view whenever you want. Most of your trip will be underground, but there are times when you will be able to see more than the walls of the tube. Now, if there are no more questions, please take your seats, fasten your seatbelts and I will authorize your departure."

"Thank you," Sabatha said. "Holiday, sit next to your brother."

Max was sitting in the back row. Holiday, who had sat at the opposite corner, frowned. "Why?" There were the beginnings of a pout there.

"Just obey your mother, Holi," Rian said. "Can you help us out here and not be difficult?"

Holiday glared at Max, but sighed loudly and moved to sit in the seat next to Max.

Max didn't want his sister mad at him, especially when it wasn't her fault she hadn't caught on to what her parents were doing—trying to get him closer to another member of the family so if his claustrophobia kicked it, he could…what…grab her hand, hug her? He wasn't sure. Something. He leaned over and whispered in her ear, "Sorry."

Holiday sniffed. She wasn't going to be deprived of her chance to pout for the next half hour. Max knew there was nothing he could do about it. After a little bit, she'd forget why she was mad anyway.

"Seatbelts," Sabatha said.

Holiday blew breath through her teeth as she fastened hers.

"Excellent, now that that's finally over with, we should be ready to send you on your way," Yuki San said, her voice sounding strangely similar to Holiday's. It was a day for pouting as well as space travel. Yuki San spoke rapidly into her cheek microphone. "Transport pod Two Sierra Yankee Lima ready for departure along pathway two one nine five. Passengers are onboard and secure. This is transport agent Yuki San authorizing immediate circuitstream insertion. Control, may I secure the door?"

The response was immediate, a calm, synthesized female voice filling the pod, ***"You may secure the door, transport agent Yuki San. Request for circuitstream insertion approved."***

"Thanks, Mother," Yuki San replied. Then to the Storm family, "Enjoy your trip, and thank you for choosing ITS." She almost sounded like she meant it. Yuki San stepped back. The doorway slid shut.

The interior of the pod was silent for a moment.

"Well, this is it," Rian said, grabbing Sabatha's hand.

"Yay!" Sabatha said. She sounded like a little kid getting a new toy. The "fun time" glasses had kicked in.

The pod shivered. Were they moving?

"Can we turn on the external cameras?" Max asked.

Sabatha, who was sitting in the front row next to Rian, turned back, nodding. "Sure, honey. Rian?"

"On it," Rian said, fingers flying across his monitor. A second later the walls of the pod seemed to fade as the digital paint began displaying a view of the world outside the pod. It was an effect that took a second to get used to since anything that protruded from the wall didn't disappear, and the wall wasn't completely transparent. The world appeared slightly distorted, but the image was remarkably effective. Max felt instantly better. He relaxed his crushing grip on the armrest of his seat. Max could see the crowded queuing platform. Looking over his shoulder, the massive switcher raised and lowered, receiving and launching pods.

A faint hum filtered through the floor of the pod, as if somebody had turned the power on. The strip that ringed the ceiling went from black to red. Arrows appeared on the strip, pointing toward the side of the pod with the counter.

The computerized female voice spoke again, *"Welcome to the Interstate Transport System. Please note that the motion indicator strip at the top of this pod has turned red, signifying that you must remain seated with your seatbelt fastened. For your safety, your seatbelts have been secured and will not be released until it is safe to do so. Trip timer begins now."* The pod began to move parallel to the queuing platform. The track, which consisted of two magnetic levitation rails, curved gently away from the platform. They were slowly approaching the switcher. It was a multi-mouthed monster, each of its pod carriers a gaping maw, ready to accept and devour incoming pods.

"Passenger seat reorientation will begin in ten seconds. Please make sure that your arms and legs are clear of obstruction."

Rian and Sabatha looked back to make sure that Holiday and Max were seated properly. Max held up his hands, grinning. Holiday did the same, her pout gone. She'd pulled out her ponytail, and her hair hung carefree around her neck and shoulders, contrasting against her shirt—a pink top with a wide collar, long sleeves, and flowers stitched on the cuffs.

All eight seats began to rotate so that they faced the side of the pod that had the luggage. The pod was still travelling in the opposite direction, so Max looked over his shoulder. With the new seat orientation, Holiday was sitting directly behind him. The pod was reaching the end of its track. There were a few seconds there where the entire Storm family held their breath because the pod wasn't slowing, yet there wasn't a pod carrier ready to accept them. But the system worked. A pod carrier swung into view at just the right time, and the pod slid smoothly into it. The Storm family emitted a collective exhale. The pod slid deeper into the dark confines of the pod carrier. The view through the carrier opening was of a spinning world that rushed past, rising and falling as the switcher moved according to its programmed sorting method.

The arrows on the motion indicator switched direction so they were pointed toward the luggage side of the pod.

The voice, which seemed to come from everywhere, spoke. *"Transport pod Two Sierra Yankee Lima, you have been approved and cleared for launch to destination Orlando, Florida. Upon insertion, this pod will experience rapid acceleration until a speed of one thousand miles per hour is attained. Please place your head against the headrest for launch. Circuitstream insertion in ten seconds."*

"Ready, kids?" Rian asked.

"Yeah," Max said.

The pod began to move forward, drifting toward the edge of the carrier.

"Five," the voice said.

"This is so cool," Holiday said.

"Four."

"Sure is," Sabatha added.

"Three. Prepare for insertion."

Outside, the world rushed by, blurring.

"Wait," Rian said.

"What?!?" Sabatha asked, her voice filled with sudden concern.

"Two."

The pod picked up speed. The pod carrier hadn't mated with their destination tube yet. The switcher was rising. Max saw sky and nothing else through the opening.

"I forgot my toothbrush," Rian said.

Holiday and Max burst out laughing. Sabatha slugged her husband on the shoulder. "Jerk!" she said.

"One. Launch!"

Max felt his body press against his seat as they tore through the opening. Their destination tube appeared, and then they were zooming through it. The sides of the tube streaked by. Still accelerating, there was a flash of something in the tube ahead of them, but they went through it so fast that Max didn't really see what it was.

"That was the airlock barrier in case you were wondering," Rian said. "We're in the airlock and they're sucking what little atmosphere there is in this part of the tube out right now. We'll hit the other end of the airlock in a second or two. There it is."

"Wheee!" Holiday said as they tore through the far end of the airlock, moving at well over five hundred miles per hour.

Since there wasn't any atmosphere in the main sections of the tube, the pod could accelerate past the sound barrier without creating a shockwave.

It couldn't have been more than half a minute after the pod's insertion that Max felt the pressure on his body ease. They were no longer accelerating. The motion indicator strip turned green, and all their seatbelts made a faint clicking sound. Max checked his monitor. A little menu advertised statistics on the pod. He touched the menu. It listed the speed of the pod as: **998 MPH.**

"We can get up and walk around now, right?" Holiday said.

"Sure can," Rian said, adjusting his seat so it reclined more. "Just fasten your seatbelt when you're sitting." Sabatha leaned her head on his shoulder and closed her eyes. Rian put his arm around her.

Max was doing well, as he hadn't yet felt that cold press of panic that sometimes caught him in small, enclosed areas from which he couldn't quickly escape. The images of the outside view helped some, but just then they were underground, barreling through near darkness. The tube was sparsely lit—a single light appeared every ten seconds or so. Max tried not to stare down the tube because it stretched into almost-darkness, and thinking about that too much could bring the panic.

Sabatha and Rian dozed. Holiday kept herself busy. It didn't take her long to discover that the list of holo feeds available included the entire *Quantum Girl!!* library.

Max got some food and Fuzz Cola and sat back. He resisted the temptation to contact Nika using the Internet connection at his seat. She was always logged onto her messenger service, so she'd certainly be available. As much as he wanted to, he didn't think he'd be able to do it without affecting his mood in a negative way. Best to keep his mind off of his girlfriend. Best to keep it on more immediate, more important things—like figuring out how he was going to get through this vacation without disappointing his entire family. Surely there was a way to think more happy thoughts…

The pod entered Phoenix, Arizona. Deceleration into a node was simply the reverse of the acceleration process. The pod entered a second airlock and decreased speed until the pod was going slow enough that it wouldn't cause a sonic boom, then atmosphere was pumped in. The seats swiveled, and they came into the node backwards. The switcher accepted them, then they were sent into another tube. That one took them to El Paso. From there, they were sent on through Texas. Most of the journey through west Texas was above ground. The view was jaw-dropping, moving at a thousand miles an hour at less than twenty feet off the ground. The above-ground portions of the tube were transparent, so they could see the landscape.

As they approached the city of San Antonio, they entered the

Zombie Fields.

The annihilation of Dallas from terrorist nukes during the construction of the ITS had forced them to abandon the planned node there in favor of one further south. However, since most of the tube had already been constructed, instead of starting a completely new tube out of El Paso, they had simply turned their construction south toward San Antonio. As such, the tube still came dangerously close to the city ruins and the mutated residents that lived there. They called them Zombies, as if they'd been dead once and then resurrected instead of the descendants of irradiated humans who had survived the shockwave and the heat. The hydrogen bomb had flattened downtown Dallas and set nearby Fort Worth ablaze.

Holiday had studied the Zombie Fields in school the previous semester, so she was curious enough that she tore herself away from episode 99—popular because it was the first episode that Captain Xeode appeared in—to stand up close to the side wall of the pod. She leaned against the wall with her hands spread, her head leaning close, watching for any glimpse of a Zombie. Max tried it and didn't think that getting closer helped. The resolution of the digital paint was fixed. The closer you were, the less clear the outside world appeared. His eyes had trouble focusing when he was that close; his eyes kept wanting to see the wall instead of the image being protected on it.

There were dark splotches on the surface of the tube.

"What are those?" Holiday asked.

"I'm not sure, kiddo," Rian said.

Sabatha shrugged. "They're blurry at this speed."

Max sat back down and scanned the options on his monitor. He looked through the menu and selected the option he'd hoped was there. The image of the outside world froze. Holiday screamed, jumping back.

There was a Zombie crawling on the outer surface of the tube.

Max had paused the image displayed on the inner surface of the pod at just the right time to catch it as the pod passed under it. The Zombie was gaunt, its flesh melted away, rot and infection evident across its green and gray skin. One of its eyes drooped, and some of its teeth had come loose, now resting on the surface of the glass in a smear of blood and saliva.

Sabatha steadied Holiday with a hand. "We're safe in here, sweetie."

"I'm okay" Holiday said, backing up, though she was shaking. "That's gross."

"Max, if you make your sister scream again like that..." Rian warned.

"Hey, it wasn't my fault!" Max protested. "We both wanted to know what those were."

"It's okay, Dad, I was just surprised," Holiday said.

"You should put this in your school report," Max said.

"Gross," Holiday said again.

Sabatha looked at Max. "I think that's enough Zombie for me for one day."

Max touched his monitor and the outside world changed, once again in motion. The black forms on the surface of the tube were gone; they were out of the Zombie Fields.

"You scream like a girl," Max said.

"I *am* a girl," Holiday said, sticking out her tongue. "What's your excuse?"

The pod continued on to San Antonio. From there it passed through nodes in Houston, Alexandria Prime in Louisiana, Jackson in Mississippi, and Montgomery in Alabama before entering Florida. They passed through Tallahassee before rocketing south, arriving at the Orlando node three and a half hours after they'd left San Diego Two.

Max couldn't help it though, when he stepped out from the pod onto the exit platform, he breathed in a big gulp of mostly-non-toxic air, and gave Holiday a big hug.

Because that's the kind of girl she was, and to let him know that everything was okay, she even hugged him back.

[CHAPTER SEVEN]

WHAT HAPPENED AT ARMSTRONG SPACE CENTER

Armstrong Space Center was a large, sprawling complex that Max saw little of. This was partly because when they entered the gates, they went directly to the departure terminal, and partly because he was staring at all the spaceships the entire time. In spite of his reluctance to come on the vacation, he found himself in awe of what he and his family were about to do. Space. It all seemed so unreal, as if this wasn't really happening to him. The enormity of his situation threatened to bring him to his knees. Space travel was common. There were daily trips to the moon. It was no big deal.

And yet it was. Really, how could it not be?

Just because it was common, didn't mean it should be treated casually. Launching oneself and one's family at twenty-five thousand miles per hour over a quarter of a million miles through space to land on your home planet's only moon was something to be *oohed* and *aahed* over, wasn't it?

Up in the sky, a pillar of smoke traced the path of a rocket launched less than thirty minutes before their arrival. The air around the Space Center carried the smell and residue of smoke.

The terminal was directly in the middle of the Space Center, which occupied an area ten miles square. The terminal was a low dome a thousand feet in diameter. Ground-based shuttles arrived and departed in a steady stream on a road that headed straight toward the west. Two gently-arcing roads extended to the northeast and to the southwest. These led to the two launch pad arrays. With almost twenty launches a day, Armstrong Space Center was the largest in the world. The second largest was in China, but it had never been used for public transportation. Named for Sandra Armstrong, the first American astronaut to set foot on the planet Mars, it handled all public transportation launches for North and South America, and ninety percent of all other launches. The only launches that didn't liftoff from Armstrong were military or private business in nature. For safety and traffic reasons, only liftoffs were handled at Armstrong. Most landings happened a couple thousand miles away, over at Sentinel Field in the Arizona desert.

As Rian and Sabatha checked the family in, Max and Holiday argued over who was going to get space sick first.

"Okay, that's done," Sabatha said, adjusting her glasses as she approached the kids. They had just come to the conclusion that Max was going to be the first to vomit in zero-*g*. Cursed claustrophobia. It would be a landmark occasion. Max had assured Holiday that he'd make sure she was close by when it happened.

"Well, we're still on schedule," Rian said, coming up behind Sabatha. "We launch in two." Sometimes Rian liked to end his sentences early, make himself sound official. Like a doctor, or a commando, or something.

"Two minutes?" Holiday asked. "Shouldn't we be rushing or something?"

Rian laughed, mussing up Holiday's hair. "Hours, Holi. Two *hours*. I see you got your funny gene from your mother."

"I totally agree, Dad, 'cause you're so not as funny as me or mom," Holiday said.

"You steal all your jokes from holos, Sis," Max pointed out.

"Hey!" Holiday said. "That was only that one time!"

"Got an idea, kids," Sabatha said. "Our ride to the launch pad doesn't leave for another fifteen minutes, and I'm due for my afternoon Fuzz Cola fix. What do you say? It's on the list of approved things we can drink this close to the launch. My treat."

Three minutes later the Storm family was sitting on benches, sipping ice-cold Fuzz Cola from insulated cups. The tiny ice pellets the machine had dispensed were Max's favorite. They kept the Fuzz Cola the coldest, and they melted more slowly than other forms of ice.

A voice came over a loudspeaker. *"Launch of lunar transport* **Moonfire** *in five seconds."*

Max turned to look out the window. The launch pads were over two miles away, but he could still see them well enough.

"Four...three...two...one! Liftoff! This launch brought to you by BioWorld Incorporated Parks and Resorts. BioWorld, where you don't have to be yourself."

The sound of the launch was a low, even rumble. The ground vibrated under the thrust of the *Moonfire*. Max saw it briefly in the distance as it cleared its gantry. He saw a flash of gold that was the surface of the vehicle and the bright glow of wide flame, but mostly he saw a lot of smoke. Even with modern ion engines, nothing could surpass a few hydrogen/oxygen boosters to get you through the lower atmosphere.

"This is going to be..." Holiday said, unable to come up with a word that properly expressed her feelings.

Max tried to slow his pulse. He didn't want to feel excited about the trip. Part of him wanted to please his dad, but another part of him still wanted to be mad—to resent his parents for forcing him to go. This ultracool, hyperawesome, and superexpensive vacation to the moon. Max felt it stirring inside him, the beginnings of being mad for *not being able to get mad*.

Sabatha leaned against Max with her shoulder. "Cheer up. It won't be as bad as all that."

Max tried to smile. "I know."

"Wait till we get into space. You'll forget about anything that's bothering you when you get up there." Sabatha lowered her voice, putting her arm around Max's shoulders, "And just let me know if you start to feel…"

"Mom…"

"Okay, just saying. I'm sure you'll go all tough guy on me and not tell me if anything's wrong, even if you should, because that's why I'm here."

"I know, Mom. I'll be fine." He hoped he wasn't lying. Wouldn't be too long and he'd find out.

Sabatha kissed the top of Max's head. "Of course."

Less than ten minutes later, they were in an enclosed vehicle, on their way to the northeast launch pad array. The land around them was as flat as they could make it, and everything was paved. The road was marked by reflectors and painted lines.

But Max wasn't interested in the road. No, the launch pad array was much more interesting. It consisted of a central tower—gray, industrial and functional. Three gantry arms could rotate out to service launch vehicles. Only one arm was extended. No ships were visible.

"Where are the spaceships?" Holiday asked.

"They're underground," Rian said. "They prep them in huge underground caverns, and then they bring them up when they're ready for launch. You can see they have three gantry arms. That way they can prep up to three vehicles down below. I don't know if it's true, but I heard they can launch ships from all three positions in six minutes."

"Not at the same time?" Holiday asked.

"Probably not a good idea," Rian said. "The danger of a collision would be too great. Most spaceship pilots like some distance between their ship and others."

"Is that ours?" Sabatha asked.

Max's heart sped when he saw what was emerging from the ground, rising up to mate with that one extended gantry arm. The nosecone picked up the sun and scattered it in a burst of brightness that forced him to shield his eyes with his hand. The effect faded, the nose of the ship slowly revealed. The surface was silvered chrome, almost mirror-like. The reflections of the tower and the launch pad structure were liquid against its smooth surface. Below the nose, the body of the spaceship flared, growing in diameter and bulk. Though it most certainly wasn't, the outside of the ship gave all the appearance of being seamless, as if it had been constructed from a single piece of metal, or carved from a single rock and polished to perfection. The body was cylindrical. The ship's four wings appeared, tapered polygons tipped by four ion engines that served as the ship's main propulsion after launch. Mated to the body, down in-between the wings, were four booster modules.

"Oh, it's an Interstellar Javelin X model!" Holiday said.

"What?" Sabatha said. "How did you know that?"

"Episode 154 of *Quantum Girl!!*. She had one just like it. She was using it to take a vacation, but she couldn't use her ship the *Quark Pony!!* because Lady Horror stole it back in episode 153."

"What happened after that?" Sabatha asked.

"Well, Admiral Dead Dread and his girlfriend Madame Sykness hijacked the ship disguised as a space tourists. Quantum Girl!! used an escape pod when Admiral Dead Dread set the ship to self-destruct. She landed on the moon and started her vacation because she assumed that Dead Dread and Sykness had died when her ship exploded. Only they didn't, 'cause they were back in episode 160."

"Oh," Sabatha said, then after a moment of thought, "remind me to limit your holo time okay, sweetie."

"Sure thing, Mom."

"Do you see what it's named?" Rian asked.

Max did. The letters changed colors, so at times, they were difficult to make out. In a vertical stripe running along the length of one side was:

STARBURST

"Okay, I guess that explains the logos," Rian said.

Max could see what his dad was talking about. The *Starburst*'s wings were covered in bold yellow and red candy logos. Each wing had a different logo on it. The fuselage didn't escape the corporate sponsorship either. As they circled the launch pad, the other side of the *Starburst* became visible. There, the logo was even bigger, extending partway onto the nosecone.

"The middle of the ship spins," Holiday said. "I bet that really messes up all those words."

Max thought that, regardless of the logos, the ship was amazing. It was a thing of beauty, and it was about to get its chance to perform.

The ship completed its ascent, mating with the gantry arm. Robotic arms and hoses began to drop from the gantry, seemingly alive as each searched for their connection point on the surface of the ship.

When they had circled the launch pad array once, their vehicle veered away, then stopped cold.

"What…" Max said.

Sabatha gave a little squeak as the ground gave way beneath them. A square seam in the ground had appeared around them, and they continued to sink down into the earth.

"It's an elevator," Holiday said.

Sabatha brushed hair from her eyes. "They could've warned us."

"Mom, don't you remember?" Holiday asked. "It was in the trip documentation."

Sabatha raised an eyebrow at her daughter. "Not all of us have photographic memories, oh prodigy of mine. You're gonna have to remind me of things like that. Help your mother out, okay?"

"Sure thing, Mom!"

The elevator descended for several minutes, the light from the surface fading above them. Then, the elevator stopped. They all exited the vehicle, each carrying their own luggage. One side of the shaft slid open, revealing a wide hallway. There were greeted by two women in white blouses and red, pleated skirts. Hair long, held back with identical red bands, one was blonde and one was brunette. Both of them had flawless skin, glowing in the bright light of the hallway behind them. Though their nametags read LAUNCH PAD HOSTESS TIMA and LAUNCH PAD HOSTESS MEG, Max's mind had already renamed them to Blondie and Brunettie.

"Welcome, family Storm," Blondie said.

"Right this way," Brunettie said.

Their voices were strangely similar. Max's teenage mind and body found them rather attractive, but also creepy. They reminded him of characters out of a sci-fi holo his parents didn't know he'd seen.

The Storm family followed the two launch pad hostesses down the hallway. They stopped at a small conveyor belt that disappeared into the wall. Above the belt was a sign that read:

PLACE ALL LUGGAGE
AND CARRYON ITEMS
ON CONVEYOR BELT.
THANK YOU.

And below that, in smaller print:

Armstrong Space Center is not responsible for luggage

and carryon items placed on this conveyor belt.
Customer assumes all risk.

Blondie turned, smiled, her lips blood red and wet, "Place all luggage and carryon items on conveyor belt. Thank you."

Max wondered if Blondie thought that nobody in the Storm family could read, or if she was just required to say that. He also wondered why her first sentence was missing an article. She'd said "conveyor" instead of "the conveyor."

Max supposed that they were assuming more risk than the loss of their luggage on this little vacation, so he hoisted his suitcase up and watched it disappear into blackness. The rest of his family did the same.

"Right this way," Brunettie said.

Further down the brightly-lit hallway, there was a sign stretching from one wall to another. The letters were lit in blue against a yellow background:

LAUNCH PREP

There were two doors underneath the sign, one on either side of the hallway. Though the hallway continued, curving left, Blondie and Brunettie halted and spun around in unison.

"Men and boys to the left," Blondie said, holding one arm out with her palm upturned.

"Women and girls to the right," Brunettie said, also holding an upturned palm, but to the opposite door.

"We will meet with you, when you have completed all tasks inside," Blondie said.

"Instructions will be given inside," Brunettie said.

Max wondered if Brunettie ever got mad that Blondie always spoke first.

Max and Rian went through the left door. The room was white and completely empty. There was a frosted glass door in front of them. Max was about to try to open the door even though it didn't have any handles, when a deep male voice said, *"You are about to enter level one decontamination. Please remove all articles of clothing and enter the room one at time when the door opens."*

Max looked at his dad, who was already removing his shirt. "Do you want to go first, or do you want me to?" Rian asked.

Max didn't really like either option, but they were the only two, so he said, "I'll go first." Heartbeat racing, his was a nervous anticipation, something he only felt when he was about to do something that he'd never done before, something he didn't really want to do. He had felt a similar feeling two months before, that one night when he was working at Galactic Taco, and those men had come in…

Rian looked a little surprised, but he nodded. "I'll be right behind you."

Max pulled his clothes off, dropping them in the corner on the floor because he didn't know where else to put them. The room wasn't cold, but bumps rose on his arms in spite of that. He walked over to the frosted glass and waited.

The door opened with a hiss of air, and Max stepped through. This room was much smaller than the previous one—more like their shower at home. Again, there was a frosted glass door in front of him. A red circle on the floor was set in the center of the room. On either side of the circle were two sets of elongated grooves. Actually, they were more like holes since they were cut through the floor, and he could only see darkness down there. Above him was a thin pipe with a nozzle on the end.

As soon as the door closed behind him, he felt the immediate press of the room, as if he'd misjudged the space available. The thought that the walls were losing cohesion, about to collapse, was difficult to shake.

He took several deep breaths and tried to think of Nika, but her face wouldn't come to him. He couldn't hold any of his family's faces either. The only thing he could latch onto was that stupid holo show that Holiday watched non-stop, so he stood there, controlling his breathing as best he could, with scenes from *Quantum Girl!!* running through his mind.

The voice spoke, ***"For your personal safety, please close your eyes during this procedure. Decontamination will commence in five seconds."***

Max closed his eyes. He held his breath, because it seemed like a good idea.

There was the groan of liquid through pipes, then it was raining. The liquid was warm, washing over and down his body, draining through the holes in the floor. The liquid started out thick and milky, but eventually ran faster as it became clearer. A minute later, the flow stopped. "Is that all you got?" Max asked the room as he stood there dripping, waiting.

A blast of air entered the room through the holes in the floor. The air was warm as it rippled over him, blowing drops of water into the air, mussing the hair on his head. He was dry in less than a minute. His skin tingled. He gulped in air, almost hyperventilated, and prayed that he could get out of the small, entrapping place.

The door in front of him opened, and he stepped through. Instead of the cold, unfriendly white of the decontamination room, this room was a more inviting, soft shade of blue. It was roomier too, at least twice the size of the first room. The walls were lined with gray lockers and plastic benches. The only break in the wall of lockers was a door on the far side of the room labeled: EXIT.

"You will find a locker with your name on it," the voice that came from everywhere said. ***"Locate it, and remove the contents from inside. Further instructions will follow."***

Max felt exposed, vulnerable, as if the person behind the voice might be watching him.

A quick tour of the lockers revealed one that had his name on a small LED readout. Max slid his thumb across a sensor mounted on the locker door, and it opened with a faint click. Inside were two packages, a pair of white boots, and a spherical object that was clearly a flight helmet. He reached in and pulled everything out. One of the packages was sealed in plastic, and the other was a medium-sized white backpack with red trim. He wasn't sure, but the sealed plastic package looked like it had clothing in it. Excellent. It just wouldn't do to go into space in your birthday suit. He was deciding which to open first when the voice instructed him: ***"The flight suit inside the sealed plastic has been designed specifically for you. It has been customized to your exact dimensions and should fit perfectly. Please break the seal on the plastic and remove the flight suit, along with the other articles of clothing inside."***

Max didn't need such detailed instructions. He was irritated, but his desire to leave his unclothed state behind was paramount. He tore the seal on the plastic and took the flight suit out. There was underwear and socks in there, as well as a shirt, gloves, and a pair of cloth shorts. The shorts were something that one might wear jogging. Everything was white and had the Armstrong Space Center logo on it. He slipped the underwear on, along with the shirt and shorts. Everything fit well, and were high-quality material, soft and snug. He had started unfolding the flight suit when his father entered behind him.

"Nothing like a chemical shower to get you going, is there?" Rian said, moving toward his own locker. "You okay?"

Max knew his father was asking *Did your claustrophobia cripple you back there in that really small decontamination room?* He tried not to be embarrassed, tried not to let his pride get in the way. He had a weakness; it was okay that his parents knew and were concerned.

Anything they said was because they were trying to help.

"I'm fine, Dad," Max said. "Really, it was no big deal."

"Good."

Rian dressed in silence while Max held up his flight suit, letting it unfold. All things considered, it wasn't anything too special. It was made out of some synthetic fiber that didn't wrinkle. It was smooth underneath his fingers. It had weight to it, but the material was thinner than the shirt and shorts he was wearing. The suit was an off-white that was still white. There was a zipper running down the left side of the chest. There was red detailing along the arms, the legs, and the neckline. There were pockets all over. In one of the chest pockets was a set of gloves that could attach to the ends of the sleeves. With the gloves, the boots, and the helmet, Max would be completely covered. There was a circular patch on the left side of the chest that had the Armstrong Space Center logo. On the left sleeve was an American flag, and on the right was a flight patch that designated a mission number of LT-6677. The patch had four symbols on it: a Space Command insignia, a pair of red glasses, a series of markings that looked alien in nature, and a drawing of a cartoon star that was winking. That last was the *Quantum Girl!!* logo, and it had been a given that Holiday would choose it for her quadrant of the flight patch. As for Max's strange symbols—they were in a code language he and a friend had invented when he was younger. They'd used it to pass secret messages in school. Nobody had ever cracked the code. If they ever decoded it, his parents might be mad at him, because the code said, "I'd rather be at Wilderness Camp." Max was beginning to regret his choice to put that on there.

He stepped into the flight suit. It fit perfectly, amazingly so. The sleeves came to the middle of his forearms, but the legs went all the way to the floor. He pulled on the zipper. It went all the way up to his neck, but not in an uncomfortable way like some of the clothes that his mother bought for him. Sitting down on the bench, he pulled his socks on, then the boots. The boots fit well, like everything else. The interesting part was that they felt like they were broken in, as if he'd been wearing them for six months already. The boots zipped at the sides. He tucked his pant legs in, zipped up the boots, then sealed them with three buckles each. When he stood, his ankles felt well-supported. He felt like clomping around, military style. His gloves went on just like the boots—zipped and buckled.

He picked up the helmet and examined it. It was shiny, gleaming pure white, but with a single red stripe running down the center of it. It had a visor that looked white from the outside, but when Max tried it on and lowered the visor, he could still see clearly. When the visor locked in place, the helmet activated. The HUD flashed to life, displaying data in Max's vision—heart rate, body temperature, hydration levels, flight suit integrity. Max played with it for a few minutes, exploring the data available to him, then he took it off. He ran fingers through his hair, hoping it didn't look too bad.

Rian was already fully dressed. He was rummaging through his backpack.

"Why is all your stuff red, Dad?" Max asked. Rian's flight suit was red with white trim—the opposite of Max's.

Rian smiled. "Even if I'm not in the military anymore, I still maintain my rank. Flight Commander always gets the red suit."

"Doesn't that make it easier for the enemy to spot the officers?"

Rian chuckled. "Yeah, it does. That's why you never let them get that close."

Max opened his backpack. It had general supplies, though most of them looked like they were samples and promotional items from various sponsors of the commercial space program. Still, some of the stuff looked like it might be tasty.

"All junk," Rian agreed when he saw Max's face.

"At least I get this cosmic backpack," Max said.

Max was considering dumping the contents of the backpack into his locker. He decided against it in the end; you never knew when stuff like that could be useful. Who knew, maybe he'd have to plug a hole in the side of the ship with some Extra Long Lasting Flavor Jupiter Gum.

"Ready?" Rian asked.

Max nodded, picking up his flight helmet.

"Let's go see the women. I've always wanted to get your mother into a flight suit. I'll bet she looks cosmically hot."

"Dad!" Max protested. "I don't want to hear stuff like that!"

"Can't be helped, Son," Rian said. "Can't be helped at all. I love hot moms. Your hot mom, specifically."

"Dad, this is completely inappropriate!" Max walked to the exit door. It didn't move.

"Hey, it's not my fault she's pretty. You should be happy we find each other attractive. We both have mediocre personalities, so our looks are what we have to rely on. And your mother isn't a slouch in the looks department..."

"Why won't this door open?!?" Max yelled at the ceiling, swearing under his breath. "Anybody up there listening to this?" He knew what his father was doing, and he did appreciate it, but he didn't know if he could take any more. It was just too embarrassing.

"Don't let your mother hear you say things like that."

Max looked over his shoulder, grinning wickedly. "I'll watch my mouth if you will."

Rian laughed. "Got yourself a deal, Max."

"Please take your flight helmet and your official Armstrong Space Center Souvenir backpack with you. Proceed through the exit doorway. Follow the hallway. Your launch pad hostesses will greet you and provide you with further instructions."

Max followed his father out of the room. The hallway curved to the right until it emptied out into another hallway similar to the one they'd been in earlier. Blondie and Brunettie were waiting for them.

"Greetings, men of the Storm family," Blondie said.

"We will wait for the women of the Storm family," Brunettie said.

It was ten more minutes before the women showed up. Rian had tried to strike up conversations with both women, but they just smiled and nodded as if they hadn't really heard him. He gave up after a few minutes.

Sabatha and Holiday arrived. Both their flight suits were white like Max's. The only other major difference he could see was that the zippers on the female uniforms were centered instead of offset.

Sabatha and Holiday twirled, showing off their suits.

Rian whistled and pulled Sabatha to him. Their flight helmets banged against each other as Rian proceeded to kiss his wife in a rather aggressive manner.

Holiday and Max covered their eyes.

"Greetings, women of the Storm Family," Blondie said.

"Your luggage and clothing has been loaded aboard the *Starburst*, and you have clearance to board the vehicle," Brunettie said.

"This is so exciting!" Sabatha squealed.

"You just wait," Rian said. "This is nothing."

Blondie and Brunettie brought them to another stop.

"This is the last restroom stop," Blondie said.

"Once you board the *Starburst*, you will not have a chance to relieve yourself until you have broken free of Earth's gravitational pull."

Nobody had to go.

"Are you sure?" Sabatha asked Holiday and Max.

Both of them denied their need, so they continued on.

The came out into an enormous underground chamber. Max knew immediately that they were under the launch pad. He could see two spaceships being prepped on large platforms. The platforms were attached to the walls on rails that would push the whole assembly toward the surface. Up above, he could see three sets of large bay doors that protected the underground chamber from the launch, but could retract to allow platforms to rise through to the surface.

Blondie and Brunettie led the Storm family toward the center of the chamber, where the central shaft was.

"We will take elevator B to the surface and up to the boarding walkway," Blondie said.

"The elevator ascension and your walk along the boarding walkway will be recorded for documentation purposes, and it will be transmitted to your home, where you can view it at your leisure upon your return," Brunettie said.

Blondie looked at Brunettie as if some of what she'd said had really been Blondie's lines.

Sabatha looked her family over to make sure they were presentable. They were, mostly, and that was good enough.

Elevator B was waiting for them. They all loaded on, including Blondie and Brunettie—who Max was beginning to suspect were androids, even though that technology didn't exist. At least as far as he knew.

They rose through the chamber. The elevator was just a platform with a rail so Sabatha made Holiday hold her hand. Max had to hold Holiday's hand as well. A hatch in the ceiling opened for them. Max felt a rush of anticipation as they broke into the open. Wind immediately buffeted them, though it was gentle and cool. The sun's light was too bright after being underground. Max shielded his eyes. The elevator platform rose along the side of the central tower, enclosed only by wire mesh. They were closer to the *Starburst* than ever before, perhaps only fifty feet away, and it was an awesome thing to behold. Max had been impressed, but he hadn't fully appreciated the sheer height of the spaceship. Rising slowly rectified that, giving him a methodical view of its height. The four ion engines mounted on the ends of the wings were tapered, pointing toward heaven with quiet solitude. Max knew that they were already active, emitting very weak ions streams in order to keep the engines working properly.

The boosters, still connected to the launch pad with segmented hoses, vented clouds of vapor. Other than the hiss of escaping gases, the spaceship made no other sounds. It waited patiently in the moment. There would be excitement soon enough.

Max could see his reflection in the surface of the *Starburst*. This gave him shivers. He found that he was short of breath and more than a little adrenalized.

They were halfway up, when Max felt his father's hand on his shoulder. Max couldn't stop himself from looking at his dad and smiling.

"She's pretty, isn't she," Rian said.

Max had to agree. The *Starburst*'s surface was polished like a mirror. *How did they do that?* "Prettiest I've seen."

Holiday said, "Not as pretty as the *Quark Pony!!*, but I do like it. It's shiny."

As they approached the pinnacle of their ascent, Max could see what he hadn't been able to see from the ground—that there were windows located just below the nosecone.

"Will we be able to look through that when we launch?" Max asked.

He'd directed the question at his dad, but Holiday—she of the perfect memory and the desire to demonstrate it at every given opportunity—answered, "No. They have the cockpit shield retracted. The shield has to be in place for launch. It's a safety precaution against debris in Earth's atmosphere."

"Oh," said Max. He supposed it made sense, but looking directly through the cockpit window might've been interesting. He supposed he could pull up some sort of video feed in his helmet during the launch.

The elevator slowed to a stop. They were looking down the lower section of the gantry arm, which provided a flat bridge leading directly to the *Starburst* entry door. Max's heart skipped a beat when he saw that the door was open.

The invitation was clear.

Blondie and Brunettie stepped off the elevator.

"Congratulations, Storm family, you are about to embark on a unique journey, on one of the most advanced spaceships in existence," Blondie said.

"Please proceed to the *Starburst* entry door, where we will assist you with boarding," Brunettie said.

The Storm family walked side-by-side, each holding their flight helmets underneath their arms. Blondie and Brunettie followed a few steps behind.

Max was grinning like an idiot, but in that moment, he didn't care. He didn't care that he was supposed to still be upset about the whole situation. What he cared about was the mad racing of his pulse and the giddy feeling circling his chest. He'd never felt anything like that, except perhaps when he'd first met Nika. Really though, this was different. This was more intense. Somewhat scary too, but his parents would never put him in danger, so any potential fear he might have had was washed away in a wave of naked anticipation.

"This is all being holoed," Holiday said. "You really want that ridiculous smile to be captured for all time."

"At least I can stop smiling, Sis. You're stuck with that face, so what are we gonna do about that?"

"Hey!"

Max laughed, and since he was walking beside his sister, he bumped her flight helmet with his hip. She glared back, but he could tell it wasn't malicious. More like a "I wish I had a comeback to that" gaze instead of an "I'm trying to set you on fire with my mind" stare.

They stopped a few feet from the entry door. Max saw that his mother had a tight grip on her husband's hand. He knew why—heights weren't her thing. He looked down and saw what she was worried about. Being almost three hundred feet in the air with only a few inches of metal keeping you up did give a person a sense of the precarious. Luckily, the gantry was solid; what little wind there was didn't have any effect.

Rian was whispering in her ear.

"I'm okay," Sabatha said. "Let's just get inside this thing so I don't have to see how high up we are. Then I can concentrate on not thinking how high up we're *about to be.*"

Max looked through entry doorway. He saw a narrow floor that they could step onto directly from the gantry walkway.

Blondie and Brunettie moved to the entry door.

"We will assist you as you enter the *Starburst,*" Blondie said.

"I will perform a brief integrity check of your flight suit," Brunettie said.

This was more a formality than anything. The entire Storm family had taken a class to prepare them for the trip. They'd all had to pass tests. Plus, Rian had several thousand flight hours, and would be performing his own set of checks once they got onboard.

Brunettie inspected each of them in turn, checking for tears or rips in their flight suits, as well as checking the seal between their gloves and their sleeves, and between their boots and legs of their flight suits. Each of them entered in turn, Rian first, then Holiday. Sabatha went next, and finally Max. Before he entered, Max turned to Brunettie, and said, "Do you always talk second?"

"No," Brunettie said.

"Yes," Blondie said at the same time, frowning.

Max smiled.

Brunettie smiled back, and there was something real about it. All the previous smiles had been scripted, all part of the act. That last one had been genuine.

To seal it, Brunettie leaned forward and planted a soft kiss on Max's cheek.

Max blushed and turned, stepping through the entry door before he got more embarrassed. His hands were shaking, and it wasn't from the excitement of impending spaceflight.

Behind him he could hear Blondie and Brunettie arguing. They stopped suddenly. Blondie's voice was suddenly broadcast through the interior of the spaceship. *"Launch pad hostess Tima confirming passenger entry. Authorization code Alpha Romeo Alpha November. I am closing* Starburst *port forward entry door."*

Max turned just in time to see the door slide closed. There was a series of loud clicks as the door sealed.

The reply that came a second later could be heard throughout the ship as well. *"This is Armstrong Flight Control. Port forward entry door closure confirmed. Thanks for showing our passengers the way. We'll take it from here."*

Max was comforted by the very real voice behind the reply. He'd expected a computer.

"This way, Max," Rian said, standing at a white metal ladder that led up into the cockpit.

"Can't I look around?" Max asked.

"There'll be time for that later. Right now we need to get seated and secured so they can clear us for launch."

Max sighed, but began to climb. It was awkward to do while holding his flight helmet, but he managed.

The ladder passed up through a hatch that Max crawled up through as quickly as he could. Sabatha took his hand and helped him up. He looked around. They were in the cockpit. There wasn't a lot of extra room—barely enough to stand when the spaceship was vertical on its launch pad. Max looked up. He could see through the cockpit window above him. The massive gantry arm partly blocked his view of bright blue sky above. Max wasn't the tallest person, but his head was halfway to the flight controls. On the floor—well, the wall when the *Starburst* was oriented vertically—were four chairs. They were very thickly padded, colored a bland gray that looked like it was designed to take abuse as opposed to entice a person to sit in them. They looked complicated and had tons of readouts, buckles, lights, and movable parts, as if they had perhaps once been used as torture devices and had been repurposed into the commercial space program.

"Max, let's help your mother and sister get seated," Rian said. "Holi, you're first because despite what Max said, you're the prettiest girl I know…next to your mother of course."

"Don't listen to your daddy, honey," Sabatha said. "He knows you're the prettiest. His judgment's off."

Rian held up his hands. "Hey, I didn't design your flight suit, babe. Not my fault."

"Oh, do you like it?" Sabatha asked, batting her eyelashes and tossing her hair in mock slow motion.

Max groaned. Would his parent's incessant flirting never end? Was it possible to be newlyweds after seventeen years of marriage? Holiday sighed, reached up, and climbed into her seat without anybody's help. And she did it with one hand since the other hand was holding her flight helmet.

Which of course wasn't really necessary since there were grooves in the floor of the cockpit that allowed one to climb to their seat.

"Show off," Max said.

"Nice to see those gymnastics lessons were good for something other than you being able to tumble out of bed and do cartwheels in the hallway back home," Sabatha said as she handed Max her flight helmet and began to climb to the front row.

Max followed her up, handing his mother her helmet back, then took his own seat. Rian was tall enough that he could check everybody out and help them fasten their harnesses. As soon as Rian had everybody secure, he climbed into his own seat, which was the front left one. Max found his seat extremely comfortable, like it had been designed, or at least adjusted, specifically for his body. The armrests were at just the right place. There were handles at the end of the armrests that he could grab onto. There was a small touchpad at each hand, as well as several buttons near his fingers. None of them seemed to be active, because nothing happened when he pushed several of them.

Max looked over at Holiday. *Now* who was grinning like an idiot? He decided not to tease her. Why risk bringing her down when she was clearly having the time of her life? There was something to be said for cordial sibling relations.

Rian was tapping away on one of the control panels. Max couldn't really move with his harness secured, but he could see lots of flashing lights, readouts, buttons and levers. It all looked properly complicated.

"Helmets on," Rian said. "I'm about to signal Flight Control that we're in place and ready to go."

Max put his helmet on, but left the visor up. The helmet connected with the neckline of his flight suit, hooking on and locking in place. With the helmet locked, it was difficult to turn his head to the side, however, he could see enough to confirm that Holiday had her helmet on properly. Max lowered his visor. Status displays burst to life in front of him. He pulled up data on the rest of the family, seeing what he could see. Everybody's heart rates were up. That was not unexpected. Holiday and his mother were breathing faster, shallower than usual. The only one who was completely calm was his father. His readings were so normal, it was almost as if he were asleep. Max began to feel a little trapped inside the helmet, so he activated the internal air circulator. The air rushing across his face helped.

"This is lunar transport *Starburst* to Armstrong Flight Control, Captain Rian Storm at the helm."

"Roger, Captain Storm," came the response. *"Glad to have you and your family with us today. Always nice to have a veteran at the helm."*

"Veteran makes me sound old, Control, but I'll let it slide today. Internal systems are secure. Passengers are secure. Pilot is secure. Confirm and authorize prelaunch system check."

"Roger that. Confirmed and authorized. System check initiated. Launch clock is set at fifteen minutes. Mark."

A counter immediately appeared in Max's vision. It was running down toward zero. Max's breathing sped up. This was it. Unless the prelaunch system check found a problem, the *Starburst* would launch in less than fifteen minutes.

Max focused on the fact that his dad was at the helm to calm himself. Ultimately, the launch was computer controlled, but the pilot did need to monitor the status of the launch and be prepared to intervene in case of emergency. If necessary, Rian could take the *Starburst* into space under his guidance. Max had never been more thankful that his father had spent time in the Space Command.

"How you doing, Max?" Sabatha asked.

"I'm fine," Max replied. It was mostly true. His unease and his excitement were at war, and he was caught in the middle. He felt vaguely sick and wondered if he was going to throw up unexpectedly. That probably wasn't a good thing to do during launch.

"Holiday, you doing okay?" Sabatha asked.

No answer.

Sabatha's voice held some concern now. "Holiday, what is it?"

There was another pause, but then Holiday's voice came in an embarrassed whisper, "I have to use the restroom."

[CHAPTER EIGHT]

WHAT HAPPENED DURING THE LAUNCH OF THE *STARBURST*

"T-minus sixty seconds. System check complete. Launch Control confirms all systems are go."

"Roger that, Control," Rian said. *"Starburst* confirms all systems are go."

"You have all the fuel you need. Hoses are retracted. Gantry retraction initiated. Six seconds till clearance. Closing cockpit shield."

Max grabbed the handles on his armrests. His hands felt sweaty in his gloves, and his breathing was on the verge of slipping out of his control.

"Relax, Max," Sabatha said. "We're all here with you."

Max gritted his teeth and shut his eyes, tried to focus. Oh, it would feel good to take his helmet off. Fighting that urge, he grabbed the handles tighter.

"Gantry is clear. Cockpit shield is secured. We see an open skyway above for you."

"Glad to hear it," Rian said.

"Cabin pressure is nominal. T-minus forty seconds."

Max forced an image of Nika into his mind, let her pretty face calm him, focus him.

"Breathe, Max," Sabatha said.

"I *am* breathing," Max grunted. He blew out a breath, fogging up the inside of his visor temporarily.

81

"T-minus thirty seconds. Initiating ion engine ramp-up."

The *Starburst* began to vibrate.

"Roger, Control," Rian said. "I see four streams. Wait. Um, got a warning light on engine four."

Max didn't like the sound of *warning light*. His father didn't seem worried, but still...

"Confirmed. Looks like you got an overzealous engine on your hands. The Javelin X models try to scare you while they're running their ramp-up calibrations. T-minus twenty seconds."

"Roger, Control. Alarm is cleared. My console's all green. I'll just sit back and enjoy the ride now."

"Good idea. Storm family, prepare for launch. T-minus fifteen seconds."

Max opened his eyes, forcing his breathing to be normal. He mostly succeeded. Now if only his heart would stop pounding so loud and so fast; it felt like it was going to burst right through his chest. He fought off the temptation to put his hand over his heart, as if that could keep it from punching through. His mom would probably think he was having a heart attack.

"Igniters active. T-minus ten seconds."

This.

Was.

It!

"We are go for booster engine start."

Hydrogen and oxygen had begun to flow into the booster combustion chambers. Then came the word that Max had been anticipating, dreading:

"Ignition!"

The *Starburst* shuddered as its boosters exploded to life. Max's helmet immediately compensated for painful noise levels that filled the cockpit. He felt as if the spaceship was moving upward, but then was suddenly pulled back. Technically, there were still six seconds to go before T-minus zero. These final seconds allowed the ion engines and boosters to reach full thrust. Additionally, the *Starburst's* thrust caused the launch pad to flex since it was still secured in place.

There was no confirmation of T-minus zero from Armstrong Launch Control, but Max felt the synchronized explosions that blew the bolts keeping the *Starburst* tethered to the launch pad.

Six million pounds of thrust from the boosters, along with another million from the ion engines, pushed the *Starburst* upward. Max felt his body pushed down into his seat. It was similar to the pressure he'd felt in the ITS pod, though that whole experience had been quiet and smooth. This was loud and shaky. This was a whole different game. This was real power.

"We've cleared the tower," Rian said, his voice calm.

"Whoohooo!" Holiday said.

Max laughed, and it felt good, even if it was the most nervous laugh he'd ever emitted. It was hard to believe this happened so many times a day. Families just like his took vacations just like the one they were taking.

"Looking good, Starburst. Rolling to exit trajectory."

Max used his helmet to pull up camera views of the launch. There was one looking down the length of the spaceship. The feed shook. He could see the massive cloud they trailed out below them. As they began their roll to a new angle of ascent, Max could see less and less, so he switched to a ground camera. It was pretty. The *Starburst* was a needle headed into the sky on a pillar of flame and smoke, gleaming in the sun, ion engines firing almost-invisible jets of blue.

"Oh, Rian! This is so…intense!" Sabatha said. "It's amazing!"

"Whoohooo!" Holiday said again.

"T-plus thirty. Ten thousand and two," Rian said. *Ten thousand feet. 2.0 Mach.*

The play-by-play wasn't necessary since Max could see all the vital statistics in his helmet. Nevertheless, his father's voice was comforting.

"Throttling down for fifteen seconds," came the announcement from Launch Control.

The buzz and shaking that was rattling Max's teeth together changed pitch slightly as the boosters and ion engines decreased their thrust in order to prevent undue stress on the spaceship while it was still in the lower atmosphere.

Fifteen seconds later, *"Throttling up."*

"Roger," Rian said. "Throttle up."

The *Starburst* seemed to leap forward. It didn't really, but it seemed like it did.

"All systems nominal. Retracting cockpit shield. Take a look around and enjoy the view."

The shield retracted. Max looked forward and saw blue sky, but he could see something else.

Stars.

Brighter and clearer than ever, twinkling against the fading blue.

"Beautiful," Sabatha said.

Max could hear his mother whispering something. He thought she might be praying.

"T-plus sixty seconds. Thirty-five thousand and five." *Thirty-five thousand feet and 5.0 Mach.*

"Booster engines at optimal thrust. Ion engines nominal."

Rian's voice took an air of solemnity as he said, "Roger, go at throttle up."

Rian had told Max the story of one tragic space flight, where those had been the second to last words that the astronauts onboard had uttered, unfortunately quickly followed by their last words: "Uh oh."

The quest for space had not been without loss of life. The concept of casual travel from the Earth to Luna hadn't been conceivable back in those days. Now, it was so common that nobody thought about it much—Max certainly hadn't until his parents had forced him to prepare for this vacation.

The *Starburst* continued to accelerate, continued to rise through the atmosphere, continued to adjust its angle of ascension. Horizontal acceleration was more important than vertical acceleration when it came to escaping the Earth's gravitational pull. The course *Starburst* took had been designed months previously, and the onboard computers were in constant communication with Armstrong Flight Control to ensure that the course was followed precisely. As a precaution, the *Starburst* also took its own readings, constantly comparing them with the data it expected. Minor course corrections were natural. These were crucial in the lower atmosphere where wind could still affect its flight path. The higher the spaceship rose, the less necessary these types of corrections were since there were fewer factors that were capable of interfering with its movement.

"T-plus two minutes. Standby for booster engine shutdown."

A second later the noise level and vibrations inside the *Starburst* decreased. The boosters had shutdown, completely drained of fuel; they would not be usable for the rest of the journey.

"Booster shutdown."

Rian's voice was as calm as ever, "Roger, Control. Booster power down confirmed."

"Takeoff looked perfect. Trajectory looks perfect. Should be smooth sailing from here, Starburst. Just sit back and enjoy the ride for the next few minutes."

Max closed his eyes and allowed his breathing to slow. This was something he was finally capable of as the sound in the cabin began to fade and the ride became calmer.

"Oh, it's so pretty," Sabatha said. Max thought she might be crying. She did that sort of thing when she was extremely happy or overwhelmed.

"What do you think, kids?" Rian asked.

"It's not bad," Max said. Couldn't show too much excitement or his parents might think he was starting to enjoy himself. He thought about calling Nika to let her know he was okay, but decided against it. It would be expensive and they still had some distance to go before they'd escape Earth's gravitational pull.

"Not bad?!" Holiday exclaimed. "You're crazy! That was the most cosmic thing I have ever done! That was even better than episode 200!"

Episode 200 of *Quantum Girl!!* was Holiday's favorite fifty minutes of holo she'd ever seen. It was the episode where Quantum Girl!! had found out that she was a space princess, in line to become a space queen, thus setting up the major plotline that would hopefully come to its conclusion in the upcoming series finale. Holiday had seen episode 200 in excess of three hundred times. That didn't count the number of times she'd replayed it all in her head. Her parents thought she watched too much holo.

If only they knew.

The constant acceleration was beginning to wear on Max. In their preparation for this trip, they'd done a little bit of time in a simulator to prepare them for close to ten minutes of acceleration. Max was glad he'd gone through the training—even if he had been a pain about it to his parents—because he didn't know if he would've been able to handle it otherwise. The handles on the armrests helped since he was able to use them to anchor his arms in place. The acceleration was kept at around three gravities, so it took three times as much effort to move as it normally would have back on Earth.

Space travel was common, but that didn't negate the laws of physics. A certain amount of force was required over a certain period of time in order to push any spaceship out of a planet's gravity pull. Since the human body was fragile, there was a limit to how fast it could be accelerated without damage or undue discomfort. They had determined that $3g$ was the highest rate of acceleration allowable. $2g$

had been considered as an alternative, since that was easier on passengers, but the amount of hydrogen/oxygen fuel necessary at the lower acceleration would've required additional booster engines. The ion engines had enough thrust to push a spaceship up into orbit and beyond, but they took their time getting a ship up to speed unless they were pulsed, and nobody wanted to wait that long. They found that passengers preferred getting into space faster and were willing to endure the higher gravity forces for the first part of the flight. The acceleration forces were extremely popular among the thrill-seeker crowd. Rollercoaster junkies loved it.

Everything would've been a lot easier if reality would just have caught up with science fiction and invented inertial dampeners. Then crushing your passengers under ungodly acceleration forces wouldn't have been a problem. Quantum Girl!!'s spaceship had inertial dampeners. How hard could it be?

"I really need to go," Holiday said.

Max looked over. Holiday was trying to cross her legs. It wasn't possible due to the harness though.

"Honey, if anybody knows how much longer it is till you can get up, it's you," Sabatha said, pausing for a moment. "So, how long till we can get up? I need to go too."

Rian sighed.

"Not my fault, babe," Sabatha said. "Sometimes we have to pee when we get excited."

"I'm not hearing this," Max said.

"How much longer, Holi?" Sabatha asked again.

"Five minutes."

"Ok, it's gonna be close."

"Mom!" Max protested. Sometimes he wished he didn't know his parents. They were determined to talk about things that 1) embarrassed him or 2) made him uncomfortable or 3) were some thoroughly diabolical mix of 1 and 2 that made him wish it was possible to instantly catch blindness and deafness. The thing was, he found himself more embarrassed and uncomfortable when it was just his family present than he did when there were others around. When he was with Nika or his other friends, he could roll his eyes and shrug, give his friends the *I'm not related to them* look and go on his way. When it was just him and his parents, there was no escape. And lack of escape had never been more real than it was while strapped into a spaceship with his family.

Max made a note to memorize the location of the escape pods once he could get out of his seat.

"Well, Starburst, *it's been a pleasure to get you on your way,"* came the voice of Flight Control. Max thought it sounded farther away than it had before, but that wasn't possible. *"Standby for ion engine throttle down. You'll be able to breathe easier in a second."*

The throttle down on the ion engines didn't resound through the cockpit, but Max could feel the immediate effect. He could take deeper breaths, and it was easier to move. He relaxed his muscles. Oh, that felt good.

Sabatha and Holiday both sighed loudly.

"Roger, Control, throttle down confirmed," Rian said.

"Starburst, you're approaching Earthspace perimeter. You ready to take the reins and let us take the next bird up?"

"Affirmative."

"Glad to hear it. Handoff in five…four…three…two…one. Mark."

There wasn't any noticeable change as primary control of the *Starburst* was transferred to the cockpit. Max could see his father's hands on the controls.

"Handoff confirmed. I have control."

"Roger that. We confirm Earthspace exit. Starburst, *you are cleared for direct transit to Luna. Good luck and Godspeed."*

"Thanks, Control. It's been a pleasure working with you."

"Can we get up now?" Sabatha asked.

"Can we take our helmets off?" Max asked at the same time.

Rian's fingers danced over the controls. "Yes, you can all take your helmets off. We have complete atmospheric integrity through the whole ship. You can release your harnesses, but be careful. I need thirty seconds to get the fuselage rotation up to speed or you'll all float away back there."

"I'm already floating, dear," Sabatha said. "Bladders don't care if they're weightless or not."

Max groaned, and the sinking feeling in his stomach wasn't his claustrophobia, but the very real possibility he'd be groaning his way through the entire stupid vacation.

[CHAPTER NINE]

WHAT HAPPENED AS MAXIMILLION EXPLORED THE SPACESHIP

Max felt much better after taking his helmet off. Unfortunately, weightlessness was a strange feeling that wasn't doing much to put his mind and body at ease about the whole trip. As big as the ship was, it was still an enclosed space, and the inability to get his body to stay in one place compounded the problem. He couldn't get still. He couldn't focus. It made for a nervous, unhappy Max.

The fact that Holiday and Sabatha—both far happier now that they had relieved themselves—were already playing zero-*g* tag didn't help.

There was a pole that ran directly down the center of the ship. Along the length of the pole, handles were placed at regular intervals. A person could use the pole and handles to pull their body between each section of the ship. In the wider portions of the ship, there were ladders that extended from the pole to the interior of the hull, allowing a person to pull themselves outward. It took some coordination to transition from the center pole to the ladders, since if the fuselage was rotating, then so were the ladders.

Max held onto the center pole and tried to steady himself. He wanted to explore the ship; he was just going to take his time. No need to rush. They had three days in space.

Behind the cockpit—Max would've thought of it as *below* the cockpit earlier, back when they were on the launch pad—was a narrow walkway that served to separate the cockpit from the rest of the

91

spaceship. There were lots of compartments in that area, most of them containing gear and supplies related to boarding or exiting the spaceship. The primary reason for this was that the next section contained three escape pods and the airlock, which could be used for docking with space stations and other spaceships. The escape pod doors were circular, with small viewing windows. Max peered in one and immediately felt like he couldn't breathe. The inside of the pod was clearly designed for two people, but he didn't see how he could ever get into one unless his life was in mortal danger. There were two long mattresses in there. It looked like the two occupants would be harnessed in a reclining position. Escape pods had very few controls. Occupants were expected to lie down and rely on the computer to get them safely…somewhere. Max didn't know much beyond that except that the escape pods were programmed to land on both Earth and Luna. However, their range was limited. If an escape pod was used too far away from either of those planetary bodies, the occupants were unlikely to be rescued.

Happy thoughts such as that were thoughts Max was best not having.

The airlock door was rectangular and bigger than the escape pod doors. It also had vast quantities of warning text all around it. Max found that interesting.

Max pulled his body along the pole, past the escape pod bay, down into the sleeping quarters. Here, the interior of the ship widened so that almost all of the *Starburst's* fifty foot diameter was available. This area rotated to provide artificial gravity. He had to look away often because watching the beds, recliners and chairs spin made him dizzy.

There were four beds, two recliners and two chairs. The beds were simple metal and mattress combinations. There were no sheets, but Max could see the straps that held a person in place. It was always safest to strap yourself down when you weren't planning on moving for a while. That way, if anything unexpected happened, you didn't float away and bounce around the ship like a human pinball. Not a good way to wake up.

He was looking forward to lying down and closing his eyes. The stress of launch and his continued unease, along with a fading adrenaline high, had left him drained and tired. His arm muscles ached from tensing them during the launch.

The next section was the galley. It was a continuous row of three-foot-high compartments set in a ring around the interior circumference of the spaceship. A few feet away from the compartments were various devices necessary to prepare food. Some of their food would need to be heated, so there was a microwave. Some of it needed to be hydrated, so there was a device for that too. Max didn't know what any of the other devices were. No doubt his father did, since he did most of the actual cooking at home. Sabatha could cook just fine when she was in the mood, but she was definitely a "let's try that new restaurant" type of woman. Max preferred the comfort of eating at home. Holiday was more like her mother, always wanting something new and exciting.

Next to the galley was a series of small booths, with tables and soft benches. The benches had seatbelts, and the table had all sorts of slots, straps, and magnetized surfaces useful for keeping a person's food down while he or she was eating it. Solid foods weren't as much of a problem as the liquids were.

A part of Max was trying to figure out how he could arrange for Holiday to spill her drink pouch at their next mealtime. He'd figure something out. He was also working on something to get his father back for all that talk about how hot Max's mom was. And he couldn't forget his mother and her bladder talk. They all needed to suffer a little—his parents because, well that was obvious, and his sister because…well she was his little sister, and a little sister needed some teasing from her older brother to keep the sibling relationship healthy.

It was his duty.

The next area beyond the galley was for recreation and exercise. It wasn't separated from the galley via a partition like most of the sections were. There were several couches with flat panel consoles as well as IIU headsets and connection jacks. There were four trampolines, spaced evenly around the circumference of the interior. Max figured one could either bounce between two of the trampolines, going back and forth across the ship, or if they were skilled, bounce between all four, tracing a square inside the circle of the ship's cross-section. Holiday, with her gymnastics training, could probably make use of all four. Max wasn't quite sure how a person was supposed to use the trampolines and dodge the center pole. There were also two treadmills. Each of the Storm family would have to spend at least thirty minutes a day using the exercise equipment. The human body didn't do well in low gravities for long periods of time since muscles didn't have to do a lot of the routine work they normally did. Exercise helped to prevent muscle atrophy, even for trips that only lasted a few days.

The pole that Max held onto came to an abrupt end in a wall that prevented his progress further into the rear of the spaceship. There were several hatches in the wall, and they were all labeled:

REACTOR / LIFE SUPPORT
AUTHORIZED PERSONNEL ONLY

Max wondered if he could get his father to let him back there. The doors were keyed, and only the ship captain would be able to open them.

Really, it was probably cramped back there, what with the ion engine reactor and the ship's electrical systems, which included lights, computer control, navigation, and life support.

Looking back through the ship, sighting down the center pole, Max could see through the entire ship. Though it was possible to completely seal each section of the ship off from each other—there were hatches that closed the openings for the center pole—he had a clear line of sight all the way to the back wall of the cockpit. Every couple of seconds, he caught sight of either Holiday or Sabatha as they practiced moving through the ship.

Max wondered if he could make it from this side to the other side without touching anything. If he held the pole and put his legs against the reactor compartment wall, he could bend his knees and use them to push off. It wouldn't be easy. Since this section of the ship was rotating, the ladders used to transition from the pole to the sides of the interior would be moving obstacles. Also, he'd have to launch his body perfectly straight. Finally, there was the totally unpredictable nature of his mother and sister. His dad probably wasn't a problem since he was still in the cockpit, not about to pass up the opportunity to pilot a spaceship again.

Max was tired, but the challenge of what he was going to attempt served both to focus his mind and to distract him from his claustrophobia.

He briefly wondered if he should go get his helmet. Might be safer that way. Still, as long as he didn't go too fast, he didn't think he'd be in any danger.

Max took a couple of steady breaths, bent his legs, then pushed off, releasing the pole at the same time. He straightened his body out, paralleling the pole. He was floating fairly straight, though he'd accidently put his body into a minor spin, the opposite direction from the rest of the interior. It was a dizzying effect, but he was happy enough to be free floating that he wasn't affected. He sailed by the first ladder with several feet to spare, over recreation and the galley, then the second ladder, which he only avoided by tucking his knees. This had the unfortunate effect of causing him to tumble slightly. When he passed through to the sleeping quarters, he was spinning on two axes. He kept his arms close to his body to avoid hitting anything.

"Hey!" Holiday exclaimed as he passed through, narrowly missing her.

"Show off!" Sabatha said, laughing.

Max tumbled through the escape pod bay, desperately hoping he could get his feet around. He swung his arms over his head trying to slow his rate of rotation. It worked, and his feet touched the cockpit wall, his knees bending to absorb his momentum. Max grinned, breathing heavily.

Maybe a vacation in space wouldn't be so bad after all.

[CHAPTER TEN]

WHAT HAPPENED ON THE WAY TO LUNA

As it turned out, it could be difficult to keep yourself from getting bored in space. The interior of the ship was filled with entertainment that they all had back on Earth. Sure, the lack of gravity thing was a nice twist, but it also made a lot of things more inconvenient. Sleeping, eating, using the restroom—all of these normal activities were major undertakings. For Max, the worst was using the restroom, since it involved numerous hoses and pumps and pouches and things of that nature. Baths and showers weren't possible in the spaceship. Instead, they all used the space-travel-approved equivalent of infant wipes to cleanse their skin. It was effective, but it never really left any of them feeling clean. Holiday was the only one who complained about this out loud though. Nobody was surprised; she took at least three showers a day back on Earth. On the spaceship, she had requisitioned a box of wipes and wouldn't put it down. She claimed she felt dirty all the time. Max thought she was crazy. After all, they'd been on the ship less than two days, and the interior of the ship was contaminant-free. She couldn't be that dirty. Max suspected she was most upset about her hair going unwashed. *Of course*, there were chemicals onboard that could take care of that, and *of course*, Holiday had refused to let them touch her hair. She was very particular about the brand of shampoo she used. Not willing to risk the shopping centers at Luna One not carrying her preferred brand, she had brought her own supply, a significant portion of her luggage taken up by economy-sized bottles of Sunspot shampoo and conditioner.

Max's suitcase was half empty, the other half filled with clothes and toiletries, a datapad that he probably wouldn't use, and his drawing supplies, consisting of exactly one drawing pad, two pens, and two pencils.

Despite his brief bout with optimism about how much fun it would be to continually zip through the spaceship, weightless and out of control, Max found that his initial melancholy was settling back in. His mind reminded him that he hadn't wanted to come on this vacation in the first place. Even though there were aspects of it that were ultimately cosmic, these didn't end up overshadowing the fact that he was drifting in a tin can through an infinite vacuum, when he should have been back on Earth at Wilderness camp with his very pretty girlfriend—the one who had kissed him rather thoroughly before he left. He saw now that she'd done it on purpose. It hadn't been that she was going to miss him so much that she'd needed to put all her passion into one last kiss, but that she wanted him to realize what he was missing. She wanted him to remember. She wanted him to ache to come back to her.

Well, it had worked.

Some part of Max was actually mad about that—that he could be manipulated so easily—but most of that was redirected toward his parents. Oh sure, he loved them and all that, but it didn't stop him from pouting in a way that would've made Holiday proud if she hadn't been slightly irritated at him for being such a party pooper.

It took about a day before Max tired of the ship and what little new entertainment it had to offer him. One would've thought that space would've been pretty interesting to look at. As Sabatha sometimes said: *Wrong-o*. Space was booooooring.

It was boring because it was mostly filled with lots and lots of space instead of extremely interesting things like planets, stars, comets, meteors, pulsars, quasars, meteors, asteroid fields, gas clouds, black holes, and wormholes. Oh sure, those things existed, but they were really far away and took a really long time to get to. Instead, they were headed to the closest piece of lifeless rock that humanity had found it could make habitable. Next to Luna, Mars was the next likely candidate for a tourist spot. And at least its surface had color. Unlike Luna, which was just a gray piece of dirt against a black background. They had a ways to go before anybody would be sipping margaritas on a Martian desert though. There had been several missions. And several accidents. On one of the first missions, four out of five crew members went crazy and started doing very bad things to the one crew member that wasn't. They'd made it to Mars, but the landing they performed wasn't the one that the space agencies had planned. Space agencies preferred landings with fewer explosions. That had not been a good year for the space program. Nobody liked to hear that long space voyages drove people insane.

The viewing windows in the G-ring were actually monitors that projected a feed from cameras on the surface of the *Starburst*. This way, the illusion of zero movement within the G-ring was maintained. If you wanted to get a clearer view of space, you had to at least go to the escape pod bay. The view was better in the cockpit though since the window there was larger. Sometimes Luna was visible right in front of the *Starburst*, and at other times, the Earth was. So, sometimes the view was actually interesting. The rest of the time, all Max could see was a field of stars. Sure, the stars were much brighter and clearer without Earth's atmosphere to get in the way, but when it came down to it, they were just glowing pinpricks of light that were all millions, if not trillions, of light years away. Really, how entertaining was that?

In Max's opinion, not very.

If that was the resentful child in him, then so be it.

Instead of spending time with his family, Max spent a good part of the second day strapped to his bed, doing his best to draw. He had several problems that hindered him at the start, all of them feeding his bad mood. First, he hadn't wanted to be anywhere in the G-ring since the rest of the family was there, doing all their family-togetherness stuff that he didn't want to do, so he went to the cockpit and strapped himself in. It wasn't the most comfortable chair. He liked to draw with his pad resting on his lap, with just pen on paper and his hand holding the end of the pen. This didn't work well without gravity because the pad kept floating off his lap. The second problem was that without gravity, his pen didn't work well. There was no force to push ink down onto the paper. And when he was able to get a small amount of ink onto the page, the paper didn't wick the ink down beyond the surface. It made for art of a different type than Max usually drew. When he closed his pad and opened it back up there were splotches everywhere, as if dozens of ink blob bugs had been squashed between the pages. He finally surrendered, switched to one of his pencils and went back to the G-ring, strapped himself to a chair, did his best to ignore his family—who were laughing and playing some magnetic dice game at one of the tables—and put pencil to paper. The only thing he could think of to draw was Nika. That wasn't good. Thinking about her was just this side of torture since he couldn't be near her—in fact, was getting less near her by the nanosecond.

When he wasn't drawing or reclining on his bed, he sat on one of the couches and watched his sister show off her gymnastics skills. It turned out that she was good on the trampolines—as he thought she would be. She could even make use of all four trampolines. It looked difficult. Oh, he'd probably been told all the intricacies of the G-ring and what was and wasn't possible in the artificial gravity, but he either hadn't been paying attention or he'd forgotten. Because the G-ring's gravity *was* artificial, a jump didn't bring a person down in the same place like it did back on Earth. Instead, a person would travel in an arc, landing in a different spot along the circumference of the G-ring. This was one reason why it was important for the Storm family to keep their feet on the floor at all times. Even the smallest jump could throw a person off-balance.

Holiday started holding onto the center pole, crouching on it with her feet and her hands. It was almost impossible to do this without moving, and her fingers were white against the pole as she struggled to keep her body from floating away. Around her, the G-ring rotated. She waited till the trampolines were where she wanted them, then she pushed her lower body away from the pole. Her body began to spin, and she tucked, spinning faster. At the last possible second, she uncoiled, her feet hitting a trampoline that had been underneath her when she'd jumped. She countered any angular momentum the trampoline had wanted to impart to her, bouncing back toward the center pole. She grabbed it with both hands, using it to pull her body around. Her feet blurred as she swung around the pole, releasing, hitting a second trampoline, bouncing straight up toward the center again. When she grabbed the pole that time, she brought her body in close, increasing her rate of rotation. When she released the pole, her body was flipping quickly, but her movement toward the side of the spaceship was slow. It took her at least ten seconds, and in that time, she did so many flips that Max lost track—at least twenty he thought. She uncoiled at the last moment, hitting the trampoline in a sitting position, grabbing fast, this time allowing the trampoline to drag her with it as it rotated. Lifting her body using only her arms, her hands grasping the sides of the trampoline, she put her feet on the surface of the trampoline and pushed off. From Max's perspective, it was a graceful jump that would not have been possible anywhere else, since she jumped in a smooth arc to the next trampoline, bouncing to the next one, then the next, and so on. There was something visually disturbing, or perhaps magical, about watching his sister bounce on the ceiling, doing gymnastics that were impossible on Earth. The smile Max could see on her face broke through his gloom, and he couldn't help but smile himself.

Fifteen minutes later, when she finally stopped and was hanging, limp and sweaty, from the center pole, she beamed over at Max. Rian and Sabatha were clapping

"Good job, Sis," Max said. "You make it look easy."

"I can't wait till we get to Luna and get to see the professionals!" Holiday said.

"You looked professional to me, kiddo," Rian said. "Maybe we should try to sneak you into performing at the exhibition."

Holiday sighed. "I totally wish I could do that!"

"Anybody want lunch?" Sabatha asked. "I'm buying."

"Can I eat up here?" Holiday asked.

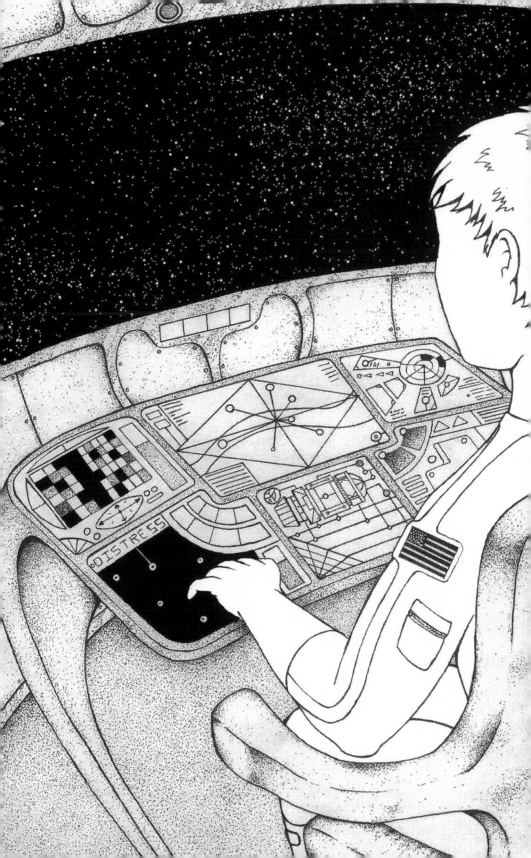

[CHAPTER ELEVEN]

WHAT HAPPENED IN THE COCKPIT

It was only half a day later—still the second 24-hour period after they'd lifted off—that Max snuck into the cockpit to get away from his family, sat down in the pilot's chair, reveling in the quiet, uneasy because the cockpit was so small, noticed that there was a blue light on the console, blinking on and winking off, and then finally saw that the inscription beneath the light read: DISTRESS.

[Chapter Twelve]

What Happened When They Stopped The *Starburst*

"We have to stop," Rian said.

"Can we actually do that?" Sabatha asked. "Will we have enough fuel to make it to Luna?"

"Well, we can't use the boosters again, but it's not necessarily a matter of fuel since the reactor can power the ion engines for years, even at full burn. The problem is distance and how fast we can decelerate without harming the ship or ourselves."

"Do we have enough room to stop?" Sabatha asked.

"The computer says we do, as long as we do it soon."

"Then we have to stop." Sabatha sighed and spoke to Max and Holiday, who were already strapped in. "Sorry, kiddos, looks like our vacation plans are changed. It's going to take us longer to get to Luna, but we'll still get there—and we'll do it with clear consciences."

Max knew the space travel code of conduct well enough because Holiday had been reciting major portions of it ever since he'd come flying out of the cockpit, yelling to his father that somebody was signaling for help. The code maintained that any spaceship should render assistance to another in an emergency as long as that assistance did not also endanger the aiding vessel. If the *Starburst* could give aid and still continue on its way to Luna without running out of fuel, exhausting the supply of food, water, and oxygen, or put the spaceship or its passengers under physical stress from rapid deceleration, then they were duty-bound to stop and help.

The distress signal had come from a small spaceship called the *Venge*. Holiday had narrowed her eyes after hearing this, but only Max saw, and he didn't think much of it. After all, his sister was the drama princess of the universe. The distress signal carried information such as stellar coordinates, time, date, spaceship model and year, origin and destination, registration, licensing, reason for distress, and amount of time remaining until life support shut down. The *Venge* was a small cargo ship. It had taken a piece of space debris through its primary fuel tank. While not resulting in the explosion that it surely would have on any good holo feed like *Quantum Girl!!!*, it had, quite efficiently, vented their fuel into space. There were secondary and tertiary fuel tanks, but they didn't hold enough fuel to get them to their destination: Earth.

The Storm family had their helmets and spacesuits back on, and they were all back in the cockpit, secure in their harnesses.

Max watched his father's hands move across the control console. "I'm disengaging computer pilot and cutting off the ion streams." The hum of the ship changed as the ion engines stopped. Technically, they were still running—they just weren't being allowed to emit ions. All Max could hear was his own breathing and the tap of his mother's fingers on her armrest. "Bringing us about," Rian said. The star field through the cockpit window began to rotate slowly. While all four ion engines rotated independently and could be used for a variety of movement, the plan was to decelerate the *Starburst* without reorienting the engines. Due to the rate of deceleration needed to stop in the vicinity of the *Venge,* Rian had decided it would be better to reorient the *Starburst*. Max had been a little disappointed. Part of him had been looking forward to watching the four ion streams shoot past the cockpit.

With the *Starburst* travelling in the opposite way it was pointing, Rian reactivated the ion engines. He increased power gradually. Max felt the deceleration forces build against his chest. It felt the same as takeoff, only it ramped up much more slowly. At takeoff, their engines had been at full thrust. Decelerating, the only way to decelerate without crushing the passengers under extreme forces was to do it slowly. Max knew—because his sister told him—that ion engines had traditionally been thought of as efficient propulsion that just required a lot of time to get up to speed. Though this was often the practice, since they were most commonly used to supplement more traditional engines, modern ion engines could also be pulsed to generate bursts of thrust, enabling acceleration approaching that of other engines. The real advantage of the ion engines was their efficiency.

"It took us a long time to get up to this speed, and it's going to take us awhile to slow down," Rian said. "It'll be a little more uncomfortable, but I'm going to have to decelerate the ship faster than I'd like. Normally, I'd keep it to 3g, and I'm still going to do that most of the time, but I'm also going to be braking harder for very brief periods—somewhere around 4g to 5g. Is that okay with everyone? If it gets too bad, let me know."

Max didn't know if it was okay or not. It didn't *sound* okay. It sounded *stressful*. But he didn't say anything. If Holiday wasn't complaining out loud, then he wouldn't.

As it turned out, it wasn't too horrible. The deceleration at 3g wasn't anything more than what he'd already felt, and the higher deceleration rates were brief—no more than five seconds at a time. That he could handle. It was physically taxing. After thirty minutes of breaking, Sabatha called for a brief rest period. According to the computer, they were ahead of their breaking schedule and could actually decelerate at 1g for a while. Since this provided them an Earth-normal gravity, Holiday wanted to get up and climb around the ship, but Sabatha nixed that idea. Max didn't think his mother liked the thought of Holiday being able to actually *fall* inside the spaceship. Through it all, Max was able to hold onto his control, pushing his unease down, sometimes just barely. Twice, he swallowed vomit down.

Then, it was back to a 3*g* and beyond cycle of deceleration. Max lost track of how long they decelerated. Finally, Rian told everybody that they were approaching the *Venge*.

Max brought up one of the outside video feeds in his helmet. At first he didn't see anything, but then he caught it—an area of space where the stars seemed to disappear. It wasn't that the *Venge* was cloaked or anything—that technology only existed in holos—simply that its surface had been painted black. Something on the *Venge* wasn't black though, and it sparkled. Max zoomed the camera in, but still couldn't tell what it was. He asked his father.

"It's fuel," Holiday said before Rian could respond. "It's frozen. You can see the ice trail leading to the fuel tanks on that side of the spaceship. It sparkles like Quantum Girl!!'s hair. I think it's kinda pretty."

"Pretty dangerous," Rian said. "It can still be ignited."

Max noted, not without some concern, that his mother's heart rate had spiked.

"Sure, but the chances of that are low, right?" Holiday asked.

Rian grunted. "Low, but not zero. We'll just make sure we don't get too close before we can assess the situation."

Watching the stars wink out behind the black form of the *Venge*, a sudden panic gripped Max, as if that dark spot in the universe wasn't a spaceship at all, but a singularity devouring all light, sucking them in with inescapable force. His breathing shortened, sped up, and he gripped his chair. Mis—

—take!

Mistake.

Mistake!

This was all.

A big mistake!

He wanted to tell his father that they should stop slowing down and start speeding up. Getting closer to that...dark place was a very bad idea. It wanted them to get closer. It was sucking them in. Maybe he'd feel better if he took his helmet off.

"Max," came his mother's calm voice in his ear. "Remember to breathe. I don't know what's bothering you, but I'm right here with you. This is on a private channel, so nobody else can hear me." His mother's voice was probably the most calming thing he could have heard at that moment. "Is there anything I can do for you?" his mother asked.

Max blew out a breath that was a mix of laughter and pent-up frustration. "Get me to Luna. Quicker the better." The last part came out through teeth gritted tight. It was the best he could do.

"We're working on that, Max, but what we're doing right now is a necessary thing. It's a good thing. It's what we'd hope others would do for us if we were in the same situation. You know that right?"

"Yeah."

"Close your eyes and just breathe. You have your air blowing?"

He didn't. He'd forgot. The air in his helmet was hot and humid, beads of moisture beading up on the inside of the visor. He activated the blower, taking deep breaths, forcing them out slowly. It was helping, sorta. He closed his eyes. His helmet felt like it was getting tighter. He really should take it off.

"I'm right here with you, Max." His mother's voice pulled him back from the brink. "Talk to me, honey, let me know you're listening."

"I am," he whispered. Again, the best he could do.

"Okay, good. Now take your hands away from your helmet."

Max's eyes flew open. What was she talking about? His hands weren't—

Only they were.

They were right there, both of them, right at the seam between his spacesuit and his helmet. His thumbs were already playing with the quick release lever. It wasn't as if taking off his helmet was lethal, but it upset him that he hadn't even known he was doing it. That was a loss of control that he rarely felt and had managed to keep hidden from his parents for the longest time.

His hands trembled and his arms resisted, but they went back down where they were supposed to be, gripping the handles on the armrests.

"That's better," Sabatha said. "And look, we're stopped. See? Nothing to worry about."

"Thanks, Mom," Max said, forcing his eyes open only through force of will.

"Loveya," Sabatha said.

"Mom…"

"Hey, I'm your mother. I'll say that anytime I want to. You'll just have to live with it. Maybe you could say it back a few times a year. Maybe even make it sound convincing."

Max felt the crushing weight around his chest and throat easing. "Funny, Mom. You know I do."

"I know. Girls like hearing it out loud though. You need to realize that. Don't say it if you don't mean it, but say it often if you do."

"Mom?"

"Yeah?"

"I love you."

"Thanks."

Max felt much better. His mother was good at getting him to relax. He was still breathing a little too fast, and he felt a little lightheaded, but the all-consuming pressure was no longer all-consuming. Raising his visor, he looked through the cockpit window.

"Cosmic!" Holiday exclaimed. "I haven't seen a Bruticon 5000 this close before!"

Max knew she'd seen exactly two spaceships that close in her entire lifetime. The other was the one she was strapped into. Max's eyes scanned the blob of black that was the wounded spaceship, wondering who was inside.

The *Venge* hovered in space like shadow on shadow.

[Chapter Thirteen]

What Happened When They Rescued The Captain Of The *Venge*

The *Starburst* hadn't actually stopped of course. Since the *Venge* was still drifting through space, stopping would have prevented them from getting close. Instead, Rian had, with the help of the computer, matched the *Starburst's* speed and trajectory with that of the other spaceship.

"Why didn't we have to stop and start back toward Earth ?" Max asked. "Wasn't the *Venge* headed away from the moon?"

"That doesn't matter," Holiday said hastily. "The best way to get from one place to another isn't a straight line out in space. We're using planetary orbits and gravity at all times. Sometime you have to travel away from your destination before you can head towards it—at least if you don't want to burn up all your fuel taking some more direct route."

Sometimes Max wanted to weld his knew-everything-about-space-travel sister's mouth shut. Either that or erase her memory. Whichever. As long as it would allow somebody else to answer questions about extremely complicated subjects that Max knew little about because he hadn't been paying attention at the time he was supposed to have learned it.

"So, basically, it makes sense," Max said.

"Complete sense," Holiday said.

Rian sounded distracted. "Yeah, your sister's probably right."

Probably? What was that supposed to mean?

"Have they seen us?" Sabatha asked. "Do they know we're here to help them?"

"Well, they *can* see us, if there's anybody still there to see us," Rian said. "I've been sending the standard response to their distress signal, but I'm still waiting for a reply."

"You don't think…" Holiday began, trailing off.

"We'll just have to see, honey," Sabatha said.

"Your mother's right," Rian said. "Since they lost their primary fuel tank, standard operating procedure says you should move to resource conservation mode. Other than the distress signal, which is a necessity, they may have decided to wait until help arrived before they responded."

"But wouldn't they want people to know that they were—" Max began.

"I don't know, Max," Rian said, then, reconsidering his tone, "let's just wait and see what happens. It's possible something else went wrong over there and they're incapable of responding at the moment. That's a worse-case scenario though, so don't worry about it. Situations like that are rare."

You mean like distress signals are rare? Max wanted to add, but knew that it would only get him in trouble. He could sulk, but if he was flippant toward his father, the vacation in space would quickly become a *hell*cation in space.

Rian, giving up on the radio response to the distress signal, opened up a wideband signal directly to the *Venge*. "This is Captain Rian Storm of lunar transport *Starburst*, hailing transport *Venge*. Do you copy?"

Ten seconds of silence finally brought a new voice. *"Roger, Starburst, this is Captain Darren Meaney of Earth transport* Venge. *I am really glad to hear your voice."*

"I can't get a response on the distress signal frequency. What's the status of your life support?"

"Ah, yeah, sorry 'bout that. Something fried when I activated the distress signal. I wasn't even sure it was transmitting. Guess now I know it was. Anyway, life support is nominal. I can go another two weeks on what I got over here."

"Roger that. Nice to know I don't have to get you out of there in the next five minutes. Now, I can see you have a fuel tank problem there. What happened?"

Darren swore, the words crackling with static. *"...bout the size of an acorn, went right through it. Happened while I was in my sleep cycle. Wouldn't have mattered if I had been awake though. We vented the entire tank in less than a minute."*

"Any fuel left in the tank?" Rian asked.

"Sensor's iced. I suspect there is some left in there actually, though it's frozen solid, just like everything that blew out. Can't figure out a way to light it up without setting fire to things I don't want to though."

"Agreed. Venting fuel from the tanks is better than venting everything else in a really big explosion. I hate to say it, but you got yourself an expensive piece of scrap metal there. It's a shame it doesn't have enough fuel to get anywhere important."

"It's also a shame that Interstellar Javelin X models don't have tow cables or carry fuel that this piece of garbage can choke down. I don't suppose you're headed for Earth are you?"

Rian chuckled. "Not for another month. I had this thing pointed directly at Luna until I picked up your signal."

Max was about to protest. *He* had picked up the signal, not his father! Why would his father say differently?

"Roger that," Darren said, his voice resigned. *"Ah well, just came from there, you see. Was looking forward to getting myself and my cargo back Earthside. Guess I'm gonna have to change my plans."*

"He's not the only one," Max said, but some sixth sense told him that he was talking only to himself. That's when he noticed that all helmet microphones except for his father's were muted. Had his father done that? He tried to clear the mute, but it was locked out. His father didn't want any of them talking. Why?

A terse, three-sentence text message flashed into Max's helmet. It was from his father, and it was blinking in small red letters: NO TALKING YET. TRUST ME.

Max didn't like it because it made him feel like a little kid, but there wasn't anything he could do about it, so he sat back and tried to keep calm. Since they weren't decelerating, he wondered if he could go back to the G-ring and draw.

"You have maneuvering thrusters?" Rian asked.

"Affirmative. Are you offering?"

Rian sighed. "Make it official."

"Captain Storm, I formally request sanctuary on your spaceship."

"Granted."

"Thank you."

"Not a problem," Rian said. Max saw his father turn his head, meeting Sabatha's gaze most likely, then he nodded, some nonverbal communication passing between them. They did that a lot. Seventeen years of marriage enabled that between two people.

"Alrighty, let's get our computers talking to each other," Rian said. "I'm too tired to do this the old-fashioned way."

"Roger that. Venge is ready for data sync."

"Initiating *Starburst-Venge* data sync," Rian said.

"Data sync confirmed," came the reply a minute later.

"Looks like you're running an older version of the docking procedure. Sending the new code your way."

"I see it. Thanks."

"We'll let the *Starburst* do all the heavy lifting," Rian said. "The *Venge* will need everything she has to stay on course till she can be recovered."

"Agreed."

"If you're not suited, get it on. You can bring your personal belongings. Keep it light. No weapons."

"Copy that. I've been in my suit since I woke up and realized my ship was vomiting all my profit out its primary fuel tank."

Darren sounded calm for somebody who had been drifting in space. Though really, these routes were travelled often enough that rescue was almost guaranteed.

"Executing docking code," Rian said.

The star field through the cockpit spun as the *Starburst* rotated to bring its airlock around to face the *Venge*. Max couldn't hear or feel the maneuvering thrusters firing, but he could see their effect in the subtle shifts the stars made. The *Venge* moved out of view of the cockpit as they made final adjustments for the docking procedure.

"Looking good," Rian said. "Extending coupling."

"Likewise."

"Connection in three minutes. Let's just take this nice and slow."

"Roger that. I've had enough accidents for one trip."

Another private message from his father. This one said: STAY IN THE COCKPIT ONCE WE'RE DOCKED. YOUR MOTHER AND SISTER WILL BE BACK IN THE G-RING, BUT I NEED YOU TO DO SOMETHING.

ROGER, Max sent back, though he couldn't prevent his breathing from quickening. Was his father worried about something? Was there something to be *worried about?* The pressure in his chest was returning, the squeezing hand that threatened to crush his lungs. No, his father needed him! He couldn't let this take him! Not this time! Max bit back curses.

Wilderness Camp would have been so much easier. The only chest-crushing pressure he'd have felt there would have been from Nika's strong hugs—the ones that made him feel like he was her lifeline, as if she were dangling from the edge of a cliff and he had been the one to reach out and catch her. That type of hug was the best.

Shame he wouldn't be feeling one for a while.

Max closed his eyes and focused. The next thing he knew, his father's voice was in his ear. "Max, let's go."

His eyes flashed open. His mother and sister were gone. He was alone with his father.

Rian stood, leaving his flight helmet on, though the visor was up. "First rule of answering a distress call is to always make sure that your ship and the people you're traveling with are safe and secure. You can't jeopardize your safety to help another ship unless everybody onboard knows the risks and are willing to assume them. I'm not willing to assume any risk when it comes to you, Sabatha, and Holi."

"I understand, Dad," Max said, though really, he only *suspected* where his dad was going with all that.

"What goes for a spaceship, goes for the people on that spaceship. So what we're going to do is be cautious. We don't know Captain Meaney. I ran a check on him and the *Venge* and nothing bad came up. We don't have anything to worry about. Still, you and I are going to greet him at the airlock and make sure before we even let him know that the women are on board."

"Okay."

"Now, there's something I need to you do. I messaged you instead of using a private channel earlier because your mom was watching me. If she had seen me talking without hearing my voice, she would have started asking questions, you know, getting suspicious."

Max wondered what there was to get suspicious about.

Rian made some small movement on the control console with his left hand. There was a *beep* followed by a *click*, then a panel in the floor beside the pilot's seat slid open. Rian reached in and pulled out the two gray cases he'd brought with him.

"Come up here," Rian said, motioning for Max to move to the front row of seats.

Max climbed into his mother's seat.

Rian looked Max in the eye. His gaze was difficult to endure for long because, well, he was a father, and it was a challenge to out-stare your father, even when you weren't on a space vacation you had sulked about for several months. "Max, you may not be eighteen, but you're a man in my book. I know you resent it, and me, but you did the right thing by coming along on this vacation. Your mother and sister are very happy that you're here. As am I. You know that don't you?"

"Yeah," Max admitted, and it was true, he did know. The part of him that was rebelling didn't like it at all though. That part of him was angry that he liked making his family happy.

"Good. I know I can't force you, so I'm not going to try, but if you could work on spending a little more time with your mother and sister over the next few weeks, I'd really appreciate it."

"Okay."

"I promise. This is the last vacation I'm going to guilt you into coming on."

Max didn't know what to say to that. Everything he thought of was going to sound bad coming out, even if he didn't intend for it to be that way.

Rian pointed toward a button on the control console. "This control opens this compartment." He pointed to the opening in the floor, out of which he'd pulled his two gray cases. Then, placing both hands on one of the cases, he said, "I should have done this before we left. I thought we had more time. That's my mistake. I don't need to spell out exactly what is in these cases to give you the password and to tell you that you are to only use them when absolutely necessary, but also that you are to not hesitate in using them when it is."

Max expected some measure of panic at this point, because when he thought about it, he *did* have some idea as to what was in those cases, and if his ideas were true, then that might mean that his father expected something to happen… No, that wasn't it. His father had just explained all that. They were just being cautious.

His father whispered a single word to him. "That password will only work for you and myself, just like the control that opens the panel. Any questions?"

"No," Max said, though he had many.

Rian smiled. "Let's go rescue Captain Meaney then."

When they got to the airlock, Max could see through the inner door, but the outer door still had a shield over its small, circular window. He wondered if his father was going to retract the shield.

"Captain Meaney, are you ready to board?"

"Affirmative. I'm in my airlock, suited and ready, with your permission."

"Go ahead and enter the chute. How heavy is your luggage?"

"Uh…less than 100 lbs."

Max could just imagine Holiday responding, "Not in space, dummy. In space it weighs *nothing! Duh!*"

"Impressive, Captain," Rian said. "You got some lead underwear?"

"Nah, just souvenirs for the wife. You know those little collectible plates that just sit at home taking up shelf space and gathering dust? Well, I have shelves at home just waiting for the seven I bought on Luna."

Rian laughed.

"In the chute," Darren said. *"About thirty seconds to your side of the fence."*

"Our airlock is vented. I'm reading zero pressure. Opening the door." Rian touched a small panel on the wall. The outer door slid open. Rian motioned for Max to back up. Max pulled his body out of the way, up closer to the ceiling. He could still see through the window, but it would make it more difficult for anybody in the airlock to see him until they stepped onboard. Rian held his body slightly off-center of the window, one hand on a wall grip to steady himself.

"Permission to come aboard, Starburst.*"*

"Permission granted," Rian responded.

Max saw movement in black.

Then a glossy black flight helmet filled the airlock window and he couldn't see anything else.

"Clear," Darren said.

"Closing outer airlock door."

All Max could see from his angle was Captain Meaney's flight helmet reflecting back a dark, distorted version of himself.

"Airlock secure," Rian said. "Let's give you some air so you can get that helmet off. Twenty seconds till pressure normalization."

A hissing sound inside the airlock slowly faded in as atmosphere was injected into the small room. When it was done, Rian said, "Atmosphere looks good. Can you confirm pressure equalization?"

"Confirmed, Captain," Darren said.

Hands came up and pushed the black flight helmet up and away. Captain Darren Meaney had a head full of short brown hair, with flecks of gray here and there. There was one patch of gray in the back large enough that Max imagined something was damaged underneath. He'd probably been hit with a rock when he was younger. A lasting reminder of some childhood accident. Some things you never forgot. Some things stayed with you.

Max thought of what had happened that night at Galactic Taco, and knew this to be true. He shivered, feeling an icy hand creeping at his throat, his chest. No. No. No. Not now. *Not now!* He needed to be strong for his father, and for his mother and his sister.

"Knock. Knock."

The private message flashing in Max's flight helmet was: READY?

Max nodded, just another lie to add to the pile, though at least this was one he told himself hoping that it might end up being true.

The airlock door opened.

Max was quick, and he had a better viewing angle than his father, so he saw something wrong right away. Though *wrong* was probably not the right word. He saw something in the airlock he *didn't expect*.

He saw a second black flight helmet.

So when Captain Darren Meaney stepped out of the airlock, Max was less surprised than his father to see a second person step out too. Though his assumptions and expectations should have been thrown out by then, Max was quite shocked to see that the second person was a young woman. She removed her helmet.

She looked about his age.

[Chapter Fourteen]

What Happened That Caused Maximillion To Forget His Girlfriend's Name

"Hi," Max said, briefly forgetting that he had a girlfriend and at the same time realizing how lame he sounded. Also, it was a little weird to be speaking down to Captain Meaney and his female companion from the vantage point of what was basically the ceiling. Not that he'd been talking to Captain Meaney. Something must've been ingrained into his hormone-infected body that required him to greet the pretty girl first instead of her...bodyguard? Father? Boyfriend?

"Hi," the girl said back, looking up at him with alert, but unconcerned eyes.

Rian held up a hand. "Stop right there, both of you."

Both of you, was directed at Captain Meaney and his female...*whatever* she was in relation to him.

"Captain Meaney, you need to explain yourself right now," Rian said, pulling his helmet off, his voice titanium hard.

"I don't understand," Darren said. He looked genuinely confused.

"Her," Rian said, pointing at the young woman, who was taking in her surroundings, looking all around. She seemed oblivious to Rian and his finger. "At no time did you inform me that there was anybody other than yourself onboard the *Venge*. That is a violation of boarding protocol, and outside of that, it's simple rudeness. I am the captain of this spaceship, and I have to know who everybody is. Explain yourself,

125

and explain who she is. Now."

Darren held up his hands, actually pushing his body backwards, as if retreating. "I'm sorry, Captain. I did not intentionally violate protocol. I assumed you received all that information in the distress signal. It should've told you that there were two people onboard."

"It did not. It indicated there was only one."

Darren sighed. "I don't know what to tell you then. Maybe the signal was corrupted when I activated it. Like I told you before, I wasn't even sure it was transmitting."

Max looked at his father's face, tried to read what he was thinking. He couldn't. He might've looked angry. He might've been happy. His face was hard and expressionless. That probably wasn't good. Masking emotion that well meant there was a hurricane inside hoping to burst into the open.

"And her?" Rian asked, pulling his arm back, and instead of pointing, jerking his head toward the girl.

"This," Darren said, putting a protective arm around her, "is Riven. She's my daughter."

Riven was stiff under her father's arm. Max supposed he often felt the same way when his father put his arm around him in front of other people.

"I'm sorry," Riven said, looking at Rian. "I didn't mean to cause trouble."

Rian's face softened after a moment. "Don't let it worry you. It's not your fault." At that last sentence, he turned his head back to Riven's father.

Darren looked distraught. "I apologize, Captain. I take full responsibility for my oversight. Irregardless of my situation and that of my ship, I should have clarified everything with you."

Irregardless isn't a word, Max thought absently, a little uncomfortable to be floating higher than everybody else. He was staring at Riven, and he didn't know why.

Okay, well, he had some idea as to why.

Now that he had a chance to look at her, she looked older than she had at first. Older than him for sure. She had to be at least twenty-five. Her hair was unkempt, falling carelessly over her ears, around her shoulders, even in front of her face. It was blonde he supposed, but the dirty type that ran dark with browns and tans that were either the work of a professional dye job or a masterpiece of freak genetics. Things like that happened sometimes. He'd once seen a girl with bright blue hair, as if perhaps she'd been hung from her heels and dipped in paint. It hadn't been a wig, and it hadn't been colored. She'd been born that way. Her eyebrows had been the hardest to accept. It wasn't that they looked bad or anything—it was just that they'd looked fake, like cartoon eyebrows.

Speaking of cartoons, Riven was nothing like one. No part of her body was cartoony, exaggerated, or out of proportion. She was real, breathing quite well, thank you very much, and her spacesuit—black and identical to the one her father wore—looked tailored specifically for her. It wasn't overly tight, and it didn't highlight any curves she might have beneath, but she…wore it well, like it was nothing more than a shirt and a pair of jeans she'd wear around her house. While Max stared, she brushed her hair behind her ear, but it didn't stay, clusters falling back to frame her chin. Riven happened to look up. Max quickly averted his eyes.

"Yes, you should have clarified with me," Rian said, "but now I know, and it's not going to be a problem. Welcome aboard, Captain Meaney." Rian held out his hand.

Captain Meaney grabbed it, shaking it firmly. "Call me Darren."

"Can do, Darren," Rian said. "And this is my son, Max."

Max pulled his helmet off and pulled his body downward to shake Darren's hand. He didn't know whether he should shake Riven's too, but she made the choice easy when she held out her hand. He took it. Her grip was strong. Her eyes, locked on, were green supernovas. Surely those had to be implant enhanced. Nobody had eyes that green. It wasn't a naturally occurring color!

"Do I know you from somewhere?" Riven asked.

Max scrambled to find his voice. "Um…I don't…think so?" Great, just great. He'd sounded like an idiot and his inflection had made it sound like a question.

Riven's eyes narrowed, and she glided forward. Yes, *glided*. Max didn't see her stop herself, but she only moved a few feet closer. She obviously had command of magical forces that allowed her to disobey the laws of physics. "Really. Then it must just be déjà vu."

"Oh," Max said, trying to remember his girlfriend's address, face, her name. Anything! This wasn't normal. Most girls didn't affect him this way, not this immediately. It wasn't her beauty. It was…he didn't know. Something was wrong. He was extra vulnerable somehow. This was ridiculous. He was panicked and dizzy. He grabbed a handhold and clenched his fist around it. *Her name! They'd been together for over a year! What was her name?*

Rian cleared his throat. "Let's get your belongings stowed. We have some maneuvering to do in order to uncouple the *Starburst* from the *Venge* before we can get back on our way. We'll also need to double-check the trajectory on your spaceship. Can we establish a remote link to the *Venge* and control it from here?"

"Yes," Darren said. "I secured all systems before we left, but I'd like to see if there's anything we can do to prevent my ship from being salvaged before I can get back to it."

"We'll see what we can do," Rian said. "Max, can you take Riven to the G-ring? Take their luggage with you. There's room in the storage back there."

"Okay," Max said. Riven moved aside to reveal two reasonably-sized, gray duffel bags floating behind her. She did a quick movement with her foot and suddenly one of the bags was moving toward Max. He caught it, the force of the bag pushing him back against the wall. Riven grabbed the other bag then waited for Max to make some sort of move.

The airlock clear, Rian closed the inner door.

"This way," Max said, though even simple words seemed awkward, as if the very syllables his mouth formed were pathetic. "You can meet my mom and my sister."

Riven stopped. "What?"

"His mother and sister, darling," Darren said. "Didn't you hear him? They're waiting to meet you probably."

Riven looked over her shoulder. "Sure, Daddy. I just…" She flipped hair out of her eyes, and her cosmic powers once again prevented her whole body from beginning a slow rotation. "I guess Mr. Storm isn't the only one surprised that there are more people on the ship than expected." Her tone was cordial, but her glare at her father was anything but friendly. It was the kind of look that would've got Max or Holiday in trouble. Darren Meaney had a different tolerance for disrespect it seemed, because all he did was force a smile without otherwise responding.

Max took that as a cue to pull his body out of the escape pod bay.

Riven sniffed and followed him.

A second later, with Riven behind him, his girlfriend's name finally returned.

Nika!

[Chapter Fifteen]

What Happened Between Maximillion And Riven

The mathematics didn't lie. It was going to take two additional days to get to Luna. That they were even going to get there at all was more a product of luck and timing than anything else. The trajectories of the *Venge* and the *Starburst* had intersected at a place that allowed the *Starburst* to continue on without having to perform a long ion engine burn or a riskier, non-standard orbit-intercepting maneuver. The first would have required everybody onboard to be strapped into their seats for long periods of time while the spaceship accelerated in order to make up for the time and distance lost while coupled with the *Venge*. The second would have required that the *Starburst* alter course and take a very fuel-inefficient path that was more straight line than curve.

Everybody was very glad that they'd found the *Venge* when and where they had. One of life's happy coincidences.

Since there weren't enough seats in the cockpit for everybody, Rian had Max give up his seat to Darren. Max found himself back in the G-ring with Riven, both of them strapped into chairs that had been designed with emergency use in mind, but still weren't quite as comfortable as the ones in the cockpit. For Max, they might have been a whole lot more comfortable if they hadn't been locked in place so close together, or if he had been sitting next to his ultra-pretty girlfriend—who had taught him that osculation wasn't just a word you could impress people with—instead of Riven, who was also pretty, but

131

in an I'm-hot-but-I-don't-appear-to-care-and-that-just-makes-you-like-me-more type of way.

But it was that way. So Max was uncomfortable. He wanted to put his flight helmet on, but Riven hadn't put hers on, so it would have been weird for him to wear his. He tried to find a safe place for his hands, but the chairs were so close together they practically shared an armrest. They'd bumped arms several times, and hands once. He eventually settled for putting his hand in his lap, as awkward as that felt.

While the *Starburst* accelerated, Max and Riven talked. With the G-ring being much larger than the cockpit, his panic didn't manifest, and Riven, for better or worse, was a very real distraction.

Riven asked him lots of questions about his family, where he went to school, how old he was, what his favorite bands were, what his hobbies were—all those sorts of questions a person asks when they're trying to be polite. Well, she was either being polite, or she was going to try to assume his identity.

"You have a girlfriend back on Earth?" Riven finally asked the question he'd been dreading and knew she'd get to eventually.

"Yeah, her name is Nika," Max said, proud of himself that he'd replied without hesitating.

"Pretty name."

"Yeah."

"Is she as pretty as her name?"

Curious question. Even if Nika wasn't present, there was only one good answer. "Yes," he said.

"Is she as pretty as me?"

Curious question number two. Only there was no good answer to that one. "Ah…" he said. Then he saw that Riven was smiling. He turned away, embarrassed that he'd fallen for her teasing so easily.

"Sorry," Riven said. "I guess that wasn't really funny now that I think about it." She put a hand on his forearm. "You're not mad at me are you?"

"No, I'm not mad at all." What was it with women and asking questions with only one answer that didn't get you in trouble? Nika did the same thing sometimes, asking questions like "Do I look good in this dress?" or "Do you think I'm fat?" or his personal favorite "Do you want to kiss me?" All simple questions that didn't need to be asked because the answers were going to be *Yes, No,* and *Absolutely!* every time. Max supposed that everybody needed their self-esteem boosted on occasion. Still, it seemed manipulative. He wasn't sure on the finer details of how it actually *was* manipulative, but it certainly felt that way.

Riven sighed, not moving her hand. "Good. Mad would be bad."

Max cleared his throat. Her hand—even though it was gloved, and his arm was covered by his spacesuit—felt hot to him, like it was burning through the multiple layers of insulated clothing separating their respective skins. "So, ah…" he began, cleared his throat again because it really was sort of dry, "what about you?"

"What about me?" Riven asked.

"I just answered a lot of questions about myself. Now it's your turn."

"Oh, I see. Well, maybe you should ask me a more specific question."

"Ah, okay. Why are you out here? Are you working with your dad?"

Riven pulled her hand back. Max found that he could breathe easier, as if she'd just stopped strangling him. "Yeah, I've been helping my father for a couple years now."

"A couple years? But you're only…" Max was going to say some age, but realized that her age might not be a good thing to throw guesses at. And because he didn't really know how old he thought she was. At first he thought she looked about his age, then later he thought she looked older. But now, sitting right next to her, she looked about

133

his age again. Maybe he was just a bad judge of those sorts of things.

Riven laughed, a quiet, melodious thing. "I'll save you the trouble of finishing that sentence and then trying to dig your way out of a hole. I'm eighteen. Actually, I'll be nineteen in a few months."

So, she was younger than she looked, younger than he'd thought. She seemed so mature to him. He had a feeling that she didn't sulk as often as he did, or Nika. In that moment, he felt ashamed of his previous behavior. He was disappointed that it took somebody in his age range demonstrating maturity and poise to make him see how childish he'd been acting.

Right then and there, he resolved to alter his behavior for the rest of the trip, and he prayed for the strength to carry through with his pledge. Sure, some of his resolve was due to his male ego, which felt the need to impress any female of his species within sight—and Riven was much closer than that. Regardless of his commitment to his girlfriend, he couldn't help his desire to impress Riven, to have her think that he was a good guy. Idly, he wondered if she thought he was good-looking.

"That look on your face," Riven said. "What? Do I not look eighteen? How old do I look to you?"

"Ah…" Max said, about to chicken out of answering, but he decided to squelch any displays of weakness. She was an outgoing person, and he needed to show her that he was strong enough to keep up with her—regardless of whether or not it was true. "You look…exactly like you should." There, he smiled, and it was genuine because, really, it was easy to smile at pretty girls. "You have nothing to worry about."

"Thanks, Max, that's really very nice of you."

Max was anxious to turn the conversation away from Riven's age and other subjects wrought with peril. "Sooo, about working with your dad…"

"Oh yeah, so I've been working with him for a couple of years, hauling supplies between Earth, Luna, space stations, as well as AMC outposts." The AMC was the Asteroid Mining Consortium. The AMC was made up of over one hundred different companies that conducted mining operations on free trajectory asteroids. It was dangerous work, but the variety of new minerals discovered had widespread applications. The operations were expensive, but there was still plenty of money to be made. Riven continued, "There's something nice about being part of a father-daughter cargo transport team. I graduated high-school a year early. I could've gone to university for another four years, but I wanted to get a job, get into space. Help out my dad. It's just me and him now, so we get by as best we can. It's hard work, but it's good work. We make an honest living. Got my level one space pilot license. Got another couple years before I can get level two, but all that means is I have something to work toward."

Max didn't know if he could spend that amount of time with any member of his family. Both he and Holiday tended to get bored, irritable, and difficult when exposed to their parents for long periods of time.

"Sounds like a good life," Max said.

"Yeah," Riven said, her voice abruptly low. She turned her head away slightly. "Yeah, it's definitely a life."

"Um, so what's your favorite movie?" Max asked.

"Wow, smooth change of topic," Riven said.

"I'm not good at this."

The hand was back on his forearm, as warm as it was before. "You're fine," she said. "And you may not believe this, but my favorite movie is *Blood Drinker.*"

"Oh," Max said, that not being the answer he'd been expecting. "Ah, which one?"

"Nothing beats the original, though I do like them all. I actually have them in my stuff if you want to watch them with me."

Blood Drinker was a science fiction holo that his parents hadn't known he'd watched when he was nine. It was scary and violent. He'd had nightmares for two weeks but couldn't admit anything to his parents for fear that he'd get in trouble. "Sure," Max said.

Riven undid her harness.

The *Starburst* was still accelerating.

"Wait, you can't—" Max began.

But obviously she could. Riven put a finger to his lips. "Don't worry, Max. I know what I'm doing." With her other hand, she glanced at a watch. "The trick is learning the acceleration cycles. Every five minutes, the acceleration drops back to…"—then she stood—"1g!"

Moving like she had been born in space, she proceeded through the G-ring, grabbing footholds and handholds in a manner Max had never seen before. She was through the galley and into the sleeping quarters in less than half a minute. Opening the storage compartment her belongings were stored in, she reached in and retrieved something with one hand, then slipped it into one of the pockets on the arm of her spacesuit. Closing the compartment, she made her way back to Max. From Max's point of view, she was climbing on the floor. The rotation of the G-ring kept her on the floor, though the acceleration of the *Starburst* continually drew her in the direction where Max was sitting.

He didn't know how long she had left. Honestly, he'd been so distracted sitting next to her that he hadn't noticed their acceleration hadn't been constant, that they were dipping back to 1g acceleration on a regular basis. She'd been out of her chair for over a minute, closer to two maybe.

It was amazing how quickly she adapted to the varying gravitational forces. He supposed that was one benefit of spending a lot of time in a spaceship.

She descended the last few feet to where the chairs were. She turned over so that she was sitting on the floor, laying back, bracing her left foot in one of the grooves she'd been using to crawl across the floor. Her right foot was against Max's chair.

Then she said, "Uh oh."

Max knew what she was talking about. He'd felt his body being pushed backward. The *Starburst* was increasing its rate of acceleration.

Riven's eyes widened a little, but her face remained calm. "Catch me," she said.

That was all the warning Max got before Riven was crouching at his feet, then her upper body was coming up toward his. He put up his arms, but despite what she had told him to do, he wasn't fast enough, her momentum carrying her not as much toward her chair as much as directly toward Max. Her hands slammed into the back of the chair on either side of his head, her body came full up against his, their legs all mixed up, her head zooming toward his, her face filling his vision, their noses actually touching for a moment.

Her face was still calm, though her eyes betrayed an intense concentration. Her teeth were clenched, her lips slightly parted. Max could feel her breath against his lips, his chin. Something minty mixed with berries. It might not have been totally unpleasant if the *Starburst*'s acceleration hadn't turned her body into a crushing weight. That also might not have been totally unpleasant if it hadn't been so overwhelmingly awkward. In reality, her weight only crushed him for the first ten seconds or so, then it lessened enough that he could breathe. He could sense the tension in her arms; his mind imagined the muscles in her forearms rippling as they strained to keep her upper body from descending down against his. She was strong. That was clear.

"Uh, hi," Riven said, her breath deep.

Max looked into her eyes because really, there weren't too many other places he could look with her at a proximity normally reserved for intimate activities. "Hi," Max said back.

"I'm not really this heavy," Riven said. Her hair was hanging in his face, tickling his cheeks.

"I know."

"I don't want you to think I'm fat."

"Do you care what I think?" Max wasn't sure why he asked that. It was a probing sort of question, too personal.

Riven smiled. "No girl wants any guy to think she's fat, Max."

"Well, you're not."

"Thanks. Nice of you to say."

After that, there were several pregnant seconds of quiet between them. Max could feel one thing: his heart beating. And see one thing: the green in Riven's eyes, like a color stolen from a rainforest. They were cosmically cool, and ultimately, the most distracting thing he'd ever seen. They were unreal. He briefly wondered if she were an alien from another planet that looked human except for being unable to hide her eye color. He wondered how long she'd be able to support her weight. If they were accelerating at $3g$ again, then she probably weighed three times as much as she normally did, which meant she weighed about…well, best not to guess about that. Still, three hundred pounds wasn't a bad estimate.

"This is a little awkward isn't it?" Riven asked.

"Yeah it is." Max found that he was breathing as heavily as Riven was.

"Well, if you wanted to get to know me, this is definitely one of the ways." Her voice was beginning to manifest signs of the strain her body was under. She really was doing a good job of keeping almost all her weight off him. Wow, she was strong.

"I guess so," Max said, immediately knowing how stupid that made him seem. Her eyes searched his for some sort of clarification. "What

I mean is…ah, is this hurting at all?"

She shook her head, which caused her hair to travel around the edges of his face, tickling him even more. He felt like he might sneeze. Riven laughed, but it was more exhale than laugh. "Sorry, didn't mean to do that. I'd get my hair out of your face if I could. Unfortunately, even if I could move one of my hands—and maybe I can—I think my hair would just come right back at you. But, no, it's not hurting yet. Though my back will probably be the first part of my body to feel it. I've done my share of push-ups, but this is going to be too much really soon."

"I doubt I could do what you're doing. My arms aren't that strong."

"Gotta be in shape to be a cargo jockey."

"Is there anything I can do to help?"

Riven looked towards her chair. "I'm not sure. I'm still deciding if I can transition to my chair without injuring myself, or you for that matter. I wouldn't want you squashed with over three hundred pounds of me."

"Think you can roll over?"

"Maybe. If you help me. Think you can do that strapped in?"

Max looked down at his harness, which was sort of difficult since most of it was being hidden by Riven's spacesuit. "No, I'll have to unhook."

"Ok, um, let's think of something el—"

"No, I can do it."

"Are you sure?"

"Yeah. It'll be safer that way. I'll hold onto you, and you can roll over."

"Okay, sounds good. Let's hurry. My arms feel like they're on fire and my fingers are tingling."

Max reached toward the harness release, which was located at the center of his chest, but Riven said, "Careful."

Max looked down, his hands paused in midair. Ah yes, discretion would be good here.

"Careful…but hurry," Riven strained through a smile. Her eyes twinkled, so Max was pretty sure she was at least partially enjoying the awkwardness of his position.

Riven arched a little and Max made sure his hands were as close to his body as possible. His fingers found the release and pressed it, causing the harness straps to retract. Max managed to retrieve his hands without causing any further awkwardness.

"I'm going to have to get closer to you to do this," Riven said. "If that's okay with you."

"Okay."

Riven let her body come against his, and for a few seconds longer than Max felt was absolutely necessary, they were cheek to cheek, her breath hot in his ear. He could barely breathe with the pressure of her body. He felt a prick in his neck, and for a second he thought she might have bit him, but that didn't make any real sort of sense. The pain faded quickly. He thought she had probably brushed his neck with her fingernail by accident.

"So, um, how do you want me to, uh…" Max began.

He felt her smile against his cheek. "Grab my waist, and steady me. I think it's going to be best if we do this fast. It'll take more strength to do it slow, and I don't know if I have enough left in me. Just hold tight. Get your fingers around my back. And don't try to keep me in your grip. When I start to pull away, let me go. The seat has enough cushion that it shouldn't hurt. I'll try to absorb most of the shock with my arms."

"Okay."

"Ready?"

"Ready." Max put his hands on her hips. Her spacesuit had enough bulk to make him feel like he wasn't going to be of much actual help.

"Here goes," Riven said.

Max may have just imagined that her lips brushed his cheek as she pushed away, but then again, maybe he didn't. At any rate, he felt the *whoosh* of her breath as she exhaled, shoving her body up and sideways, rolling as she did. Max rolled his hands on her hips, pushing her away, then guiding her over towards her seat. She slipped from his grasp, her body slumping into her seat, the cushions groaning at the arrival of her mass. Her elbows came down first, taking the brunt of the impact, along with her buttocks.

"Ow," Riven grunted.

"Are you okay?" Max asked.

"Yeah, not too bad actually. I'd prefer not to be forced to pull a stunt like that again though. I'll just stay here until we stop accelerating. What do you think?"

"Good idea." Max worked to secure his harness again as Riven did the same.

"Thanks for the help," Riven said, her head resting to one side.

Max felt self-conscious suddenly, though it didn't make any sense for him to feel that way *after* the whole awkward situation had passed. "It was no problem."

Her face looked a little sad. "You're a nice guy, Max."

Max wasn't sure if he ever blushed, but he sincerely hoped that he wasn't blushing right then. "Thanks," he said, smiling, suddenly feeling sleepy. The adrenaline that had been rushing through his body for the past several minutes had drained, leaving him weak and limp. It had taken him by surprise how abruptly it had hit him. He wouldn't have minded talking to Riven some more, since she was sort of fun to do that with, not to mention sort of fun to look at too.

"It's a shame, really," Riven said.

"What's a shame?" Max asked, though his words came out slurred for some reason. Weird. He was more tired than he thought.

Adrenaline crashing could really sneak up on a guy.

"That we won't get to watch this." She held up a small data card about the size of her thumb. "*Blood Drinker*. It really is the real thing, and it is my favorite holo. That part was true."

What was she talking about? Max couldn't figure out what she meant. Maybe she was talking to somebody else. "Not gonna watch it, huh?" he asked, the words barely comprehensible that time, sounding more like "Nagowatuh?"

Riven shook her head, reaching out to smooth hair from his forehead in a move that looked tender, but maybe she was just checking something because her hand moved to his neck, where he had felt that brief pain earlier, pushing his head to the side a little. When she pulled her hand away, her glove had spots of blood on it. "No, Max, we're not going to watch it. You're going to go to sleep now."

That sounded like a super, extra-fantastic idea with the way Max felt. Sleep was just what he needed. He shut his eyes and found that he couldn't open them again. But that was okay, since he didn't want to open them anyway. Sleep was what his body wanted, so sleep was what he was going to let it have.

Some distant part of his consciousness did realize that she had lied to him, made up a story about who she was and what she did, then, using the *Starburst's* acceleration as an excuse to get close to him, she'd drugged him—which was super, extra-cosmically bad considering that if Riven Meaney wasn't who she said she was, then Captain Darren Meaney probably wasn't who he said he was either.

And that meant that the Storm family space vacation was in serious trouble.

[CHAPTER SIXTEEN]

WHAT HAPPENED WHEN HALF OF THE STORM FAMILY LEFT THE *STARBURST*

Max ascended from his drug-induced, unconscious state like a person swimming through honey, which is to say, not quickly and in a sweetly sick way that had his stomach rolling.

His eyelids kept closing in spite of his best efforts. It took a couple minutes, but he finally got them open. Then his problem was that the room was spinning, and it wasn't just because his chair was inside the G-ring. He had to shut his eyes again, though at first that didn't help much—the darkness behind his eyes was spinning too. He almost threw up. And even though he'd joked about it back on Earth with Holiday, vomiting wasn't something he wanted to follow through on.

The chair beside him was empty. Curious. He wondered where Riven had gone. There wasn't any pressure on his body, so that meant that the *Starburst* had stopped accelerating. It was probably safe to get up and walk around. He released his harness. That told him that the G-ring was spinning, since he didn't immediately float out of his chair. He tried to stand. That was a mistake, resulting in a wave of dizziness that had bile in his throat, his head between his knees, and prayers on his lips. When the dizziness passed, he tried again, moving slower. He was able to stand without passing out or vomiting, so he claimed victory. A few tentative steps forward revealed that things were much better if he just took it slow. Deliberately, he made his way toward the galley. There, he searched the compartments. Finding a water pouch, he greedily opened the tube on one end and began to suck. Thankfully, his body didn't reject the liquid. Disposing of the empty pouch in the waste receptacle, he made his way toward the front of the spaceship.

It was quiet. Normally, somebody was talking. Sound carried well inside the *Starburst,* especially within the confines of the G-ring. Weird. Maybe everybody was asleep.

[Max!]

Oh, he could hear Holiday…somewhere. He wasn't sure which direction her voice had come from. He thought maybe from the direction of the cockpit, maybe closer, like the escape pod bay.

He wondered again where Riven was. He thought he remembered something about her saying she wanted to watch a holo with him. *Blood Drinker.* That would be sort of nice, though he would have to make sure that his sister didn't come and try to watch it with them. That might upset his parents, and he'd already resolved to do less of that for the rest of the trip. Yeah, watching a holo with Riven would be nice. He was sure that other girl—his girlfriend, what's-her-name—wouldn't mind.

Max passed through the sleeping quarters, didn't find anybody there, though it looked like Holiday and Sabatha had spilled some paint—there were red splotches on the floor between the beds. He then moved into the escape pod bay. Coming out of the G-ring wasn't something he was particularly skilled at—he always felt like the room was spinning—which was weird because in reality, the escape pod bay was stationary, and it was the G-ring that rotated.

Once his body had acclimated to the lack of gravity again, he looked around. From the center of the room, he could see both the airlock and the three escape pod doors. They were all closed, just like they should be. Max didn't always notice everything about a room the first few times through it, which is why he saw the lights next to each escape pod door for the first time just then. Next to each circular door was a single light, about half a foot in diameter. Two of the lights were red. One was green. Interesting. He wondered if there was some sort of test going on. From his point of view, the escape pod with the green light was above him, and he couldn't see through the window. Using handholds, he pulled himself closer.

That's when he saw the soles of two pairs of boots through the window.

His first instinct was to turn away since he realized, with no small amount of horror, that he'd come upon his parents making out, but he stopped himself since that didn't make any sense. Those were the boots of their spacesuits. They were probably just sleeping. In an escape pod. Half cringing, he looked closer.

There were drops of blood on the inside surface of the window.

Like a close friend returning from a long separation, panic grabbed his body in a crushing hug and attempted to squeeze all the air from his lungs. His vision began to fade, and he realized he wasn't breathing. He forced air into his lungs, made his arms pull him up and closer.

Those *were* his parents in there. He was looking up their bodies. His father was moving. His mother wasn't. She was on her side. He could see red stains on her spacesuit, but her head was lolling to one side and he couldn't see her face. Her arms, bare because the sleeves of her spacesuit had been torn off, were stretched behind her back, where he could see her wrists were strapped together with plastic ties. Her wrists were bleeding. Black and blue bruises dotted her arms.

What was going on? What had happened? Had they been attacked by space pirates? Who could have done this?

Max had stopped breathing again, blackness threatening to close in around him. He clenched his teeth and sucked air in through his mouth and nose. He slapped his hand against the escape pod window.

His father looked up, wide-eyed. There were bruises on his face and an angry red cut across one cheek. He was mouthing something, but Max wasn't a lip reader, and the window was double-layered, with a vacuum between the two layers, so no sound could pass through. Rian's hands were bound as well, so he couldn't make any useful gestures. The frustration showed on his face, but he jerked his head violently to one side, as if trying to point Max toward something, telling him to go somewhere.

It was useless. Max decided he had to get his parents out of there. They would know what to do. Max backed off from the window and looked at the controls next to the escape pod door. The door could be voice-activated, but some portion of Max's mind told him it would be better to keep silent. There was a single, glowing touch panel, right beneath the green light. Max reached for the panel, but he noticed a decal next to the door. It read:

!! CAUTION !!

ESCAPE POD
DOOR CANNOT
BE OPENED ONCE
LAUNCH DOORS
ARE OPEN

!! CAUTION !!

Max choked back a sob when he saw that the green light was labeled:

LAUNCH DOOR STATUS
RED = CLOSED
GREEN = OPEN

Max looked back through the escape pod door window. "I can't open the door," he said to his father. Tears came into his eyes then, only serving to blur his vision and tighten the crushing sensation in his chest. His hands were shaking. His father shook his head, then once again jerked it to the side, following the movement with his eyes. Max wiped the wetness at his eyes with the sleeve of his spacesuit. What was his father trying to tell him? He looked sideways, in the general direction his father was jerking his head. There was only one thing in that direction: the airlock door.

There was a white-gloved hand plastered against the window.

Max thought of Holiday, and his heart seemed to stop beating, only to then resume its normal routine, but at triple speed, before finally trying to exit his body through his throat. It hurt a ton, just about crippling him. However, the thought of his sister's hand against the airlock door window shook his paralysis from him. He launched himself across the room. Teardrops shook loose from his eyes, hanging in midair like suspended rain. He reached out, and in a different time, he might have felt a little like Superman, stretched out prone like was. He hit the wall with his hands, almost rebounding off before managing to snake his fingers through a handhold. In one swift motion, he rotated his body down till his feet were resting on the floor. Face to the airlock window, he stared in. Holiday was there, in her spacesuit, her helmet on, visor down, and that was because...

Oh God save her, the outer airlock door was open!

Max knocked on the glass. Holiday looked up, not because of the sound—the airlock door had the same double-layer window as the escape pod doors, not to mention being filled to the brim with a complete vacuum—but because of the movement of his hand. Holiday had her visor in transparent mode so Max could see her face. Her eyes were wide. She brought her face as close to the window as she could. The window was about even with the middle of her forehead when she was standing flat, so she had to push up on her tiptoes to see through. Some of her hair hung down in front of her face, as if her helmet had been shoved down onto her head by someone else.

Holiday was mouthing something, but Max had no clue what she was saying. Why did everybody assume that he could read lips?

But this time he didn't need to read lips to know what she wanted him to do. And unlike the escape pod door situation, he could actually do something about his sister's plight.

He ran his hand across the airlock door control. The outer door slid closed. Holiday managed a weak smile, giving him a look he'd never forget. *I love you, Max,* was encoded in that smile. Also, *Thanks for saving my life, I suppose I'll owe you forever now. Does this mean you're going to tease me endlessly when this is all over?*

Or course, Max thought. Inside the airlock, the hiss of inflowing air became audible. He took a couple of deep breaths and exhaled.

He looked around. If it had been space pirates, they hadn't discovered him yet. He wondered where his flight helmet was. Something like that was going to become pretty important if anything else happened. He hoped they hadn't got to Riven and her father. There weren't a whole lot of places on the ship to hide, so Max's mind raced for places that the Meaneys might be held. The cockpit at the front of the ship. The reactor and life support chambers at the rear. The cockpit door was only a couple meters away. The hand around his lungs tightened when he thought of who might be on the other side of that door.

As soon as the air pressure in the airlock was equal to that of the ship, Max hit the control that opened the door. Holiday came flying through the doorway at him, capturing him in a tight embrace that sent them both backward across the room. Max grabbed a handhold to stop them.

"Oh, Max!" she whispered when her visor had flipped up. "Thank you! Thank you! Thank you!"

"What happened?" Max asked. "Where are the space pirates?"

Under different circumstances, Holiday may have had the presence of mind to ask her brother what drugs he was on to ask a random question like that, but the very real trauma of the situation held her back. *"What?!?* Space pirates? No, don't be stupid! It was Darren Meaney and that evil tramp daughter of his! We can't let them find us! What are we going to do, Max?"

Wait, what was she saying? Darren and Riven? That didn't make any sense. He had just been talking with Riven a little while ago. She had mentioned that they were going to watch *Blood Drinker*. Then he'd fallen asleep for some reason. After that...he couldn't remember...maybe if he could just get the—

Wait.

Wait.

Wait...a...minute...

Yes. He. Could. Remember. Oh. Wow. *Oh. No!*

The dam broke. It all came flooding through. Riven had been close, really close, and he'd been distracted, really distracted. Then he'd felt a pain in his neck, as if he'd been stabbed with something. Riven had watched him drift off. She'd drugged him. That little wench had shot him up with something so she could help her father hijack the *Starburst!* The drug must've caused some kind of short-term memory confusion, otherwise he would have immediately assumed that Darren and Riven were the culprits, not space pirates!

"I don't know. Quick, tell me what happened."

Holiday looked stricken. That's how Max's mind thought of it: *stricken.* She looked around, as if Darren or Riven might pop out at any moment. It was a valid concern. It was exactly the sort of thing that could happen. Her eyes went all liquid then. Max hugged her closer. He would've smoothed her hair to comfort her if she hadn't still been

151

wearing her helmet.

"Just tell me," Max said.

"It was my fault," she sobbed. "It was during one of our $1g$ breaks. Captain Meaney had left the cockpit to…well, I guess I'm not sure. Anyway, I needed to go, you know, to the restroom. Dad told me to wait till Captain Meaney came back, but I didn't listen. I went anyway, and when I left, I slammed the cockpit door, just so Dad would know how mad I was." Holiday sniffed, her nose beginning to run. "After I was done, I caught a glimpse of you and Riven. At first I thought you were asleep, but Riven was kissing you, so I was a little shocked. I mean, she was all over you."

Kissing him! Max didn't remember that at all! That meant she'd done it when he was knocked out! The tightness in his chest was changing to something a little less debilitating—the seeds of anger planted, taking root, and beginning to grow. "I was asleep," Max said.

"I know," Holiday said. "Because I was angry you were cheating on your girlfriend, I confronted you. Riven came out of her chair at me, but you were obviously unconscious. I knew something was wrong. Riven's good in space, but I—" and here Holiday's voice became more confident, less wavy, "—have the power of gymnastics on my side. She couldn't catch me. I went straight for the cockpit, but Captain Meaney caught me as I was coming out of the G-ring. He…he took my helmet from me and forced me…into the airlock. Then he used the intercom to tell Mom and Dad what he'd do if they didn't come out of the cockpit. If they did anything wrong—send a distress signal, turn the ship, pull a weapon, or just not obey him fast enough— he was going open the outer door. I think he did something so that Dad couldn't override the airlock controls from the cockpit." Fresh tears sprang into her eyes. Max wiped at them, her makeup smearing at the edges of her eyes, staining Max's fingers. "I don't know if they did any of those things, but Mom and Dad came out really quickly."

"Do you know where Mom and Dad are right now?"

Holiday nodded, pointing at the escape pod.

"Okay, what happened next?" Max asked. "Do you know what they want? Why is the *Starburst* so important to them? I mean, we're just on a family vacation. There's nothing special about what we're doing."

Holiday shook her head. "It's not this spaceship that they want. It's Dad."

"What?"

"It's true. Captain Meaney let me out of the airlock once he had Mom and Dad tied up. He took us all to the sleeping quarters. He put Mom on one of the beds, and he made Dad kneel on the floor. Then he kept asking Dad about coordinates and some discovery. He made it sound like somebody had found something on Luna, and he thought that Dad knew where it was."

"That doesn't make any sense. Dad's just does freelance security work. Why would he know anything about things on Luna?"

"I don't know, Max. That's exactly what he kept telling Captain Meaney over and over. Captain Meaney didn't believe him. That's when he started hitting Dad. But Dad still wouldn't tell him anything. So he…" Holiday's voice caught in her throat, drowned in a river of tears that no amount of wiping on Max's part was going to stop.

Max knew what his sister was going to say, and it broke his heart.

Through tears and a voice thick with hurt at the memory, Holiday said it: "He started hitting mom."

Max turned away, anger in full bloom now. His thoughts turned to the single word his father had spoken to him in the cockpit. He knew now what his father had been talking about, had been preparing him for, making sure he was ready to do what he needed to. He wasn't ready, not really, but with his father trapped in that escape pod, the only person that could help Max was Max himself. And he had a responsibility to protect his sister.

Max steeled himself. "Then what?"

"He hurt her, Max. Bad. She was unconscious the last time I saw her." The tears weren't stopping. And nobody could blame her for that. "We can't get them out of the escape pod can we?"

"We don't know that yet, Holi," Max said, holding the sides of her helmet, making sure she was only looking at him.

"I want to see her."

"Tell me the rest. Hurry. We don't know how long we have, and we have to come up with a plan to get the *Starburst* back."

Holiday searched his eyes, desperate for reassurance that her brother knew what he was doing, desperate for hope, desperate for salvation. She must have found what she was looking for because she continued, "Dad told Captain Meaney that he'd tell him whatever he wanted to know as long as he'd stop hitting mom."

"What did Dad tell him?"

Holiday wiped at her tears. Her face was a mess of makeup now. "I don't know. Captain Meaney took him in the other room. Riven stayed with me and mom. She didn't look happy about it, but she stayed. She let me help mom, but all I could really do was dab at her cuts with a damp cloth. I called Riven all sorts of names, but she never reacted. She just looked at me and Mom without saying a word."

It burned Max that all this had taken place while he'd been unconscious. If only…

No, he couldn't let regret hold him back now. There would be time later to beat himself up over being seduced by a pretty girl.

Holiday said, "When they came back, they put me in the airlock and threw my helmet in after me. Dad must not have seen my helmet come in after me, because he went willingly when Captain Meaney told him to put Mom in the escape pod and then to get in with her. After that, I barely got my helmet locked on before he'd opened the outer airlock door. He...he did it without depressurizing the airlock too. He just opened the outer door! I grabbed onto one of the handholds in there, but if I hadn't, I would've been sucked out along with all that air."

Holiday looked more angry than anything after that last part. Good, that was good. Tears—though there were still plenty of those to be shed—needed to be suppressed and saved for later. In that moment, anger, lots of rage, and a good dose of fury were better suited to the task of taking back the *Starburst*, saving their parents and bringing Captain Darren Meaney and Riven to justice.

Three things that Max intended to do. If only he could come up with a workable plan. His hands were still trembling. He was still panicked, sort of. He was...*whatever* some unsettling mix of terror and anger was. One second all he could think of was that his family might not survive their vacation, and the next second, he was so violently angry that he was clenching his fists and gritting his teeth. Then the next second he felt like he should crawl into a corner and close his eyes till it was all over.

But looking into his sister's eyes clarified things. It was time to fight his fear. It was time to man up. It was time to do what needed to be done. And even if he failed, he wouldn't have to live with the regret of not trying at all.

"Listen, Holi," Max said, trying to keep his voice from wavering. He was successful, mostly. "We're going to get through this. You and me. It's just us now. Mom and Dad are counting on us to do whatever we have to. And whatever we end up doing, we're going to do it together. I can't do this without you."

"I'm scared."

"I'm scared too." Max didn't know if that was the right thing to tell her at that moment, since he needed to be stronger for her than he'd ever been, but it was the truth. He hoped it was easier to cope with being scared when you were being scared right next to somebody else.

"I want to save Mom and Dad," Holiday said, setting her chin. "I want to make the Meaneys pay. I want our vacation back."

Max knew that the Storm family space vacation was over and that there was no real way to salvage it. He kept this knowledge to himself though, nodded, and brought his forehead to Holiday's helmet. "I love you, Holi, you know that right?"

She nodded back, "I love you too, Max."

"Ok, we need to get to the cockpit. It's the only place we have a chance of getting more control of this situation than they have. Did either of the Meaneys have any weapons?"

"Not that I saw. Captain Meaney just used his..." Holiday clenched her eyes.

"Don't think about that right now," Max said. "Did you bring anything that could be used as a weapon?"

Holiday shook her head. "I don't think so."

"Me either. I have some drawing pens, but those probably aren't dangerous enough. That means we'll have to either overpower them or outsmart them."

"Outsmarting them is easy," Holiday said simply. "Bait."

"What?"

"We need to lure them away from the cockpit. To do that, you need bait. That's me."

Max didn't like the thought of his sister putting herself in direct peril like that. Then again, she already was, so perhaps it was just a different sort of danger. She'd already been threatened with being evacuated into space, and she didn't seem traumatized. Max knew then that his sister was a lot tougher than she looked, and she was light years tougher than he was.

"You're the genius, Sis. What are you thinking?" The score on Holiday's latest IQ test had been 155. Sabatha and Rian thought it would be higher if she didn't spend so much time watching *Quantum Girl!!,* but when your daughter kept testing in the *genius* category, you were inclined to let her have one or two vices. History had shown that many geniuses were perceived as crazy—some used the word "eccentric" when they were trying to be nice—talking to tables and walls in Latin, or mowing their lawn naked, that sort of thing. Watching too much holo seemed tame by comparison. Besides, Holiday's IQ was rising as she aged. She'd been tested two years before and had scored only 140. *Only 140,* as if that didn't place her in the *highly gifted* category as it was. Nobody knew how high it would go before it stopped. They had unspoken fears about it going high enough that the government would notice. Then they'd do something that neither of her parents wanted, like try to recruit her. For this reason they administered the tests themselves privately.

"It doesn't take a genius to steal ideas from holos," Holiday said. "Were just going to do what Quantum Girl!! and Captain Xeode did in episode 100."

"Tell me."

"Simple plans are the best ones, right? Fewer things to go wrong. Anyway, you hide somewhere. I create a diversion in the G-ring. When they come to get me, you sneak into the cockpit, get control of the ship back, save our parents, and then we think seriously about shoving the Meaneys out an airlock without spacesuits."

There was a hardness in Holiday's voice that Max wasn't sure he liked, but that just might be necessary. *Whatever it takes* were the three words of the hour. Holiday had realized and accepted that a whole lot easier than Max had. Despite his emerging bravado, he was still coming to grips with the whole direness of their situation.

"Okay, but you need to get into the cockpit with me, Holi. I don't have anything to bargain with if you get caught."

"I know. I need a signal."

Max wasn't thinking clearly enough to come up with anything fast. "What do you think I should do?"

Holiday looked over her shoulder at the escape pod their parents were held captive in. Max saw that she really was scared. Her anger hadn't totally taken that from her. Smart or not, brave or not, the inescapable fact was that she was still a girl who was in danger of losing her parents. Max didn't know how she was holding herself together. He was on the verge of breaking. He wanted to cry, and he wanted to breathe normally. Neither of those things were happening though.

"Turn out the lights," Holiday said. "All of them. Even the emergency ones."

"But you won't be able to see."

"I won't need to. I have this spaceship memorized. I know exactly where everything is. I can navigate it with my eyes closed."

"Are you sure?"

"Yes."

Max sensed that she might be lying. Still, she had the best memory he'd ever seen, and it wasn't like he had a whole bag full of better ideas. "Okay," he said. "I just need a place to hide."

"Easy," Holiday said. "Pick the one place that they won't expect."

Holiday stared into his sister's eyes, and right then and there, he believed that she was already walking down the *eccentric* route, because what she was suggesting was craziness. He only hoped that he and Nika would have settled down out of state when his sister took up mowing the lawn naked. "Good idea," he said, because really, it was useless to protest at that point. Besides, it would work. Probably.

"There's a helmet for you in that compartment," Holiday said, pointing. Max reached up, opened the compartment and pulled the helmet out, put it on, locked it in position, then double-checked his glove and boot seals.

"Ready?" Max said, then inclining his head. "Do you want to see

Mom and Dad?"

"No, not now," Holiday said. "I did, but now I don't think I can do that without crying. As long as they're in the escape pod they're sorta safe. And we can't help them from here. I think I can do this as long as they're safe in there."

"Okay," Max said, happy that she was almost as talkative as she normally was, answering his question with an essay when a simple "yes" or "no" would have done the job. He hugged her one last time, their helmets bumping. They lowered their visors. Max opened up the private channel between his helmet and Holiday's. He checked their statistics. They both had spacesuit integrity and adequate oxygen. Hopefully they wouldn't need any of that. Unless their spacesuits detected a lack of oxygen on the outside of the suit, they'd use external air before switching to internal reserves. "Remember, if you get in trouble, just ask yourself, 'What would Quantum Girl!! do?' "

"Max, that's how I live my life."

With that, Max pushed off towards the airlock. He opened the inner door, transferred door control to his suit and sent the verbal command to close the door. Holiday raised her thumb at him, then her visor went dark. The door closed, cutting off his view of her. Max sat down, getting out of direct view of the airlock window.

"Max, there's nobody in the sleeping quarters. Okay, I just thought of something."

"What?"

"I know how I'm going to make a diversion."

"Is it dangerous?"

"Yes."

"Don't blow yourself up."

No response.

"Holi?"

"I heard you. I was deciding whether what I'm going to do will produce an explosion of a catastrophic nature."

Catastrophic nature. Only Holiday would put it like that. Max didn't know what to say. "Um, will it?"

"Probably not."

"Probably?"

"It won't. I'm sure."

"You don't sound sure."

"Too late, I'm in the galley already. Nobody here, and I don't see anybody in the recreation area. The door to the reactor and life support chambers is open. My guess is Captain Meaney is back there. That would mean that Riven's in the cockpit."

"Well, it's either that or the other way around."

"Hah, funny. You know, if the Meaneys were more observant, they probably would've discovered us already. They underestimated us."

"Be careful, Holi."

"This thing's insured right?"

"I'm sure it is."

"Just make sure you turn those lights off quickly, Max."

"All I need is for you to let me know that you can see both of them."

"I put three bottles of Sunspot shampoo in the cooker."

Max was speechless, but responded anyway, "Um, okay. That stuff is flammable?"

"Explosive is the word you're looking for, Max."

"And how is that safe to put in your hair?"

"I don't heat my head up to five hundred degrees. Ever. That would be dangerous regardless of what shampoo I use. Anyway, it should be more smoke than flame. As long as the cooker itself doesn't catch fire, any flame should be mostly contained within the cooker. Ready or not, here goes. Okay I've turned the cooker on. It's all the way up. This will only take a few seconds. I'm going to hide beside one of the couches. Hopefully they'll see the smoke before they notice me."

"Or that fact that I'm not there anymore."

"Yeah, that. Behind the couch now. Still don't see either of them. Ok, the cooker is smoking."

Max felt the *Starburst* shudder, as if something had hit the hull.

"Was that—?" he asked.

"Oh yeah," Holiday replied.

Max decided to take a chance and stand. He moved toward the front of the ship, making sure he had some view through the window. As long as Riven—if she was the one in the cockpit—passed by without checking the airlock, he'd be fine. Then, a brief moment of panic seized him. When he'd found Holiday, the outer door had been open. It wasn't anymore. If Riven noticed...

Nothing he could do about it. Holiday's diversion had already been triggered. Besides, he wouldn't have time to fill the airlock again if he opened the door now. If Riven looked in, he'd open the door and deal with her. Punch her in the face or something. Max told himself that he could take her. He had to tell himself two to three times because the first couple times he didn't sound convincing.

"Max, Mr. Meaney came out of the reactor chamber. Riven's probably up there with you. He hasn't seen me yet. There's smoke everywhere, lots more than we could've hoped for. Perfect." Then Holiday swore. It was a word Max hadn't realized she knew. "He sees me."

"Is he armed?"

"Busy."

There was a flash of black across the airlock window. Riven. Max counted to five, then triggered the door. It slid open. He looked down the center pole and caught sight of Riven's backside as she pulled herself through into the galley. Her body was swallowed by black smoke.

"Max, he has a knife. Hurry."

That was bad. Riven might have one too. "Riven's on her way to you, Sis."

"Roger that. Get those lights off for me, pretty please."

"On it," Max said, already pulling himself through the cockpit door. His heart was a rolling thunder in his chest. There was sweat beading on his forehead. He activated the helmet blowers. Much better.

Through the cockpit window, Luna dominated the view. It was bright and beautiful, but Max didn't really notice.

Coming down into the pilot's seat, Max frantically searched the control panel. He knew where everything was, but his recall was delayed due to the stress of the situation.

"Come get me, you ugly wench," Holiday's voice said in Max's ear. He could hear her breaths, deep and quick.

"Computer, all internal lights off. Emergency lights off. Exception for the cockpit."

"Thanks," Holiday said. "Just in time too. Headed toward you. I'm feeling good. Kicked one of them in the head. I think it was that witch Riven."

"Bad kiddies," Darren's voice said. He had either managed to locate the intercom on one of the walls, or he'd connected his spacesuit to the intercom earlier. Max was thankful there were certain controls that weren't possible to transfer out of the cockpit. Navigation was one of them. *"You made a big mistake. We were going to let you all live. Now I have to do something very bad to your mommy and daddy."*

"I'm sorry, Max," Riven said, her voice diabolically calm.

The *Starburst* shuddered.

"No!" Holiday screamed.

Max stared in horror at the control console, not wanting to believe the indicator light that had just lit up.

The escape pod containing Rian and Sabatha Storm had just been launched.

[Chapter Seventeen]

What Happened In The Cockpit When Holiday Revealed Her Secret

Max turned just as Holiday's helmet popped through the cockpit door. She shot through, her hands up, body trailing smoke. Her hands hit the ceiling. She pushed off, widening her legs, travelling back towards the door, only her feet landing on either side of it so she didn't go through. Her body absorbed most of the shock, so when she bounced off, she didn't go far. She ended up hovering several inches above the door.

"Close the door!" she yelled.

Max waved his hand across the control console, and the door closed, then locked. Nobody else was coming inside.

"Where are they?" Holiday asked, her voice choking. She tumbled forward over the chairs, stopping her forward movement with a handhold before swinging down into the copilot's seat.

"There," Max said, pointing to a display on the control console where he'd brought up one of the external cameras.

"Are we locked down?" Holiday asked, raising her visor.

"What?"

"Is everything locked down? Can the Meaneys control anything from out there?"

Max swore at his oversight. He quickly locked out all systems from external control. He closed the reactor chamber door. One of the two remaining escape pods wasn't accepting his commands though. He hit his hand on one of his armrests.

"What is it?" Holiday asked.

Max told her. She merely nodded and went back to staring at the hurtling escape pod their parents were trapped in.

"I can't communicate with the pod, Holi. I'm sorry. The Meaneys can't control an escape pod remotely, but I think they did something to the radio—the one here, not the escape pod. I can't contact anybody on Luna for help either."

"I can't read them either," Holiday said. Then she took off her helmet and put her head in her hands, her fingers on her temples, rubbing in circles, as if she was concentrating, trying to move the escape pod back into the spaceship through force of will.

Max was confused. "Yeah, the radio and all."

Holiday looked over at him, and for a second, she looked about ten years older than she was. She looked weary. "Take off your helmet, Max."

"Why?"

"Just do it, okay?"

Max took off his helmet.

"This has been happening for as long as I can remember, but it's been pretty much constant since we've been up in space. I don't really have a lot of control, but I should be able to show you."

"Hello, kiddies!" Darren's voice taunted through the intercom. *"Now that your parents aren't here, you don't have to follow their rules anymore. Why don't you let us into the cockpit? We promise we won't hurt you!"*

"Computer, mute intercom," Max said. There, now they wouldn't have to listen to their hijackers. There wasn't a lot of damage Captain Meaney or Riven could do to the *Starburst* without putting their own lives in danger, so he figured they had some time to collect their thoughts and figure out their next move. He turned back to his sister, who was now staring intently at him. She looked like she was trying to read his thoughts. Max's mind laughed at that idea. Now wouldn't that just be something so like her? She was already a certified genius—it only made sense that she was pushing her intelligence to the next level. Great, so much for privacy.

Holiday laughed, but it looked like it hurt. "I won't read your thoughts unless you ask me to."

Max's mouth dropped. No. No. No. He'd been joking.

"This is no joke," Holiday said, smiling, though her smile was pained. She was ready to start crying again. "I really can hear what you're thinking."

"Ah...wonderful?" Max suggested, too stunned to have any decent sort of reaction. Really, it was wonderful, but also it really wasn't. What kind of messed up world was it where your sister announced that she was telepathic while your parents were adrift in space in an escape pod, and you and your aforementioned sister were in the middle of a spaceship hijacking? A super ultra mega messed up one.

"It's sorta neat," Holiday said, "but it comes and goes. It usually happens when I'm not thinking about doing it. I just sorta pick up other people's thoughts. It's almost like somebody's talking in another room, and I'm just overhearing their conversation."

"And you were trying to hear Mom and Dad?"

"Yeah. I could before, sometimes. It was helpful to know they were alive. Now I can't. I think they're too far away."

"They'll land on Luna, you know," Max said. "That's what the escape pods are programmed to do."

"I'm worried we're too far away."

Max studied the console. "No, I think we're good." This was one of the first outright lies that Max had told his sister in a long time. The console didn't indicate any such thing. Then he realized that his sister was probably still reading his mind. He stared out into space and filled his mind with thoughts of Nika. It worked. Thoughts of the escape pod were quickly replaced by images of his Nika and the memory of her insistent kisses. If anything could replace all other thoughts in his male mind, it was thoughts of her. "They'll be fine. We'll meet up with them on Luna." Max almost found himself believing it, in large part because he intended to make it happen, just as soon as the invisible ropes around his neck were removed and the urge to vomit had finally passed. Should happen any minute. Max thought some more about Nika and tried to slow his breathing.

"What are we going to do, Max?" Holiday said. Max saw drops of liquid on the control console. Holiday was weeping silently. She was being as brave and as strong as she could, but her limits were being tested.

WHAM!!

Something had slammed against the cockpit door. Holiday squeaked in fright. She buried her head in her hands.

It didn't take a telepath to know what she was thinking.

[We're not going to make it!]

Max had to stop that line of thinking, and he had to do it quickly. Gently, but quickly. He rotated the pilot's chair and turned the copilot's chair so that he was knee-to-knee with his sister. "Holi, listen to me. We *are* going to make it, and I don't want to hear you say anything like that again. I know this is difficult, but I am not letting anything happen to you. I swear to God."

"Okay, I believe you, but I didn't say anything," Holiday said.

"Yes, you did. You said, 'We're not going to make it.' "

"No, I didn't."

"Yes, you did."

"No. *I didn't.* At least not out loud."

"Yes, *you*...wait..."

Holiday leaned forward, searching his face. "You could hear that?

I only *thought* it."

Nothing came out when Max tried to speak next. Either his vocal cords had vanished, or somebody had sucked the atmosphere out of the room, and there was just no medium for sound waves to travel through.

WHAM!!

WHAM!!

Again, Holiday squeaked. Max made sure the door was holding. It was. He checked the console for the status of the escape pod. It was indeed headed toward Luna. The cameras showed the escape pod's maneuvering thrusters firing, making slight adjustments to its trajectory and speed.

Max said a prayer for his mother and father. The thought of his mother, beaten unconscious, simmered like an underground lava flow, dangerous and deadly, but still hidden beneath the surface. Until it broke through, it was just a warm threat, held back only by Max's own fears, his anger and his inability to deal with the emotions that pushed and pulled inside him. Fear for his parents. Fear for his sister. Fear for himself. Fear of pain. Fear of death. Anger at Darren and Riven Meaney. Anger at his parents. Anger at himself. The desire, the need to panic. The need to stay calm, for himself and for his little sister. All these things warred within him. He wanted to cry. He felt like laughing. He needed to crawl into a bed and fall asleep. Then hopefully, he'd realize that this was—please, God let it be—only a dream. Only a really bad, horrible nightmare that he could wake up from and laugh about after the chill of drying sweat faded from him.

A nightmare, though, it was not.

"You can hear my thoughts too?" Holiday asked, breaking through Max's dark reverie.

"I...don't...well, maybe."

"What am I thinking right now?"

Max listened for a few seconds. "I have no clue."

"Try again."

Max listened again, wondering if this was really what they should be spending their time on. Dealing with the hijacking of their spaceship and finding a way to reunite with their parents were more important. He shook his head. "Nothing."

"Well, maybe you can't really hear my thoughts. Maybe I'm broadcasting. Maybe I can put my thoughts in your head. Then, you wouldn't really have to have any telepathic abilities."

Now Max was sure their focus should be elsewhere. They should be figuring out how they were going to get Darren and Riven Meaney off the spaceship. Telepathy probably wasn't going to be the answer. Not unless Holiday could make their minds think that the airlock door was the entrance to the cockpit.

"If I've been broadcasting," Holiday said, "then it's been happening without my knowledge. I guess I don't know how to control this. And if I can't control it, then it's useless at the moment." She swore, bending her head over the display that showed the escape pod spinning in an elegant spiral. Her shoulders sagged. "I guess I was hoping that I had some useful ability—something that could save Mom and Dad, or get the Meaneys off this ship."

Max put a hand on his sister's knee. "I know neither of us has the time right now to process what you can do, but it is special, and it is useful. Let's not worry about it right now though. We need to deal with the Meaneys. They've probably found the emergency lanterns, so the darkness back there isn't slowing them down much."

"Okay." Holiday nodded her head.

As if in answer there was a KA-WHUMP!

That time, the hull of the *Starburst* quivered in reaction. Thankfully, the cockpit door held. The computer indicated the maneuvering thrusters had to make a minor course correction. Max's ears were ringing.

The Meaneys had detonated something inside the ship.

[CHAPTER EIGHTEEN]

WHAT HAPPENED WHEN MAXIMILLION AND HOLIDAY TRIED TO ESCAPE

Max held Holiday's hand, and she seemed to appreciate it. She squeezed his hand, even attempted another smile, though she was only a little more successful that the last time. Even though her thoughts weren't being beamed directly into his brain, Max knew that they were of their parents. That was like her though, empathetic enough that her concern was for others first rather than herself.

The panel in the floor slid aside when Max touched the control that opened it. He reached down and pulled one case from the compartment. Holiday took the second case.

"What are these for, and how did you know they were there?" Holiday asked.

"Dad showed me. As for what they're for—it's better to just show you, but I'm pretty sure you already know."

"Yeah," Holiday said. "But even if I couldn't, I can see it in your mind."

"Holi, I love you, but stay out of my head."

"Sorry, I can't help it. I'm not doing it on purpose."

"Okay, well then just don't tell me when you're doing it." The last thing Max needed at that moment was to know which particular thoughts his sister was hearing.

Max spoke the password, then unlocked the first case. There was a brief hiss of air as the case equalized its internal pressure with that of the cockpit. He did the same with the case Holiday was holding. They opened them simultaneously.

"I don't know if I can do this," Holiday said. Her face betrayed the distaste she bore for real-life weapons.

"You don't have to do anything," Max said. "I'm the only one who knows what these are and how to use them." He thought that a month at Wilderness Camp would've improved his skill, but he wasn't a bad shot. Well, at least against unmoving, paper targets.

"Just because I don't like shooting guns, doesn't mean I don't know about them. For example, your case has two Remington Pyros and a Mark Seven Neural Disruptor. My case has an older weapon in it. A Reaper."

Max's eyes widened. He hadn't ever heard of a Reaper.

Holiday continued. "It's also illegal to own one. They're restricted military issue. How come Dad has one of these? And how did he get it?"

Max was wondering the same thing. He thought about his father's service in the Space Command. He thought about the weapons his father might have been familiarized with during his tour of duty. He thought about his father stealing a weapon such as the Reaper, and his mind couldn't accept it. His father wouldn't do something like that. If he had these weapons, there was a good explanation.

Max picked up one of the Pyros and loaded it. The ammo was in a clip that slid in through the grip. The clip clicked into place and the readout on the side of the weapon read: **100%.**

"Give me the Reaper," Max said.

"Give me the other Pyro," Holiday said. "I'll trade you for the Reaper."

"You don't like guns," Max said, handing the second Pyro over anyway, taking the Reaper. It didn't have much mass to it. In spite of the lack of gravity, the weapon seemed to drift into his palm and stay there, as if that's where it belonged, where it wanted to be.

"Yeah, well I also don't like the spaceship I'm on being hijacked. Nor do I like having my parents shot out into space. So, what I like doesn't really matter, does it?" Holiday said all this while sniffing, a tear on her cheek.

"No, it doesn't," Max said quietly. His sister was older than she was. He'd known that for a long time, but sometimes it was so evident, so overwhelming that he felt a strange kind of pride to be her brother.

"I'll take that too," Holiday said, pointing.

"This?" Max asked. She wanted the Disrupter.

"Yes. That way I won't be forced to use the Pyro unless something really bad happens. The Disrupter should be enough." Holiday held out her hand.

Max slapped the silver cylinder into her palm. "If you never let Dad teach you how to shoot, what makes you think you know how to use the Pyro?"

Holiday answered by taking an ammo clip from the case Max was holding, pushing the quick release, and watching magnesium-tipped bullets stream into the open. She caught them in quick succession, reinserted them into the clip, then slammed the clip into the grip of her Pyro. Her fingers flew across the delicate control surfaces on the grip, running it through the self-cleaning and diagnostic process that ensured complete firing reliability. Two seconds later, the Pyro beeped and the readout on the side glowed a green: **100%.** Her thumb switched the safety lock off. The gun was ready, like a hand grenade with the pin pulled.

"Careful," Max warned. "That thing is dangerous like that."

"No, it's not," Holiday said. *"I'm* dangerous like this. I don't like guns, and I don't like touching them. I feel queasy and a little sick holding this thing. But all these things are not the same thing as not knowing how to use it. I took the safety off because our current situation is anything but safe. If I have to use this, I'm not going to waste a nanosecond disabling some safety feature. The only safety anybody needs to worry about is not doing something that would make me point this at them."

Max made a mental note never to make his sister mad. Ever again. He kept reminding himself that his sister was only twelve.

"And I don't need Dad to teach me how to shoot," Holiday said. "I learned all I need to know through other sources."

"You don't mean..."

"Hush, Max, you don't watch *Quantum Girl!!,* so you have no clue what type of useful information can be learned from it."

Fantastic. His sister had learned to shoot guns by watching an animated holo feed. Max had a moment of panic about this, but quickly pushed it away. He had enough to worry about without adding trust to his list. If his sister said she could do something, she was telling the truth, flat out.

The ammo for the Reaper was comprised of clear vials. All of the vials were connected to each other, each filled with a black liquid that appeared not to know that it was in a zero-*g* environment, since the liquid kept pooling to one side of each vial. It was as if they'd managed to contain and liquefy shadow.

Max saw that his hand was trembling as he picked up the vials. Holiday reached out to steady him. Together, they slid the vials into the ammo slot of the Reaper. The weapon didn't make a sound. It just accepted the ammo without comment. It didn't begin to hum. Lights didn't flash. And yet, it looked somehow more ominous.

There weren't any controls on the Reaper other than the trigger. There was no safety, no readouts, no writing. Absolutely nothing. It didn't need any of these things to get in the way of its intended purpose.

Which was to end life.

Max felt like putting the Reaper back in its case. He wasn't sure he was ready to use a weapon that didn't bother with flashing lights, readouts and safety features, but readily acknowledged what it was and what would make it happy.

Instead, he kept it in his hand. Because he had to. The Pyro he attached to a clip on his spacesuit. Max secured his helmet, and lowered the visor. Holiday did the same.

Max sighed, staring at the Reaper in his shaking hand. Images of Captain Meaney and Riven flashed in his mind. The thought of pointing the Reaper at either of them and squeezing the trigger was repulsive, but that was precisely what he was about to do. If only he had an idea of what their real plan was.

"What's the plan?" Holiday asked through the private channel. "I don't like the idea of going out there guns blazing if that's what you were thinking."

"No, we can't do that," Max said. "Somebody would get hurt. Probably us." He looked out the cockpit window and saw the ever-growing moon. The display on the console still showed the loosed escape pod. He looked back to Luna, then back once again to the escape pod.

And there he had it. The Plan.

"I don't know how to land the *Starburst*," he said.

"Is that supposed to comfort me?" Holiday asked.

"No. What it means is that even if we can somehow hold off the Meaneys, we still have two problems. First is that we can't land, and the second is we can't help our parents in a timely manner."

"Max, stop it. Don't make me cry with my helmet on." She meant it too; her voice was cracking.

"Also, at this point, Captain Meaney and Riven probably think we're going to attempt to land this spaceship. Either that or alter its course to rescue Mom and Dad. That means we can't do either of those things. Instead, we have to do something they won't expect."

"And that is...?"

Max voice faltered, making it sound like he didn't have faith in his own plan. Which, he supposed, was somewhat true. Making hard decisions was the only alternative to giving into his base nature, surrendering to his panic, curling into a fetal ball in the corner and just waiting for fate to do with him what it would. He cleared his throat. "We're going to use one of the escape pods."

"What?!?"

"It makes the most sense, Sis. They're already programmed to land on Luna. We can let the Meaneys have the *Starburst,* and we'll get to Luna just like we need to. The escape pods have all the supplies we need—oxygen, food, water, radios. We might even be able to help Mom and Dad. At least we'll be in a better position to get help for them. Remember, these escape pods are mobile when they reach the surface."

Holiday was silent.

"What are you thinking?" Max asked.

"That your plan is probably the craziest thing I have ever heard in my entire life. It has a high chance of getting us both killed."

Not exactly a rousing endorsement. Max felt the constriction in his chest tighten. He switched the Reaper to his other hand, hoping that simple movement might serve to focus his mind and prevent a complete panic attack.

Holiday sighed. "And it's exactly what Quantum Girl!! would do!"

Great. Just....great.

"That means it's going to work," she declared. "All we have to do is make sure that the Meaneys don't interfere with our entrance into the escape pod."

"We have the bigger guns," Max said. "They'll do what we tell them to. If not…" He left that unfinished. It didn't need to be said. Holiday knew what he meant. Even if he still didn't know if he could go through with it when push came to shoot. "Okay, is there anything we're forgetting?"

Holiday's helmet shook from side-to-side. *No.*

Max's helmet dipped then raised. *Roger.* He danced his fingers across the control console. Then, he pushed out of his seat. "I have the escape pod control transferred to me, and I've locked the *Starburst* controls. If we can't have control of the ship, then neither can they." Max couldn't believe the command in his voice. It almost sounded like he knew what he was doing. He floated there for a few moments, and when he found that his eyes were on his sister, he kicked off and hugged her. She had her leg braced, so they didn't move too much.

"I'll be right behind you," Holiday said.

"Computer, remove intercom mute," Max said as he reactivated the lights throughout the interior of the spaceship. "Captain Meaney."

There was only the briefest of pauses, then, *"Thanks for turning the lights back on, kiddo. The lanterns only had seventeen more hours on them, and Riven was starting to get a little worried. Now, are you gonna let us in so we can work this out, or do I have to blow the cockpit door in?"*

Max's ears burned at the word "kiddo." Darren didn't have the right to call him that. "We're not letting you in, but we are coming out there. We're ready to talk."

Max brought up an internal HUD that showed one of the cameras in the escape pod bay. He could see Riven hovering near the cockpit door. Her hair free-floated around her, making her look like some wild space creature. Captain Meaney wasn't visible there. All the other cameras were offline. Max cursed himself for not checking to make sure they hadn't been tampered with earlier.

"Good to hear it. You're making a smart move, you and your sister. Less people get hurt this way. We'll be waiting for you."

"No. No you won't. Get out of the escape pod bay. Get back into the rear of the ship. We'll come out of the cockpit and meet you in the back of the ship, where there's plenty of room for us to all watch each other."

"Not going to happen, kiddo. You just come out and let us get into that cockpit. After that, we'll discuss what needs to be discussed."

"This isn't a negotiation," Max said.

"Open the cockpit door, or when we get in there, I'm going to make you watch while I throw your sister out an airlock without her spacesuit on. You can watch while her veins freeze and her blood boils."

Max couldn't help it, the image of his sister being expelled from the *Starburst* hit him, and it was beyond horror, her body swelling, her futile attempts for air. It was almost impossible to survive for longer than ninety seconds in a vacuum. People usually went unconscious within the first fifteen seconds due to oxygen-deprived blood. Max shuddered at the images, shaking his head to try to banish them from his mind.

"For a person who spends as much time in space as you do, you know nothing about space, loser," Holiday said. "You don't freeze because your body heat doesn't go away quickly, and your blood doesn't boil because it's not exposed. Why don't you read a book or something sometime if you're going to be out here hijacking spaceships? Nobody wants to be hijacked by an uneducated moron."

"Just wait, you little tramp!" Captain Meaney roared.

"Max," Riven said, her voice suddenly sultry. *"If you come out, I'll let you—"*

The rest of whatever she was going to say was lost in her screams.

Max looked at his HUD, the image from the camera in the escape pod bay showing Riven holding on for her life, the airlock doors open. Both of them. Max watched Riven struggle to maintain her grip, each hand on a different handhold. He looked and felt nothing except fear that this plan wasn't going to work. There was some amusement as her helmet, which had been floating somewhere in there, exited the spaceship, clipping Riven's boot as it went.

The warning klaxon that sounded a few seconds later was quickly muted by Max. He didn't want to hear the ship's voice repeating, *WARNING! AIRLOCK MISCONFIGURATION! INTERNAL PRESSURE DROPPING BELOW SAFE LEVELS!* over and over. Things like that could really get on a person's nerves.

Satisfied that his point was made, Max closed the airlock doors. Riven was gasping for air, frantically searching compartments for another helmet. Her tears looked like floating rain. Max found he didn't care.

"Get out of the escape pod bay, or I will depressurize this entire spaceship," Max said. "You have three seconds to move."

He watched as Riven located a new helmet, shoved it on her head. Still coughing, she grabbed the center pole and pulled herself out of the escape pod bay.

"You're hardcore," Holiday whispered, no small amount of awe in her voice.

"We have to do this fast," Max said, grabbing one of the ceiling handholds, pulling his body toward the door. Holiday was right behind him. "Cover me."

Max opened the door and looked into the escape pod bay. Traces of smoke wafted into the cockpit, but he didn't see any movement. Cautiously, he pulled his body through, leading with the business end of the Reaper. He was pretty sure that if either Darren or Riven came at him, he was going to shoot them from pure reflex. He was an unsettled guy with a gun, and it would be best if nobody spooked him. He came into the escape pod bay, where everything looked clear. He motioned for Holiday to follow him.

She came though, head first, tumbling at the last second so her feet landed properly, her hand shooting out to grab a handhold. She had one hand free to hold the Disruptor.

Max noted that the walls around the cockpit door were scorched black, blast patterns radiating like rays from a sun. Whatever they'd used, it hadn't been enough—though they'd probably been cautious, not wanting to blow a hole in the hull.

Keeping the Reaper trained on the opening to the sleeping quarters, Max moved toward one of the remaining escape pods. He looked inside. It was clear.

"Maaaax," Riven's voice said through the intercom. *"That wasn't very nice of you. It may affect our relationship. We may have to work on a little thing called trust."*

"What my daughter is trying to say is that we're back here waiting for you and your sister to hold up your end of the bargain," Darren said. *"Why don't you come back here, and we'll work all this out. I'm sure we can come to a mutually beneficial arrangement."*

Max opened the escape pod door. It swung open.

Over the private channel, Holiday said, "You know she's not his daughter, right?"

Max hadn't known that. Hadn't suspected it. But he knew Holiday was right, like she always was, about everything. He felt duped. He felt stupid. He felt angry. He readily embraced this anger, but found that there was also a certain amount of sadness in there. And he was surprised that the sadness was aimed at Riven. Actually, the sadness, now that he considered it, felt more like pity. It kind of hurt. All that youth, all that beauty, all that vibrancy—wasted. The beauty on the outside was stained by the corruption within. He wondered what sequence of events had led her down this path. Part of him wondered the same thing about Captain Meaney, but Max's connection to Riven's—what?…her partner?…*her lover??*—wasn't as strong. What dark influences had twisted her mind, guiding her choices till they had her participating in the hijacking of a spaceship? The small cut in Max's neck itched. He thought of Nika and her sweet spirit and how she was waiting for him back on Earth. These thoughts drove tears to the edges of his lids.

"Riven," Max said. "What's your real last name?"

"What're you playing at, boy?" Darren asked.

"Tell me," Max implored. He waved to Holiday. She pushed toward the escape pod door.

Silence on the intercom.

Then: *"I can't tell you that, Max."*

Darren's laughter came through the intercom, loud and clear and mocking, killer clown-like, as if he were some animated cartoon character. Max set his jaw.

"I'm disappointed in you then," Max said.

"What are you doing?" Holiday asked. "Stop talking to that bimbo and get in the escape pod!"

Max nodded. "It's not too late for you. For either of you, but especially you, Riven."

"I'm sorry, Max," Riven said, her voice quiet. Max imagined her crying, but that was wishful thinking if it was anything.

Me too, Max thought, looking over his shoulder, where he could see Holiday crawling through the escape pod door.

Of course, that's when Captain Darren Meaney attacked.

He came fast, real fast, shooting through the opening, pulling his body along the center pole. Somehow he managed to redirect his trajectory so he barreled right at Max. Holiday was yelling something, but Max was too confused and surprised to comprehend what she was saying. Some reflex had Max trying to get the Reaper into firing position, but his hands and arms were paralyzed, the panic detonating inside him like nuclear bomb, tearing at his skin. He felt like he might come apart right then and there. Darren's body slammed into Max's, the momentum carrying them to the floor, where they both rebounded back into the air. The Reaper went tumbling away. Darren had both of Max's forearms pinned, his fingers tightening like bands of steel. Their helmets collided. Darren was too strong, much stronger than Max. Though Max was no slouch in the muscles department, wrestling with Darren was not a fight he could win. His mind raced for an option— any course of action he could take to turn the fight in his favor. Max twisted sideways as Darren released one of his arms in an attempt to pull the Pyro from him.

Some movement flashed behind Darren.

"*Stop it!*" Holiday screamed, broadcasting to everybody.

Darren and Max were still bouncing around the escape pod bay, but Max caught a glimpse of Holiday bracing her back against the wall, her feet set in a wide stance. She had her Pyro in one hand, and the Reaper in the other. The Disrupter was down on her waist. Max realized why—the Disrupter wouldn't work through the spacesuit materials. How had they not realized that earlier? Stupid.

Darren brought their tumble to an abrupt stop, swinging Max around in front of him, holding him secure in place with his other arm clamped around Max's neck, making sure that any shot taken would have a good chance of hitting Max.

"Careful with that," Darren said. "Your brother might get hurt. The type of hurt that means you need buried."

"Riven, your partner is about to die," Holiday said. She sounded tough as spikes, but Max knew that she was crying. The sight of his twelve-year-old sister with two deadly weapons in her hand, threatening to inflict mortal damage on somebody was enough to break his heart. "You can either save him by telling him to let my brother go, or you can tell him goodbye."

"You're not that good of a shot, girlie," Darren said, but his voice didn't sound sure.

"If I squeeze this trigger, you will die," Holiday said. It was that simple. It was fact. It was a promise. It was inevitable. She wouldn't miss. In that moment, Max knew this to be truth.

"You might want to let Max go," Riven said.

Darren shook his head. "I don't think so. Go ahead and shoot. I want to see how big a hole you burn in your brother."

Max could see movement at the entrance to the sleeping quarters. Riven was hovering right there, biding her time presumably.

"I tried," Riven said. "He's pretty stubborn. Perhaps as stubborn as Holi is."

"Don't call me that," Holiday said. "You don't have the right."

"Boy, tell your sister that she needs to put those weapons down, or I'm going to break your neck. C'mon, be smart."

Holiday's voice came over the private channel. Her voice was cold, distant, and sounded strangely like Sabatha's. "In two seconds, you need to jump."

"What?" Max asked, but by then, he already had his feet in the air.

The Pyro in Holiday's left hand spoke, loudly and brightly. She fired a burning star right through Darren's right boot. Max didn't feel the heat from the shot, but his mind imagined it—an intense fire that melted spacesuit and skin and bone with reds and blues and greens.

Two things happened then, more or less at the same time. First, Darren, caught in the all-consuming agony of his wounded foot, screamed and released Max. Second, an alarm began to sound through the ship. Along with the deafening alarm, the ship was speaking. What it said went a little something like this: *WARNING! IRREPARABLE HULL BREACH DETECTED! INTERNAL PRESSURE DROPPING BELOW SAFE LEVELS! ENTER ESCAPE PODS IMMEDIATELY!*

"What have you done?!?" Riven yelled.

Max was frozen for a second, as immobile as if Darren was still holding him. The *Starburst*'s atmosphere raced to get into space. The whine of the escaping oxygen was strangely complementary to the sound of the alarm.

"Get in the escape pod, Max," Holiday said, now pointing the Reaper at Darren and the Pyro at where Riven lurked.

Max pushed off, sailing toward the escape pod, pulling his body forward, through the door, then onto one of the mattresses. He turned on his back, looking back through the door. He couldn't see Darren, but he could hear him screaming. He didn't think Darren could still be a threat with a hole in his spacesuit.

Riven was a different story.

Max could only see the top of Holiday's helmet from his position.

"I need to get in that escape pod," Riven said.

"Oh, you mean that escape pod?" was all Holiday said before brilliant rainbow light filled the bay for the second time. "*I think it has a hole in it.*"

"*Nooooo!*" Riven screamed.

Riven must've made a move for Holiday, because Holiday said, "That will get you hurt. Back off."

The next thing Max knew, Holiday was through the escape pod door, pulling it closed with her boot—a maneuver that Max didn't think he could've pulled off. When the door closed, atmosphere began to fill the pod.

Riven's helmet filled the glass, her fists pounding on it. Her frantic voice filled Max's helmet.

"*Max, please let me in! Please, oh please, I'm so sorry! Don't leave me here! I thought about it. You're right. I can change! I want to change! Please, oh please! I don't want to die!!*" Her voice choked in a perfect sob that Max didn't think she'd faked.

"Launch us, Max," Holiday said, her voice drowning out Riven's continual pleas.

Max checked his suit, verifying that the atmosphere in the escape pod had reached an acceptable level. It had, so he raised his visor. He did this so that Riven could see his eyes as he slowly shook his head at her. He couldn't see her face since her visor was down and opaque, and he wished he could. Or maybe he didn't. The whole situation was wrong and confusing, he didn't know what to feel. Anger was the easy emotion, and it was certainly there, but it was jumbled with so many others that nothing really made sense.

Riven's visor went clear. Max could see the panic in her eyes.

Then she was accelerating away, fading into the distance.

Max couldn't remember if he had been the one to launch the escape pod or if Holiday had done that. Though, it didn't really matter who had done what. The important thing was that the escape pod was loosed from the *Starburst*. They had escaped. Lying on the mattresses next to each other, they took off their helmets, just staring at each other, just breathing.

And neither was surprised when, as Max pulled his sister into a desperate embrace, they both began to weep.

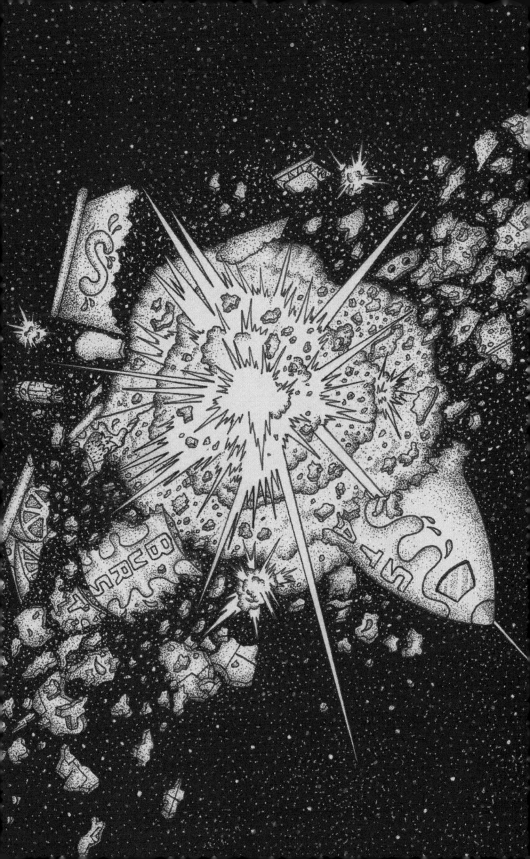

[CHAPTER NINETEEN]

WHAT HAPPENED TO THE *STARBURST*

Both Holiday and Max were wiping at their tears, trying to verify that their escape pod was indeed on a course to rendezvous with a safe landing site on Luna, when the *Starburst* did something that neither of them expected:

It exploded.

Holiday sucked in a breath of surprise.

Max was too shocked to do anything but watch. His heart seemed to fill the pod with a telltale beat.

It was silent, but the flare of light as the reactor exploded was blinding and unmistakable. Max watched one of the displays, which showed the view from a camera mounted on the surface of the escape pod. The core of the ship had disintegrated, spewing debris in a sphere from the center. One of the ion engines was still firing, accelerating away from the explosion on a brand new trajectory. It would use up the mass in its engine, and then it would shut down, but it would continue on unless it hit something, which was rather unlikely. Space was full of lots of planets and moons and asteroids and suns and comets, but between all those was a whole lot of nothing.

One of the most fascinating aspects of the explosion was that it was moving through space at the same speed that the *Starburst* had been the second before it had come apart. Max tracked the explosion's course. The fireball faded out quickly as the oxygen feeding it was consumed almost instantaneously.

They had only been away from the *Starburst* for a few minutes, and Max was worried that a shockwave from the explosion might throw their escape pod off-course. He didn't have to worry. Though pressurized air that hadn't been consumed in the explosion did buffet the escape pod, it only had to make a minor course adjustment.

Holiday was breathing heavily. Her eyes were wide, fearful, and guilty. "I…" she whispered.

Max didn't know what to say. He didn't know what to feel.

"I…I didn't mean to…" Holiday tried to start again, her voice sputtering, then giving out altogether, devolving into a gulping sob.

Max found his voice. "You didn't do that, Holi. Don't think that for a minute. There is no way the Pyro could've done that."

"Maybe…"

"Nothing *maybe* about it. You did not cause the *Starburst* to explode. No way. Your first shot went through the hull, and your second shot went through the last escape pod, and right out into space."

Holiday shook her head, tears falling to her mattress. "No. No, the escape pod shot was clean, but the other one…it could've gone through the hull and hit one of the ion engines."

"But that wouldn't cause an explosion like—"

"You don't know that!"

"Listen, you know as well as I do that Darren had been in the reactor chamber. Do you know what he was doing back there? No, and I don't either. I suspect he was going to destroy the *Starburst* anyway."

"That doesn't make any sense."

"Sure it does," Max reassured her, placing a hand on her shoulder and squeezing. "We don't know what information he wanted from Dad, but if we assume he got what he needed, then he didn't need any of us anymore. He could've just killed us all, but he didn't, which means that he had other uses for us, or he was just making sure he got everything he needed before he did. He used you to get at Mom and Dad, and he had Riven drug me. We were all under control. All it would take is for Darren and Riven to set the *Starburst* to explode, then use the escape pods to get away. They would have their information and the *Starburst* would look like it had some sort of accident. I think I threw a wrench in their plans when I woke up earlier than they intended. Then, when you and I took the cockpit, we really messed things up. We forced them to take more aggressive action against Mom and Dad. They launched the escape pod instead of killing them outright. If they had killed Mom and Dad then they never would have got us out of that cockpit. They needed them alive so we would devise a plan to rescue them instead of trying to land on Luna or something like that."

"That doesn't explain the explosion, Max. They had control of the *Starburst* at that point. Even if you locked out the controls, they would've found a way around that. Why did it blow up?"

"I don't know. Maybe they couldn't stop it. Maybe what they did was irreversible. Or maybe something simply went wrong."

Holiday wanted to believe something along those lines; Max could see that clearly in her searching eyes.

She rolled over on her back and sighed. "Are Mom and Dad going to be okay?"

"Yes."

"Are we going to be okay?"

"Yes."

"Okay. I believe you."

Max monitored the displays and readouts, but while the pod was drifting there wasn't much for him to do. The pod computers had been programmed with the idea that in an emergency situation, human interaction wasn't necessary for a safe landing. It was better, easier, and safer if the computer did all the work. Max assumed there was some sort of emergency override somewhere, but he didn't know where, and he wouldn't have used it if there was.

"All my clothes were on the *Starburst,*" Holiday said.

"Mine too."

"I guess we'll have to go shopping when we get to Luna One."

"Yeah, as if you and Mom weren't going to do that anyway."

Silence, only broken by the sound of their breathing and the occasional beep from the pod computers, fell between them like a shroud for several minutes.

Max found that he was extremely tired. He dozed, and Holiday did the same.

He woke when he heard Holiday speaking. Groggy, he didn't know if she'd been talking for a while or if she'd just asked him a question.

"What did you just say?" he asked.

"I was just watching episode 154."

In my mind was the end of that sentence, Max knew. "Sure. Is this important?"

"Maybe."

"Tell me."

"It's the one I told you about earlier."

"Okay," Max said. He didn't remember anything like that, but then again, he did tend to tune his sister out when she mentioned *Quantum Girl!!.*

"Well, I think we need to be careful when we get to Luna."

"I agree, but why is that?"

"Well, in episode 154, Admiral Dead Dread and his girlfriend Madame Sykness die."

"Sounds like a fitting end to the bad guys."

"Of course. Only that's not how it all turns out, because they're not really dead. They show up six episodes later and give Quantum Girl!!

a very hard time."

"So what are you saying?"

"That what if when we get down there, it turns out that Darren and Riven aren't dead?"

Max looked over at his sister to see if she was serious. She was, deadly so.

"This is real life, Holi. Nobody can survive an explosion like that. And even if they did, you know exactly how long they could survive in the vacuum of space."

"I know, but…"

"No *buts* about it. Let it go. They're gone. It wasn't your fault, and there's nothing you can do about it. They chose their path in life, and it ended badly for them. We can feel sorry for them, but we shouldn't fear them anymore." Max hoped he sounded like he believed what he was saying—which he wasn't sure he did. He hoped she wasn't reading his mind.

Holiday thought about that. "Okay, but when we get to Luna, let's be careful. Nothing wrong with that, right?"

"Not at all," Max said, thinking of Riven's frightened face as it had zoomed away. Not an image he'd be forgetting in his lifetime. He turned over on his side, away from Holiday, and tried to shake off the unease that Holiday had resurrected. He shrugged and sighed. Darren and Riven were dead. Extremely sad, but extremely true. What worked in cartoons didn't work in the real world. In the cartoon world, explosions launched people miles into the air. In the real world, explosions blew arms and legs and heads off. The explosion of the *Starburst* had been of that second type. Nobody could survive an explosion like that.

Nobody.

[CHAPTER TWENTY]

WHAT HAPPENED IN THE ESCAPE POD

If Max and Holiday had been outside the escape pod as it hurtled toward Earth's only moon, here's what they would have seen:

A vehicle that looked vaguely egg-shaped. The surface was glossy silver, just like that of its recently discorporated parent. The orphan—for that's what it truly was, though at least it still had one sibling left—reflected the stars, the Sun, Luna, and Earth. Reflecting these celestial bodies as it did, the orphan pod was barely visible and seemed merely to warp space as it traveled, much like the *Venge* had. The pod was superior in its stealthiness though, since it reflected instead of blocked. Every so often, the flare of a maneuvering thruster disturbed its chrome surface. These thrusters were scattered around on the skin of the pod, making adjustments on three axes. There were more thrusters near the belly of the pod. If one were to look closely, one would see the outlines of hatches. These housed the landing stabilizers and the wheels that enabled it to become mobile once it had landed safely on the planet to which it was escaping.

The interior of the escape pod wasn't too bad all things considered. Max had been staring at it for several hours, and he'd just about memorized every square inch of the thing. There wasn't much to do. In fact, there was nothing to do except wait for the escape pod to fulfill its mission. To Max, it seemed like it did this extra slowly, but he didn't have much cause to complain. They were, after all, still alive, unlike their two hijackers. There wasn't a lot of room to move around inside the pod. The mattresses were bumped up right against each other. Max couldn't seem to turn over without elbowing Holiday. It might've been more comfortable if they hadn't been wearing their spacesuits, but for safety reasons it was best to keep them on. It also didn't help that they needed to keep a seatbelt—or was it a *mattress*belt?—around their bodies at all times. The escape pod did its job, but it was cramped and uncomfortable.

It had been okay at first, due to adrenaline he supposed, but it didn't take too long for Max's claustrophobia to kick back in at levels that he'd hoped he could avoid on vacation. Then again, hijacking had also been on his list of things to avoid while on vacation, and hadn't that just been a miserable failure? Every wall was so near. Every wall was closing in. Every wall felt like it was leaning toward him, about to collapse on top of him, bury him in rubble. He was able to turn on blowers in the ceiling, and Holiday held his hand—something that comforted him more than he would ever have admitted in public. He did his best to distract his mind with the computer displays, but they were fairly uninteresting after a few minutes, since as he had previously experienced on the *Starburst*, space could be ultra-boring. He took deep breaths. He closed his eyes. He did his best.

Around the mattresses, there was a half ring of controls and readouts built into the walls. There were several displays, and most of the controls were related to different systems you could monitor on the displays. The ceiling contained all the interesting stuff as it turned out. That's where the steering controls were. The ceiling was close enough that it wasn't a strain to reach up. The controls were duplicated, one for each mattress position. It would be easy for either of them to steer the pod once they landed.

The light inside the pod was soft and warm. For the most part, they kept the lights dim, so that the pod was cast in the reds, blues, and yellows of the various readouts and indicators.

Max listened to the soft, rhythmic sounds the escape pod made, finding some small amount of comfort in them, as if it were alive and he was hearing its heartbeat. *A womb in space,* he mused.

He drifted then, perhaps falling asleep, because when he opened his eyes, his sister's helmet filled his vision. The interior lights were up.

"Wake up," Holiday said. "We're almost down."

Max turned over, looking at one of the external camera feeds. Luna's surface completely filled the screen.

"Do you know where we're landing?" Max asked, cranking up the air in his helmet and tilting his head from side-to-side, working out a tense muscle. Wearing a helmet while lying down stressed the neck.

"Near Luna One?" Holiday suggested.

"You didn't check already?"

"I don't know how to do that."

Max stopped his jaw from dropping. He was pretty sure he'd never heard those words from her mouth before.

"I don't know everything, Max."

Max's heart sank. He heard the fear and resignation in her voice, as well as the threat of tears. She really was young—too young to be dealing with anything of this. At the end there on the *Starburst,* she'd been as hard and cold as one of the villains in her holos. She'd done what she'd thought she had to in order to help save their parents, and to save him. She'd done more than Max, in fact.

Max propped himself up and pulled his sister closer. Their helmets clanked together. "Love ya, Sis. Can't wait to see Mom and Dad, huh?"

Holiday nodded, her face shield squeaking against his. Even though her eyes were moist, she smiled, hugging him back as tightly as she could with the both of them wearing their spacesuits.

When Holiday let him go, Max looked at the ceiling monitors to see that they were indeed almost down. The countdown monitor indicated they had less than twenty-seven minutes left. The last two digits of the countdown timer changed so fast they were just blurs.

"Where are we landing?" Holiday asked.

"There," Max said as a topographical map of Luna appeared on one of the monitors.

"How far is that from Luna One?"

Max zoomed the view out, displaying more of Luna's pockmarked surface. The graceful curve of Luna One's dome appeared in one corner of the map. The city beneath twinkled as if it were a dark sky full of stars.

"Uh, that seems really far," Holiday said. "Is that right?"

Max didn't know if it was right. It didn't seem right, but he also didn't know what he could do about it. He didn't know how to reprogram the landing site—if such a thing was even possible. He debated what to say to Holiday.

"Do we have enough supplies to make it that far?" Holiday asked.

"Yes," Max said.

There was a sudden, sharp pain in his shoulder. Then Holiday was leaning over him. There were tears at the corners of her eyes. "I'll just hit you again if you lie again."

Max sighed, forcing himself to hold her gaze, which was somehow comforting despite the fear and the tears he saw there. He took a deep breath and blew it out. "Sorry. It's far, but we'll make it. We have enough oxygen, food and water for a week."

"Not with two of us we don't."

Max swore. Nothing ever got by her. He wasn't sure why he ever tried. "No, you're right, with both of us we have half that. But this thing is already sending out a distress signal, so they'll pick us up when we get down. We won't have to do this all by ourselves."

Holiday pushed back and away, laying her head down.

The pod was silent for several minutes before Holiday asked, "Do you think the Meaneys reprogrammed the landing site for the escape pods?"

"Maybe," Max said, though that's exactly what he'd been thinking. It was the only reason he could think of that explained why they weren't landing closer to Luna One. A quick check of the computer let him know that there wasn't a trajectory problem that would have prevented them from landing closer to the city. Left to its own programming, the escape pod would have set them down as close to civilization as possible.

"Why would they do that?"

Max shook his head. He had no idea. "I'm sure it wasn't because they wanted to do some lunar sightseeing."

Holiday was quiet for a few moments, then said, "We don't know enough to figure out what their plan was. If they reprogrammed the escape pod, then we could assume that they were planning on using it themselves."

Max could think of another reason they'd reprogram it.

"Unless they were just trying to sabotage any escape attempt we might make," Holiday said, giving voice to Max's thought. He still didn't like discussing scenarios where they ended up dead, though it was obvious that she didn't feel such restraint.

"Yeah, well," Max said, "that didn't work out so well for them." He tried not to think of the terror on Riven's face as the last escape pod had accelerated away from the *Starburst*. He couldn't shake the oppressive feeling that he'd altered the universe in some inescapable, damaging way by leaving Riven and Darren behind. That there was no way either he or Holiday could have known the *Starburst* was going to explode didn't matter. It didn't matter what Riven and Darren had done to his parents and what they had been trying to do to him and his sister. What mattered was that the two of them were dead, and he'd been responsible for taking their only method of salvation.

He was afraid Riven's face was going to haunt him for the rest of his life.

Something gripped his chest and began to squeeze. It was as if he was adrift in the vacuum of space without his suit—he sucked in a breath, but there was nothing there.

He rolled his body away from Holiday as much as his belt would allow so she couldn't see him struggling. Grabbing the side of the mattress, he willed air into his lungs, but it was like the air was used up, stripped of oxygen. Black spots began appearing, blotting out the interior of the pod. He felt the full force of the panic, but he also felt angry and frustrated. It was stupid, so utterly stupid to let the situation overtake him like this. His sister needed him, and he was letting her down. The world faded. Somewhere in there, he knew that passing out might actually be good because his body's natural reflexes would kick in, relax his muscles and allow him to breathe again. In the last few seconds, as everything went so apocalyptically dim, he managed a few desperate thoughts of Nika. They were good thoughts, but they didn't help.

There was a blast of cool air on his face, and suddenly he was looking up at Holiday. His helmet was off, and so was hers. "I'm here, Max." Her hand was cool against the side of his face.

"Sorry," he said. If he said anything more he was going to cry.

"It's okay." She looked so much like her mother, and in that moment, that was the greatest comfort possible. Her hair was streaming down to one side like a waterfall made of a midnight sky. Something in her hair twinkled. He focused, seeing that they were tiny stars. He hadn't noticed them before. Why was that? Oh, yeah, because he didn't pay much attention to her most of the time.

After all this, he resolved to do something about that. He wasn't sure what, but…something. She deserved better. He owed her more.

"Put your helmet back on, dummy," Max said, feeling curiously calm in spite of his panic of only seconds ago. But that was the way of it. It came, strong, overpowering, but then it was gone, and he could never remember exactly where the debilitation actually came from.

"You first, Max."

Max sighed, but did as his sister ordered. The panic didn't return. Max turned up the air circulation, making sure cool air was flowing over his face.

"Okay," he said, "let's do some system checks to make sure we're ready for landing. We have—" He looked at the ceiling monitor. "—thirteen minutes." Using the HUD in his helmet he went through all systems on the escape pod, making sure that everything was running properly. He let Holiday see everything he was doing. He hoped the process was as comforting to her as it was to him.

Everything checked out, so he grabbed his sister's hand, and they watched the monitors as the pod descended.

Luna's surface was as pockmarked as any picture Max had ever seen. But none of the pictures could ever really convey the true nature of the landscape. Even the virtual reality simulators hadn't been as good as what he could see on the pod's monitors. In spite of their situation, there was a part of him that was looking forward to getting closer.

Part of him wanted to get out of the pod when they landed.

Only a few minutes from landing, Holiday asked, "Can you track the escape pod Mom and Dad are in?"

Max couldn't. He tried, but from what he could tell, the escape pod was pretty much designed to ferry its occupants down to the nearest habitable planet, emitting a distress signal all the while. He would've thought that tracking other space vehicles that could rescue it would've been a good idea. Then again, it was always possible he simply didn't know what to look for. He wasn't an expert at the escape pod's systems. Or maybe the Meaneys had done something to the escape pod, crippled it in addition to reprogramming its landing site. He felt a sudden burst of anger at himself for not being more prepared. How hard would it have been to learn the intricacies of the escape pods? Not hard at all. But his anger at his parents had distracted him from what was really important—his family and their safety.

Still, maybe everything was working exactly like it should. Maybe it didn't matter. They were almost down.

The landing site—set next to the ridge of an enormous crater— was now clearly visible on the monitor as a thin, blue circle.

"Two minutes," Holiday whispered.

Max concentrated on not squeezing her hand too hard, because the threat of another attack was there. He could feel it prickly inside his chest, an irritating caress, like a shark circling its prey.

It'll grab me. If I let my guard down for even a second, it'll strike. And this time, it's not gonna let go. I'll be useless.

Max cranked the air in his helmet up as high as it would go. He squinted his eyes, and still they were drying out. He blinked repeatedly.

There was a beep in his helmet. Sixty seconds till touchdown. He closed his eyes. Watching wasn't an option. It was either close his eyes and focus on maintaining control or open them and freak out.

"It's beautiful," Holiday said in a quiet, awestruck tone that she normally reserved for things involving *Quantum Girl!!!.*

Max knew it was beautiful, and he regretted missing it—this, his first moon landing. He would only get one first time, and he wanted to scream because he couldn't let his eyes open.

Another beep, followed by another. Those were counting down the last ten seconds. In those final few seconds he first noticed the subtle force of gravity that was now pulling at his body. It had surely been in effect for some time now, but he hadn't noticed before.

His helmet chirped, somehow happier this time. At the same time, he felt the pod shudder. Briefly fogging his visor, the breath he'd been holding came out then, and with it went the threat of paralyzing panic. He turned the air in his helmet down and slowly opened his eyes, rotating his head toward his sister, seeing that her eyes were sprinkled with tears. And then his were too, though that was okay. It seemed, in those few moments, he wasn't able to summon any embarrassment about crying in front of her.

As the escape pod whirred and hummed, hatches opening, wheels reaching out to kiss the cold, dusty surface of Luna, brother and sister shared tears, yes, but also quiet, comforting smiles.

[Chapter Twenty-One]

What Happened On Luna

Max assessed their situation. Two kids, on the surface of Luna, separated from their parents. The escape pod—that had surely saved their lives—moved slowly but steadily over the rocky, cratered skin of Earth's only moon. Power reserves were at full—so said the onboard computers in their monotone voices. Max didn't like to admit it, but when the computer talked, he felt an overwhelming comfort. It was almost as if there were three of them in the pod.

Communications weren't working. At least, they couldn't broadcast. They could pick up broadcasts from terrestrial and lunar sources, but they weren't able to initiate any sort of communication with anybody in the vicinity of Luna One. Max was suspicious that the Meaneys had done something to the pod, just like they had maybe reprogrammed the landing locations. No way to prove anything though. It was also possible they'd taken some minor damage when the *Starburst* had exploded—some small antenna sheared off. He hadn't seen anything on the external cameras, but he certainly wasn't an expert in escape pods.

Other than the lack of two-way communications, he had no serious concerns with the pod. It was working. It would get them to where they needed to go. It was on a rendezvous with Luna One according to the computer. It would get there in six days. They had enough supplies for one person for a week, less with the two of them. They were going to have to ration, especially the water, though the spacesuits had water recyclers in them, which reclaimed water from sweat and urine.

There might be some awkward moments when it came to bodily waste, but they'd get through it. The spacesuits actually handled all the dirty work anyway.

Speaking of their spacesuits, they had double-checked them and they were intact. In spite of everything, there was no damage. If something happened to the pod on their way, they could survive on the moon's surface for as long as they had oxygen, food, water and the strength to put one foot in front of the other.

Max adjusted his leg, his foot bumping Holiday's Pyro at the far end of the pod. The Reaper and the Disruptor were there too, resting on the floor and against the wall. Somehow, Max's Pyro had been damaged in the struggle with Darren. They'd unloaded and disassembled it, storing it in an empty compartment they'd found. Max shook the image of Holiday holding those weapons from his mind. He tried to banish the memory of her shooting a hole through Darren Meaney's foot. It was his fault she'd been put in that situation. If only he hadn't frozen. When this was all over, he was going to talk with her about it, make sure she was really okay. He knew she wasn't going to be. How could a little girl be forced to do that and *not* have it affect her? They'd have to deal with it. Together though; he'd help her, any way he could. He owed her that. He owed her his life. He owed her *everything*. She was much more his savior than he was hers.

That just proved how backwards the universe could be at times.

Holiday was on her stomach, staring out the forward view screen that gave them live video from the cameras positioned across the pod's outer skin. She was switching the feed every minute or two, watching as the moonscape passed by or faded into the distance behind.

Now, she watched the view in front of the pod. Max's HUD inside his helmet overlaid a translucent green graphic over the view screen that illustrated the path the pod was going to take toward Luna One.

Max turned toward Holiday, tapping her on the shoulder. "Hey, I bet the Low-G Gymnastics Exhibition—" Max saw that Holiday was waiting patiently for him to finish. He sighed. "—Sponsored by Energistix…is going to be pretty fun."

He could see that her face was on the verge of lighting up. "Do you think we're still going to get to go?"

"I do. Even if it takes us a week to get to Luna One, we'll still get back in time for the main competitions."

Okay, now her face was lit, and she was beaming a smile that made him want to do anything to keep that look on her face. Nika had a similar look that turned him into an oozing pile of alien goo when she aimed it his way.

"Oh, it's going to be so great, Max! I really can't wait to get there and watch with you and Mom and Dad! The stuff they can do is so cosmically amazing!"

Max nodded. "Yeah, they're amazing, but so are you. The stuff you…" He trailed off, reconsidering whether he should be bringing up anything about what she'd done on the *Starburst*.

"You mean all that stuff I did on the Starburst? Oh, that was nothing." Whew, her happiness was undisturbed.

"It wasn't nothing, Holi. I don't really need to see any exhibition. Not after what I saw you do. Nobody's going to top that."

"Really?"

"I mean it."

Then Holiday was giving Max a one-armed hug that felt pretty darn good. She turned back to the forward view screen, her head bobbing to some remembered tune. After a minute, she tapped Max. "Do you think Mom will let me get a tattoo after this is all over?"

"Um." Max knew she was serious.

"I want a tattoo on my arm, just like Dad has, only I don't want a skull or a Space Command logo. I want Quantum Girl!! And I want her to have her space princess crown, though if she gets to be space queen in episode 300, I'll want her to be wearing her queen's crown. Also, I want her to be wearing the outfit she did in episode 217, because that one is the best out of all she's ever worn. Do you remember it? I showed it to you that one time. It's her black spacesuit, and the Uranian women made it for her after she saved them from the Space Caterpillar Invasion in episode 215. That suit makes her invincible every time she uses it." Holiday paused, thinking. "But episode 217 was the episode where Baron Edward Blaze kissed Quantum Girl!! And he's not supposed to do that! Ever! Because Captain Xeode is her real boyfriend, and when they get married, he's going to be space king! Oh, that Baron Edward Blaze makes me so mad! I don't know why Quantum Girl!! even lets him hang around. He's not right for her! He never does anything wrong, and Captain Xeode is always messing things up at exactly the wrong moment."

"Of course," Max said.

"But Captain Xeode loves Quantum Girl!!, and he even proposed to her, and they're gonna get married in episode 300, I just know it."

"Did she say *yes?*"

Holiday hesitated. "Well…not exactly."

"So, she turned him down then?"

"She didn't exactly do that either."

"Holi, it's not a question you answer with a *maybe*. You either say *yes* or *no*."

Holiday frowned. "I know, but she had to think for a second, and then she didn't get a chance to answer because Commander Klarg jammed the signal."

"Wait," Max said. "Are you saying that Captain Xeode proposed to Quantum Girl!!, and they weren't even in the same room? Were they in different spaceships?"

"Yes," Holiday said in a whisper.

"That's a little weird don't you think?"

"Her life is complicated!"

"Where was Baron Edward Blaze during all this?" Max asked. He knew that if he didn't use the character's full name, Holiday would correct him, or worse, wait patiently until he corrected himself.

Holiday's answer was so quiet that Max didn't actually hear her. Instead, he got a *[That jerk was on the* Quark Pony!! *with Quantum Girl!! He heard the whole thing.]* from her, loud and clear, as if her mind was trying to shout.

Max smiled. "That must've been awkward."

Holiday nodded. "It was. And that's not the only—hey!" She glared at him.

"You sent me your thoughts."

She sighed, long and drawn out. "Stupid Baron Edward Blaze," she muttered.

Max didn't feel like teasing her, so he let it drop. He'd watched the show with her before, when he was feeling particularly brotherly. Before she'd let him do that though, she always had to get him caught up with the story since he's last watched it. This often took more than half an hour, and she talked so fast it could be a chore to keep up with her. Still, her passion for the holo show was infectious and he usually found himself caught up in it with her.

Maybe he'd watch the last episode with her. If it was anything like last time, she'd try to hold his hand the whole time, squeezing really hard at the most exciting parts. It was difficult not to get sucked into the experience when she was like that.

She really was something. A little nuclear bomb packaged like a twelve-year-old girl. If people only knew.

Time passed, and the two settled into a routine of sorts. Sleep, eat, talk, watch holos—*Quantum Girl!!* of course. Holiday was determined to make the most of the lack of parental intervention in her holo watching, and she wanted to make sure Max was completely current on Quantum Girl!!'s latest adventure. Max indulged her. Besides, there wasn't much else to do.

Two days passed.

When Max woke up on the third day, an alarm was sounding in the interior of the pod, letting him know that all was not right with the universe.

[CHAPTER TWENTY-TWO]

WHAT HAPPENED WHEN MAXIMILLION AND HOLIDAY FOUND THE WRECKAGE

A thin, blue light flashed in Max's peripheral vision, accompanied by an alarm that throbbed dully, like the beat of a punctured drum. He tried to wipe the sleep out of his eyes, but his hand slapped against his visor. Sleeping in a spacesuit and helmet was annoying.

Next to him, Holiday groaned. "What is it?" she asked, but didn't roll over. Max was amazed at how quickly she adapted. Even though they were alone on the surface of the moon, and there was an alarm, she felt safe enough with him and comfortable enough in the escape pod to attempt to go back to sleep.

Max thought about taking his helmet off—he really wanted to get that crud out of the corner of his eyes—but he figured it wasn't a good idea until he found out what was wrong. It just wouldn't do to find out the hard way that the escape pod had no atmosphere.

His right arm was tingling because he'd been sleeping on it. He tried to move it, but it wouldn't respond. Grunting, he shifted so he could bring his left arm forward, tapping the console. The alarm cut off. Holiday sighed, murmuring a muffled, "Thanks."

What is so important? Max thought. He rolled over, wincing as the blood returned to his arm. He hated that feeling, the numbness that wasn't really numbness at all, but a prickly pain that seemed to go on for far too long. As Max flexed his right hand, the pain drowning any panicky feelings, the HUD in his helmet flared to life.

"Max, what is that?" Holiday asked quietly, awed. Well okay, so she hadn't been asleep after all. That's how she was. Always on pace with him, often ahead.

Max stared at the image his HUD displayed—presumably the same image that his sister was looking at. "Ah…" wasn't a good response, but it's what came out.

"Is that a…a spaceship?"

Max squinted at the HUD as if to bring the object into better focus, knowing that it wasn't going to work, but unable to stop himself. The image on the HUD vibrated, going slightly out of focus as the pod rolled across some particularly uneven terrain.

Whatever it was, it certainly wasn't native to the moon. The part of the object that wasn't buried in the lunar surface was a mass of metal superstructure that reminded Max of the playground equipment at that park down the street from where they lived—beams and struts forming triangles and hexagons—the bisected sphere of an insect's eye. To one side was a cylindrical main body. Long, flat panels protruded from the object at angles seemingly chosen at random. Circular antenna arrays littered the object's body, their concave surfaces filled with dust and other assorted debris.

The object had suffered massive damage from the crash. Everything was bent or fractured. The solar panels—if that's what those were—looked like broken arms, the once pristine surfaces now splintered, as if some giant had attempted to crack them over its knee. The main body was punctured by one of the object's own supports. The gaping hole it had made was ragged, like the work of an unskilled butcher with a dull knife. Electronic viscera and the bulging fat of insulation spilled from the ugly wound, wires and tubes hanging like intestines.

Max didn't know how large it really was, but he imagined that at least half of it was buried in the ground. Every surface was completely coated in dirt.

"Max?" Holiday prodded.

"I think it's a satellite."

"Oh."

"I don't see any place that looks like a cockpit. Also, I don't see any large propulsion system." Max took another look at the satellite, then highlighted areas on the HUD, passing the data over to Holiday so she could see what he was talking about. "See, there are maneuvering thrusters, but nothing big enough to do much other than to adjust its trajectory."

"A satellite, huh? I guess that makes sense."

"Yeah, but as to why it's here…I'm not sure."

"It's triple wrecked. I wonder what caused it to crash."

Max wondered that too. He also wondered why he hadn't heard the phrase *triple wrecked* before. Had she heard that on her holo show, or did she just make it up?

He felt something on his shoulder. Looking, it was Holiday's hand. Her eyes were wide and bright behind her visor. Then, unexpectedly, her eyes glazed over and she looked away, her expression darkening. She looked like she was listening to something she could barely hear. Max was about to ask her about it when she shook her head and reaffixed her gaze on him. "We should investigate it," she said with an all-too-serious look that she'd probably copied from some scene in *Quantum Girl!!*.

Max should've seen this coming. Holiday's curiosity was paramount, overshadowing any adverse situation, any peril. Still, it wasn't a good idea. "Absolutely not. Our priority is to get to Luna One and find Mom and Dad. We can't let anything get in the way of that."

"Is it out of our way?"

"That doesn't matter," Max said, letting just a little bit of frustration creep into his voice.

"Fine." Holiday turned away from him.

The escape pod moved across the moon, each second filled with more silence than the previous. Max couldn't get Holiday to look at him, even when he tapped her on the shoulder. Internally, he sighed, but this was how it had to be. It was better for her to be safe in the pod and upset with him than out exploring the wreckage of a crashed satellite and thinking that he was the best brother in the universe.

"It could be important," Holiday said quietly.

"What could be important?" Max asked.

"The satellite."

Max debated how to proceed. He could ignore her, or he could try to win her over. Neither seemed all that attractive, and neither promised simple success. He settled on at least interacting with her. "We'll tell Dad about it as soon as we see him."

"If we're going to report it, shouldn't we at least make sure we have some way to identify it?"

"I'm sure the computer has a scan of it." Max hoped he sounded convincing.

There was another pause, and when Holiday spoke next, Max knew that she was going to be trouble all her life. "Is the satellite still sending any signals?"

"I...I'm not sure," Max said.

"Check it, please."

Max knew then exactly what she'd been doing in that brief pause, and that her question was infinitely rhetorical, but he checked for himself. He swore in his mind.

"I heard that," Holiday said, and she was gloating, just a little.

There it was, right in his HUD—a red, pulsing circle. Next to it was a single word: DISTRESS.

The wrecked satellite was calling for help.

And even if it was just a lifeless machine, that signal meant that you were obligated to provide assistance if you could do so safely. Rules of the universe; everybody knew that. *Safely* was the key word here though. And, that was the question, wasn't it? Could they investigate the wreckage without putting either of them in more peril?

Max shook his head. "It's not a good idea to go out there. We have much more important things to do. I want to get you to someplace safer than the inside of an escape pod. And besides, I'm worried about Mom and Dad."

"I'm worried about Mom and Dad too," Holiday argued, and then a hint of that distracted look washed over her again, "but we have to do this. I feel like..."

Max waited for her to finish, curious why she was so interested in getting a closer look at the wreckage.

"I can't explain it exactly. I just think we have to go out there and check it out."

"That's not good enough." Max could tell she was holding something back from him. He wasn't sure why. "Tell me what it is. Are you embarrassed or something? I won't laugh or anything like that if that's what you're afraid of."

She sighed loudly. The look in her eyes said: *Brothers are so stupid!* She sighed again, quieter the second time. "It's not embarrassing. I just don't think you're going to believe me."

Max didn't think he would either.

"You believe I can read your thoughts, right?"

"Yes," Max choked out because, well, it was true. He did, even though he felt guilty for believing something so ridiculous.

"It's sort of like that right now. I can't exactly read the thoughts, but I can sense...something...or someone." Holiday pointed at the forward screen, directly at the satellite. "And whoever or whatever it is...is right there."

Max's heart sank even as he searched his sister's face for any sign that she was lying just to get her way. No such luck, but he already knew that. She wasn't a liar.

Great, his conscience wasn't going to let him ignore the distress signal now. When it had just been a lifeless machine, it was easy to be adamant. Now…it was more difficult. He could still argue that they wouldn't be able to provide adequate assistance even if there was something or someone alive, that there was no more room in the escape pod, but he wouldn't be able to do it with any conviction.

Max checked the statistics. At their current rate, their course would take them closest to the satellite in just under fifteen minutes. It would take the pod an hour to navigate the rim of the crater, and after they'd investigated, another hour to resume their course. It would deplete some of their resources, but not enough to be of any concern as long as nothing went wrong during the rest of their journey to Luna One.

Even as Max instructed the computer to plot a course toward the satellite, he tried to think of scenarios that could explain the situation. Sure, there were satellites in orbit around the moon, but it seemed unlikely that any single one of them was going to be abandoned like this one seemed to be. Usually they knew when a satellite had reached the end of its life, and when they did, they brought it down when and where they wanted to. Usually. But not this time. Something had reached out to this particular satellite and pulled it from space.

That nobody had recovered it yet was of some interest. Even if it had crashed unexpectedly, they tracked everything between Earth and Luna. They would have calculated its impact location ahead of time, made sure it wasn't a threat to any existing installation and been waiting for it. All the satellites were owned by governments or corporations, and they all had to make sure their technology wasn't stolen.

"That thing crashed today," Holiday said, "didn't it?"

Today was a term that people used when they were on a planet that had a day and night cycle. Even though their trip had been only a few days so far, Max had lost track of what *day* it actually was. Still, he supposed she meant within the past twenty-four hours.

"Maybe," he said. It was the only possibility he could think of that even began to make sense. It didn't make sense that the satellite had been there for much longer and that *nobody cared about it.*

He found that he couldn't draw his attention away from the red pulsing circle in his HUD and the word next to the circle that demanded his attention. *Here I am!* it seemed to say. *Pay attention to me! I'm calling for help, and you have to save me! Even though you probably shouldn't because you're alone on the surface of the moon in what, for all you know, is a rolling casket. That, and you don't know where your parents are. But still, you have to come and save me, all because you can't bring yourself to disbelieve that your sister is telepathic.*

The tightening in his chest grabbed him fast and firm. He couldn't help it, he reached for something—*anything*—close, and that just happened to be his sister's arm. He shut his eyes, but not before he saw that she'd seen his face. He clamped down on her arm harder than he wanted to, but it was through the spacesuit, so maybe it didn't hurt too much.

Not again, not in front of his sister again, not when she needed him the most!

He felt her free hand on top of his. She didn't say anything, just let him know that she was there and that he was okay.

Max sucked air through clenched teeth and desperately sought to fill his mind with the emptiness of space, with all those twinkly lights adrift in a sea of peaceful black. The fear, the panic, they could be replaced with the calm and the beauty of billions of stars, each positioned precisely, a wonderful, peaceful garden of lights, patterns upon patterns arranged in endless fractals. He let himself get obscured by the black, lost in the infinite.

His breathing resumed. His heartbeat slowed. His body relaxed.

"Sorry," he muttered when he regained his ability to speak. He was embarrassed again.

Holiday nodded, but didn't say anything. Max was grateful.

"This is so cosmic!" Holiday shouted just a short while later as the pod approached the wreckage.

Max brought the pod to a halt when they were roughly one hundred meters away. Now that they were closer, the forward monitor showed detail they hadn't been able to see before.

Holiday inhaled sharply, a finger stabbing toward the monitor. "Look! It's one of ours!"

Max had seen the same thing. The red and white stripes, the white stars on a field of blue. The flag was partially obscured by dirt, the surface it had been painted on broken, tearing the flag symbol nearly in half. The flag was upside-down, which was entirely appropriate given the condition of the satellite. *Right-side-up, it's a symbol of freedom, but upside-down it's a sign of distress*, Max thought.

Max waited for a full five minutes, intently looking at the monitor for any sign of life. Holiday kept sighing, louder each time. Waiting did not thrill her.

In the tortured, twisted wreckage of the satellite, nothing stirred.

Max looked at Holiday, questioning her with his eyes. He could tell she was going to sigh again, louder than ever, but then she reconsidered. She nodded, "I can still sense…whatever, or whoever it is."

"And it's in the wreckage?" Max asked.

Holiday cocked her head, as if that would allow here to *sense* better, then after a few seconds, she closed her eyes, completely focused. When she opened them, she said, "I can't tell now. It's stronger than it was before, but I can't tell where it is."

Max barely knew what to ask, but he tried, "Are you sensing

any…uh, words or…feelings?"

"Well, I don't think so."

"What does that mean?"

Holiday wrinkled her nose. "It'd be like if you were in your room talking to yourself, and I could just barely hear you while I was in the living room. It's all the way across the house, and I've got good hearing, but I wouldn't be able to understand what you were saying. I'd just sense that somebody was in your room. That's the closest I can come to describing what it's like. I don't think I'm hearing words, but I could be wrong."

"But you're hearing something."

"Definitely."

"Okay."

A pause. "Okay what?"

Max exhaled. "Okay, let's do this."

The smile his words put on his sister's face warmed Max's heart. It almost drowned the unease he was feeling and was easily enough to push aside any immediate panic.

Max brought up a checklist for exiting the escape pod. First on the list was to make sure their spacesuits were intact. Each inspected the other, making sure that their helmets were sealed and secure, then they double-checked their suits, just to make sure they hadn't been damaged in any way during the journey.

"All secure," Holiday said, saluting, smiling.

Max laughed. "Internal air systems are all green. Circulation on. Oxygen levels are at 100%. Without carrying spare tanks, we can each last for ninety minutes out there. That's not going to be a problem, since we'll be quick about our business."

Max scanned the pod, making sure that everything inside was secured and tied down. Everything important was.

Holiday was practically vibrating with excitement. Despite

everything that had happened, she was caught up in the moment.

To avoid any loss of oxygen when they opened the door, the pod was going to reclaim all the interior air. The vacuum inside would match the vacuum outside. At that point, both environments would be hostile—a thought Max was determined not to dwell on.

"Holi, when we're out there," Max began, "you need to do whatever I say. I don't want any arguments. If I say get back in the escape pod, you get back in, no questions. If I sense any danger to us, we're going to get back in the pod and leave. If you pick up any threat...*anything*, you send me your thoughts. Our safety is our top priority. We come first, no matter what."

"Okay."

"We're going to check out the wreckage, and then we're going to leave. That's it."

"Got it."

"I need you to promise."

"I promise," Holiday said, and it was almost a sigh of exasperation.

Max hugged her, if a bit awkwardly. His hand moved to the console. The sound of sucking air filled the cockpit at first, but quickly faded.

The red light above the hatch turned green, indicating that the pressure inside the pod was the same as on the outside of the pod. Max paused, staring at the hatch and the window in the middle of it. Through it, he could see the jagged surface of the moon set against a field of stars beyond. *Nika, if only you could see me now,* he thought. *If only you could see this with me.* Thinking of Nika made him feel better. And well, maybe a little worse if he let himself do it for too long. The feel of her last kiss was still vivid. His lips went all tingly, a little numb at the memory. He felt lightheaded, but that was probably just the lower gravity.

The Reaper, the Pyro, and the Disrupter rested on the floor next to the hatch. Max's vision flicked to the weapons as he debated what to do.

"Well, are we doing this or what?" Holiday interrupted, her voice, carried over their private communication channel, clear in his ears.

Max swallowed. "Yeah, we're doing this." Max issued the commands in his helmet's HUD that transferred all pod system controls over to his spacesuit. As a precaution, he did the same with Holiday's. Then he sent the command to open the pod.

The hatch swung open.

"Cosmic," Holiday breathed.

Max disconnected the belt that secured his body to the mattress, while Holiday did the same. It felt weird, no longer tethered, his body weighing only a fraction of what it did back on Earth. Somehow, it was more awkward to deal with than being weightless in space. For some reason, it hadn't bothered him while he'd been strapped into the pod, rolling across the moon's surface, but now, his body free, he found his fingers gripping the sides of the mattress, unable to let go. He had the irrational thought that if he relaxed his grip, he was going to float away.

Beside him, Holiday was sitting up and scooting her body toward the hatch.

Max blew out a breath and stopped thinking about the infinite possibilities lurking in the situation, and he just *moved*. He sat up and pushed toward the door. His momentum was greater than he'd expected and his helmet banged on the pod's ceiling. The sound reverberated in the small confines of his helmet.

"Deft," Holiday said.

Max bit back a retort and reached for the Pyro. He handed it back to Holiday, then took the Reaper for himself, saying a silent prayer that they'd never be used. *Just a precaution*, he reminded himself.

He went feet-first through the hatch. Perhaps not the best from a tactical perspective since his weapon wasn't going to clear the escape pod until the rest of his body did, but at least he wouldn't look like a complete idiot in front of his sister by coming into direct contact with Luna's surface for the first time on his hands and knees. The Reaper was making it awkward enough as it was. He didn't want to drop it.

One boot touched down. A shiver went through his body. The other boot followed, and then he was able to extract his torso from the escape pod. He stood, immediately bringing the Reaper up in both hands. He scanned the area, but saw nothing. The satellite wreckage was off to his left.

The sun was behind them. He saw Holiday's shadow moving with his, and then she was out, standing beside him. One gloved hand held the Pyro. The other she used to grab his hand, which was still supporting the Reaper. He let the Reaper fall to his side and held her hand.

"One small step for Holiday and Max," Holiday said. "One gigantic leap for Storm-kind."

Max squeezed her hand. *Very funny, Sis.*

"Max, we're walking on the moon! Look at that!" Holiday was pointing straight up. There was Earth. A blue marble swirled with white, spinning in an infinite expanse of stars and void. It was an unfathomably beautiful thing. He'd never forget it.

Then again, it was unlikely he'd ever forget anything about this particular space vacation, no matter how hard he might try. No, this was going to stick with him, in his dreams and in his nightmares.

Feeling very small and overwhelmed, Max took deep breaths. With the Earth hanging up above, so large and close, the threat of panic was an undercurrent that wasn't lessening. But, just then, neither was it rising.

Max should have known what Holiday was going to do next. He saw her give an experimental hop, then the next second her feet were higher than his head. Her arms were out, providing balance, the Pyro flailing beside her. She landed square, her feet sending up twin dust clouds.

"Did you see that? That was at least ten feet!" she said.

It was impressive, and he briefly wondered what he should tell her. On one hand, any acrobatics carried a certain amount of risk. Any sort of injury would be really bad. On the other hand, they were on the moon. The moon! Even though travel to the moon was common, it certainly wasn't common in the Storm family. Well, except for Rian, but that had been a long time ago. Max didn't want to kill even small amounts of joy she could draw from the experience.

Then again, there'd be plenty of time for low-G fun once they were safe at Luna One with their parents. Assuming that's where their parents would be. That line of speculation, Max shut down quickly. Dwelling on the *what ifs* of their situation was a fast train to Panicworld.

He resisted the urge to tell his sister to be careful. "Okay, get it out of your system," he said, sighing.

Holiday giggled. She jumped again and landed perfectly again. "Here, hold this," she said, handing him the Pyro. Max took it from her, watching as she took a couple steps, then leaped forward, her body curling. She was able to do four flips before her body unfurled.

She landed on her butt.

"Ow!" she exclaimed, but she was laughing.

"Ok, that's enough for now," Max said, helping her to her feet, checking her suit for any surface damage. She had a brilliant smile on her face when she took the Pyro back from him. She grabbed his hand and squeezed.

Max pulled her with him, starting toward the satellite. It was awkward to walk. He had to temper every movement or risk losing his balance. Every step carried the threat of sending him into the air. Holiday adapted almost instantly, moving like she'd been born on the moon. She was pretty amazing to watch, and Max found himself studying her movements, copying her. After only a few minutes, he was a whole lot more confident and was wobbling significantly less.

Halfway to the satellite, he looked back. The escape pod was a small and lonely thing, a shiny silver anomaly resting on a field of gray. The top half of the pod was black, reflecting the lights and void above. Though it was only fifty meters away, it seemed a lot farther, almost as if he were looking at it through the haze of a dream, and if he tried to run back to it, he would never actually get there.

Max brought the Reaper up to a more ready position, his finger resting above the trigger guard, his other hand cradling the grip on its underbelly. Holiday had done the same with her Pyro. He looked around, seeing no movement. He tried to remember how far they were from Luna One, how long it would take help to arrive at their position if something happened and they got stuck there. He found he couldn't remember, the last position readout from the pod momentarily escaping him.

An enormous crater descended into the moon's surface to their left. Max could see the ridge of it, and a part of him wanted to go closer to the edge and peer down into it, but again, there would be plenty of time for exploration after they were safe at Luna One.

Closer now, the true mangled nature of the satellite began to reveal itself. It rested no more than ten meters from the edge of the crater, one bent strut rose up and over, looking like a broken arm, reaching toward some unseen salvation. From the monitors in the pod, it had looked small, and now Max could see that he'd seriously underestimated the size of it.

"It's huge," Holiday whispered.

The cylindrical body, if it hadn't been crushed and half-buried in the moon's surface, would have been at least six meters in diameter. And there was no way to really tell how much of it was under the surface. Max's mind briefly told him that what appeared to be a satellite was really the tip of some bigger device, and the rest of its long body—a hundred meters or more—lay coiled deep below, patient and waiting, like some mechanical worm, grotesque and bloated with some ancient, alien technology. It didn't matter that there was a United States flag painted there. No, the satellite had been found and taken over by some alien race. Then they'd sent it back, booby trapped it. Now, it rested, waiting patiently to be found by humanity.

Max shook his head and sighed, banishing his incoherent, paranoid musings. He wouldn't be in this situation if he'd been allowed to go to Wilderness Camp. Oh yes, Wilderness Camp was way better. It had river rafting, singing, cookouts, nature hikes, and best of all, a pretty girl who smelled nice and sometimes let you kiss her. It was difficult to have your spaceship hijacked at Wilderness Camp. You didn't have to threaten people with guns at Wilderness Camp. And best of all, your mother didn't get bludgeoned unconscious at Wilderness Camp.

When it all came crashing down, Wilderness Camp beat out Space Vacation on pretty much every level. Space Vacation was the underside of the desk where Wilderness Camp wiped its boogers. Space Vacation was the gum Wilderness Camp scraped off its shoes. At the beach, Wilderness Camp kicked sand in Space Vacation's face. Space Vacation was for losers.

"Sensing anything else?" Max asked, desperately trying to focus.

"No, nothing more than before, but I'll tell you if I do."

So, whatever it was, it hadn't been a glitch. It was still there. That didn't make him feel any better.

"Seriously," Holiday said as they approached, finally standing in the shadow of the satellite, "how old is this thing?"

"It can't be that old," Max said, but now that he'd said it, he wasn't so sure. Looking at the faded, dust-covered flag on the torn panel directly in front of him, the paint was cracked and peeling.

"Well, it sure looks old. Look at this." Holiday was pointing toward what had once been an antenna array. Now, it looked more like what a sculptor might create if their only source of materials was a scrap yard. Thin metal rods were bent at odd angles, and the antennas that had been smooth, concave shapes were now little more than crumpled shells.

Max looked at the mess and saw what Holiday did. "Is that rust?"

"I think so," Holiday said.

"That doesn't make any sense." He hadn't meant to say that out loud. "I mean, assuming this is even a metal that can rust, there isn't enough atmosphere in space to allow this to happen."

"What if the satellite had oxygen inside it?"

Max took a quick glance at the satellite. "Even if it was filled with oxygen, it's not big enough to hold enough for this much oxidation." Now that they were closer, he could see that the rust damage was extensive, covering large areas of the satellite. Had they really made it entirely out of material vulnerable to rust? It didn't seem right, but then again, rust in space also seemed like a big improbability. And yet, there it was.

"I thought this thing was going to be cosmic, but it's just a huge, rusted piece of junk," Holiday said.

"Stop!" Max shouted.

Holiday froze, her hand outstretched where she had been about to idly flick the end of one protruding antenna.

"Don't do that," Max said. "It could poke a hole in your suit."

She pulled her hand back, then took a step backwards.

"Let's not touch the satellite, okay, Sis?"

"Okay," she said. Max knew she was going to sulk for a minute.

"Besides, you don't want to get your suit dirty."

"Right."

They walked around the satellite, carefully avoiding coming into contact with anything while they peered into the wreckage.

"What do we do now?" Holiday asked. As Max had predicted, she had only pouted for a minute.

Max's HUD let him pinpoint the exact location of the distress signal. It was coming from the center of the main cylinder, which was at least a meter beneath the surface. Max couldn't see a clear way in. There were a couple of openings to be sure, but they were either filled with debris or too dangerous to risk crawling through. At least for him. Holiday might fit. Still, he wasn't going to risk it, and there was no way to be sure that the inside of the satellite had ever been made to accommodate a person.

A second trip around revealed nothing new.

"Okay, that's it," Max said. "We're done. I'm not detecting any heartbeats or heat signatures that would let us know there was a person in there. There's nothing living here. Outside of the distress signal, this thing is dead."

Max checked their air supplies. Fifty-seven minutes left on Holiday's, and fifty-three on his. He was consuming more oxygen, though he wasn't sure if that was natural or if she was simply calmer than he was. Probably the latter. He looked back at the escape pod, wondering how fast they could make it back if there was an emergency—like if one of their suits was damaged. The image of air leaking from Holiday's spacesuit, her mouth open, her throat convulsing as she gasped for air, entered his mind for a brief second, and it was enough to constrict his own throat. A weak, strangled sound escaped. *"Nika,"* he pleaded, his voice almost prayer-like in its fervency. This time, he was able to summon her image quickly, and the pressure weakened enough for him to continue breathing. It didn't go anyway entirely though, as if the hand around his throat was still there, squeezing gently.

"What did you say?" Holiday asked, though Max knew she'd heard him.

"I was thinking about her, that's all," he muttered. "Let's get back to the pod."

Max waited till Holiday was in front of him, then followed her. She hadn't taken more than ten steps before she stopped. She was shaking her head, bringing one arm up, her gloved hand resting against her helmet as if she could massage her temple. Max moved around her, grabbing her shoulders. His HUD told him that her heart rate was accelerated.

"It's changed," she said.

"What's wrong?" Max asked.

"The feeling—it's changed."

"What do you mean?" The hand on his throat tightened.

"It's clearer now. Stronger. It..."

Max didn't want to shake his sister, but he couldn't help himself. She glared at him, and he stopped. "Tell me," he demanded.

She was shivering. "It was only words with you and Dad, but I'm getting feelings from it now. It has emotion now. Oh, Max! It's...*it's getting angry!*"

Despite the ever-tightening grip on his throat, Max was spinning, yanking the Reaper up to shoulder level, eyes searching the area for any sign of movement. He studied his HUD, but it simply wasn't showing him anything to be worried about. Still, that panicky part of him trusted his sister more than a computer, and it was screaming at him to curl up in a ball and hide in the nearest crater until the danger was passed. "Stay close to me, Holi," he whispered. He reached behind with one arm, his fingers spread wide. A second later, he felt her take his hand.

"I can't use the Pyro like this," she complained, fumbling for control of the weapon with her one free hand as he dragged her forward, toward the escape pod, their feet kicking up explosions of dirt.

Max gritted his teeth, thinking of Captain Meaney's foot burning, and what his sister had done because he couldn't. "You don't need to use the Pyro. We're not in any danger."

"Then why are you feeling scared?"

Max looked up and tried to fill his mind with thoughts of stars and the void they were set in. Earth hung there, close and beautiful and oppressive. It was easy to let thoughts of Nika flow in when looking up there. He thought of how her hair floated against her neck, and how her skin shone in the sun. His throat relaxed and his pulse eased.

"C'mon," Max said. "I-I'll just feel better if we're back in the pod." He tried to take another step, but Holiday resisted, her hand tightening on his. Angry, he didn't turn around, but instead let her hand drop, continuing to walk. "Fine, you don't have to hold my hand. Let's just keep moving."

Holiday didn't answer. Great, she was going to sulk. Max let angry thoughts run through his mind, hoping she was eavesdropping. He whirled on her.

And standing there was Captain Darren Meaney, who was very much not dead, holding Holiday close, pointing a gun at Max with one hand and fingering the quick release latch of Holiday's flight helmet with the other.

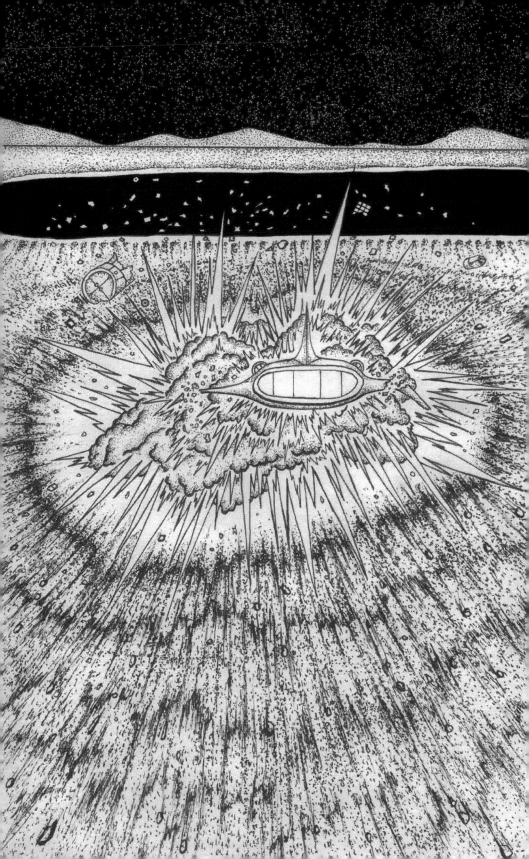

[CHAPTER TWENTY-THREE]

WHAT HAPPENED TO DARREN MEANEY

"If that Reaper moves, we all get to see how long your sister can hold her breath," Darren said.

Max could see his sister's mouth moving, but he couldn't hear her. That meant her communication system was down. Had Darren damaged her helmet in some way? Max's mind raced. Darren was alive! How was that possible? It didn't seem that Darren would have had enough time to get off the *Starburst* before it had exploded...but clearly he had. Did that mean that Riven was alive too?

Max froze as best he could considering his legs were about to crumble underneath him. "Don't hurt her. Please." No, no, no, this wasn't happening. And there it was, the fear, the panic, the paralysis that had overwhelmed him so completely that night at Galactic Taco. Even now, with danger present and clear, the memory of that night burst into his mind. Images of broken glass and drops of blood. His nose had bled, and had continued to leak for hours after it was all over. The memory that overshadowed all the others was that of Emy's cheek, tear-stained and dented with the barrel of a gun.

"That's up to you, Max," Darren said. *"Do what I tell you, and you'll both live through this."*

"What do you want?" Max asked, but his thoughts were stuck trying to figure out how Darren had snuck up on them.

[Max!]

Holiday's voice was so loud, he flinched. Darren's arm tightened around Holiday. Her eyes were wide in some crazy mix of fear and anger.

"Bad idea," Darren said.

"But I didn't—"

"Just shut up. Drop the Reaper."

[Don't do it, Max. Just shoot him.]

Max tried to imagine it, actually raising the Reaper and trying to shoot Darren without hitting his sister. Max's imagination didn't think he could do it. He wasn't quick enough, he barely knew how to shoot, and he had certainly never fired the Reaper. Max's imagination was quite graphic in depicting the results of what would happen when he failed.

He closed his eyes and shuddered. Slowly, he lowered the Reaper to the ground. Some part of him ached when his fingers were no longer touching its smooth skin. Even with his relative inexperience around weapons, there had been no small amount of comfort in being armed against his enemy.

He couldn't look at Holiday; he didn't want to see what might be in her eyes.

"Smart move," Darren said.

Holiday's Pyro was half-buried in the dust half a meter behind where Darren stood. He was wearing a different spacesuit than before. This one was black like the previous one, but with a thin red mesh covering the entire surface of the suit. The mesh extended up onto Darren's flight helmet as well.

[I think that's how he snuck up on us. I never saw anything. One second everything was fine, and then the next second his arms were around me. It's some sort of cloaking system. I tried to send you my thoughts, but I don't think it worked. Anyway, if his spacesuit can cloak, then maybe he's got his spaceship nearby. It can probably do the same thing. It's the only way we wouldn't have seen it.]

Much like her voice, her thoughts had tone and inflection to them. Max knew there was more. Most likely it was going to be about—

[Quantum Girl!! went through something similar in episode 56.]

Max steeled himself and asked, "What do you want with us?"

Darren motioned with his weapon—a snub-nosed, grey thing—for Max to move forward, back towards the satellite. *"Holiday here has a task, a little mission, she needs to complete for me."*

"What is it?" Max asked.

"Both of you, start walking," Darren said, waving the barrel of his gun toward the satellite. *"Max, you walk out in front of your sister. Your sister's level of pain is directly related to how well you follow instructions. Right now she's not in any pain, so her level is zero. If you do anything other than walk, her level will increase. Holiday, the same goes for you. Just follow after your brother now."* Darren pushed her forward behind Max. *"Move it."*

[He's telling the truth, Max. He'll hurt us if we don't obey.]

Max led the way back to the satellite, each step feeling more hopeless than the last, aching for the claustrophobic comfort of the escape pod, but not daring to turn around and look. He watched as his feet dug ugly furrows in the moon's surface, scars that would remain for years. He couldn't stop the sense of loss that filled him, the yearning for his parents and for home. It was strong enough to block out any panic that might have taken him then. He didn't even try to stop the tears when they came. The satellite became a blurry mess in his vision.

[Max, we gotta figure something out. Mom and Dad are depending on us.]

And there it was. The difference between the way Max looked at the universe and the way Holiday did. Scared as she might be, she was still more concerned about her family than she was about herself. If that was something she'd learned from *Quantum Girl!!*, then maybe he should start watching it with her. Max was ashamed and embarrassed that her thoughts weren't his thoughts, that what came naturally to her required persistent effort on his part.

[I need you to protect me.]

Her words were soft, but felt like a slap to his face. Either one of them alone wasn't going to be enough; it was going to take both of them supporting each other if they were going to have a chance of surviving.

Okay then, Max thought, *this has got to stop.* Everybody was depending on him. His parents were depending on him to get Holiday and himself back to Luna One safely, and Holiday needed him right now to be strong, to be somebody she could look to and lean on. He needed to be that person for his parents. For his sister. And for himself.

And he needed to do it *right away.*

Max took a deep breath, willing the tears to stop. Increasing the air flow in his helmet dried his cheeks in a matter of seconds. He flexed his fingers into fists, letting anger and frustration seep into him, watching his pulse speed and his blood pressure increase in his HUD.

They were approaching the satellite again. It seemed gloomier now, inkier, dirtier, more scarred, the rust an overwhelming, oppressive force, a reminder of an inescapable, entropic demise.

[He hacked my computer, Max. Somehow he hacked it! Life support is working, but my computer's not responding to any commands. Even though I can't broadcast, or hear you, for some reason I can still hear Mr. Meaney. And he can hear me, I think. Weird. I hope he doesn't do the same thing to yours. Anyway, if I couldn't listen to your thoughts and broadcast mine to you, we'd be in trouble.]

As if they weren't in *other* sorts of trouble.

Leave it to Holiday to not let the impending doom in any particular situation get to her. Max was envious of her resilience. Where Max was hamstrung, she was free. No doubt fueled by the plot of some *Quantum Girl!!* episode, she probably already some crazy idea of how to turn the tables on Captain Meaney and get back to the escape pod.

Max, honestly, had nothing. He was keeping the panic at bay through anger and frustration, but it was taking all his effort, and there didn't seem to be much left with which to formulate escape plans.

Darren's voice broke though, *"That's close enough, Holiday."*

She stopped. Max was a couple meters ahead of her, but he stopped too.

Max felt a hand on his shoulder, then felt a *thump* as the barrel of Darren's gun was pressed against his helmet. He was pushed forward toward the satellite until he was only a few steps away. *"Why don't you sit yourself down there, Max,"* Darren said. Max lowered his body and sat in the dirt, his back to the satellite. There was something poking him, so he shifted, realizing he had come down on a curved ridge of metal that had only a thin layer of dirt coating it. He didn't see any rust. He was curiously comforted by that. The mangled piece of metal hanging in his peripheral vision was red and black with the stuff.

Looking at the satellite, one of the larger wounds in the satellite's skin was just over his shoulder, though from his sitting position he couldn't see far inside.

Darren pushed Holiday directly in front of the hole, then released her, walking over beside Max. Again, the gun went to Max's helmet, hard this time, forcing Max's head almost to his shoulder. Max steadied himself with one hand, his fingers disappearing into the dirt, mere centimeters away from a razor sharp twist of metal that protruded from the ground.

If my hand had come down on that...

When Darren spoke next, he was addressing Holiday. *"I'm going to pull this trigger if you don't do exactly what I say. Do you understand?"*

Holiday nodded. [*What should I do, Max?*]

Exactly what he says, Max thought. Without a plan, he had to wait for an opportunity to present itself. Neither of them had any real weapons, and the ones they'd had were now hanging at Darren's back.

Max didn't see any way to get them. He could just barely see Holiday if he turned his head in his helmet. She was at least three meters away. But it really didn't matter—with a gun to his head he wasn't going anywhere. He thought about the large crater on the other side of the satellite. *Maybe if I could figure out some sort of distraction…*

"Holiday," Darren said, his voice lowering to a rumble. Max didn't like how his sister's name had sounded that time. *"I need you to climb into the satellite and get the object your dad was sent here for. I need you to retrieve the Crux."*

Holiday's thoughts came through loudly. *[Oh, Max, I don't know what he's talking about, but I can't tell him that or he might hurt you! I'm just going to have to climb in there and get him what he wants. I think he'll let us go if we don't cause him any trouble.]*

Max didn't know what a Crux was either.

"What does it look like?" Holiday asked. Even though Max couldn't hear her voice in his helmet, she'd sent him thoughts to mirror her words.

"Use this to find it," Darren said, reaching into one of the pockets on his spacesuit and pulling out a circular piece of what looked like glass. It was small enough to fit in Holiday's palm when he handed it to her. She held it between her forefinger and thumb, turning it slowly. The outer edge was chrome, the center transparent.

"What am I supposed to do with this?" she asked, and even in her thoughts, there was just a hint of whiney twelve-year-old in there. Max wanted to snicker.

If Darren cared how she responded, he didn't show it. *"When you get inside, look through it. The Crux will glow red through the Oculus."*

"Oh," Holiday said, not hesitating in turning toward the satellite and looking for the best way to reach the hole.

Max had a billion questions, but everything was moving so quickly. Holiday put her hand on the satellite, looking for a foothold.

Don't touch the rust, Max thought, though he wasn't sure why. *It's not safe.*

Darren grunted. *"Good girl. I like it when my girls obey."*

[What a creep. I am so not his girl.]

Max had never felt like punching somebody in the face as much as he did in that moment. He wanted to ask Darren about Riven, but he didn't dare.

"One more thing before you go in there and get me what I want," Darren said and then did something that Max didn't see. For a second he could move his head again, letting it return to a more vertical position, only to have it shoved back down against his shoulder. He could feel something vibrating against his helmet.

[Max, that's the—]

But he didn't need her to tell him that it was the Reaper.

"Holiday," Darren said in a quiet, whispery tone of voice that Max had only ever heard from his father. It was strange and out-of-place. *"You need to hurry. You don't have much time. You're running out of oxygen."*

Her scream careening through his mind, Max watched in horror as his sister's air supply began to vent, spewing into the vacuum from a release port somewhere between her shoulder blades.

"Stop it!" Max shouted, barely stopping himself from making an attempt for the Reaper, knowing that there was no way he'd be able to get the weapon from Darren.

[No!No!No!No!No!No!No!No!No!No!]

"Not another word, Max," Darren ordered. *"Better tell your sweet little sister to hurry. At that rate she's leaking, she only has…oh, let's say less than eleven minutes of air."*

"Hurry, Holi," Max choked out, though he assumed that Darren was still blocking her from receiving his audio. *Please hurry, and be careful!*

The litany streaming through his mind stopped abruptly, almost as if Holiday had switched the channel she was broadcasting her thoughts on. Max had just enough of a view to see her, instead of grabbing onto the satellite, bend her knees and jump. She went straight and true, one hand still holding the Oculus, the other hand coming around a bar of metal just inside the opening. Her feet swung wildly, but they landed directly on the uneven bottom edge.

His sister was amazing. No matter the difficulty, she always rose to overcome it. Max was envious.

[Thanks.]

"It's a mess in here. There's not much room for me to move around," Holiday said.

"I'm sure you'll find a way to get me what I want," Darren replied. He sounded annoyed.

Max felt a shift somewhere in the deep recesses of his mind, and then he was desperately trying to deal with the rushing stream of Holiday's consciousness:

[Keep calm. Control breathing. Jerk! Jerk! Jerk! Hate Darren. Hope he falls into a crater. Don't breathe deep. Got to conserve. Scared. Wow, messy in here. Think I can squeeze through though. Wish I knew what a Crux was. What does it even look like? Stupid Darren. Looking through the Oculus. Nothing. Probably just a stupid piece of glass. No way this thing does anything. All wires and electronics in here. Smashed. Everything's ruined. This is nothing like Quantum Girl!!'s ship. Hers is so much prettier and pinker and has lots more glitter. Tons of glitter. Ick, what is that? Getting grease all over my glove. Gross. At least I think that's grease. Okay, keep moving. Can slide through there I think if I just…okay, not working, maybe if I move these cables out of the way. There, much better.]

Max's throat caught a little when his sister disappeared fully into the satellite.

[No rust here. Good. Uh oh, lots of sharp stuff though. Cosmic, avoided that one. Would've put a hole in the arm of my spacesuit. Don't have time to deal with field repairs. Better here now, more room. Better look around again with the Oculus.

Nothing. Again. Dumb old piece of glass. Dumb Darren. He'll pay for making me miss the Low-G Gymnastics Exhibition Sponsored by Energistix!]

Life-threatening danger or not, Holiday was still Holiday.

[Okay, what's that? Need more light. There, that's better. Back there, behind all that mess. Doesn't look as damaged as the rest. Looks interesting. Looks way more cosmic than anything else in this wreck. Looks like it belongs in the engine room of the Quark Pony!!. *Oculus says no, though. Maybe I'm not using this thing right. As if there's a wrong way to look through a stupid piece of glass.]*

There was a long pause.

[Dumb! Dumb! Dumb! So dumb. Can't believe I was looking through it backwards. Can't believe it actually works. There's the Crux glowing red through the Oculus, just like dumb old Darren said it would. Know what it looks like now. Still don't know what it is. Just a white plastic sphere with curvy lines on it. Sort of pretty. Just a little closer so I can reach it. There. Wow. Didn't expect it to come out that easily. Weird. It feels warm even through my spacesuit. Not radioactive though.]

There were little strips on the arms of their spacesuits that changed color when exposed to elevated radioactivity levels. Max checked his. It was blue, which meant he wouldn't be growing a third arm today.

[Max, I got it. I'm coming out. I'm okay. I have less than eight minutes of oxygen left. We have to hurry back to the escape pod. Get ready.]

There was something in the tone of her thoughts that alarmed Max. *Get ready for what?* he thought.

[I lied. He's not going to let us go.]

Despite his resolve to be strong for sister, suddenly Max couldn't breathe. He jerked as if he'd been punched.

"Watch yourself, kid," Darren said. *"This is almost over. You wouldn't want to blow it when you're so close. Holiday, honey, you'd better hurry. I don't think your brother's doing so well."*

[We have to do something. So, let's do what Quantum Girl!! would do if she was in a situation like this. When I give you the signal, run for the escape pod.]

I can't, Max thought. *I can't do it, Holi. He'll blow my head off if I try anything. We have to think of something else. This won't work.*

[We don't have any time to debate this, Max. He'll be distracted in a second. When you see your chance, take it. I need you to do this. Mom and Dad need you to do this.]

It was embarrassing to be ordered around by his younger sister, but Max knew she was right. They were out of options and out of time.

Holiday's arm emerged from the hole, followed by her helmet.

Max's arm tingled from the pressure he was putting on it. He looked there, where his gloved hand was buried in the gray, lifeless dirt, his eyes coming to rest on the thin twist of metal he'd narrowly avoided earlier. His fingers were only a few centimeters away. He adjusted his hand and pressed against the metal with his finger. The metal moved. He pressed a little more, pinpricks travelling up and down his arm from loss of circulation at his wrist. The metal shifted again, turning slightly. Holiday's entire torso was visible now as she methodically extracted herself from the interior of the satellite wreckage. Max concentrated on moving his hand without shifting the rest of his body too much. He thought that Darren might be more fixated on Holiday, but his restricted view didn't let him look directly up.

"I found the Crux, Mr. Meaney!" Holiday shouted, though Max didn't see her holding it.

"Let me see it," Darren demanded. Max's helmet shifted as Darren pressed the Reaper closer, emphasizing what he would do if Holiday tried anything.

"Sure, got it right here!" Holiday said, reaching into one of the rear pockets on her spacesuit. Her fist reappeared, holding the white, spherical Crux. Holiday looked down to keep her balance, steadied herself, then readjusted her footing.

And slipped.

Her arms flew out wildly, the Crux sailing high into the air.

Darren shouted. Max felt the Reaper shift, come away from his helmet ever so slightly. And then, consciously, deliberately, he swallowed his crippling fear and acted.

He grabbed the metal shard at its base and yanked. Simply imbedded in the dirt and not attached to anything underneath, it came loose easily. Gritting his teeth, he swung his arm around, burying the shaft of metal into Darren's leg. Along with a blast of escaping air, and Darren's shout of pain, there was a wet, fiery pain in Max's hand. His HUD flared to life with a furious, reddish alarm. An overly calm female voice in Max's helmet made sure that he was aware of his EXTRAVEHICULAR MOBILITY SUIT INTEGRITY COMPROMISE. Glowing numbers, swiftly decreasing, hovered in his vision, letting him know how many minutes of oxygen he had left. He felt the chilled rush of air along his body as his spacesuit began to deflate. His palm felt slick, somehow both warm and cold at the same time.

That. Was going to be a problem.

Darren disappeared from Max's field of view, but his grunt came loudly over the communication channel.

[Run, Max! Now!]

Max pushed up, seeing that Darren was on the ground at his feet, and oh, Holiday was crouching on his back, her hands furiously working at the weapons there. Max's mind imagined her faking her fall, throwing the Crux as a distraction, jumping from the satellite, right onto Darren, at precisely the same time that Max had stabbed him in the leg. Clearly, the combination had been enough for the takedown.

Run for the escape pod, now! Max thought.

The Reaper was out of Darren's hand, but still within his reach. Max dove for it.

[No, Max!]

Max knew his sister only had a little oxygen left, but he couldn't let

Darren have the Reaper. The other weapons were dangerous, sure, but if he could get the Reaper, he would have firepower superiority, and just maybe, some semblance of control of their situation.

Now, Holiday! Max's thoughts screamed as he planted his foot hard between Darren and the Reaper.

Using her full name got her attention. She jumped to the side, and when she did, she took the Pyro with her. She was fast, real fast, running with an ease and grace that was years beyond her twelve-year-old body.

Mouthing a quick prayer, ignoring the decrementing numbers in his vision and the insistent alarm filling his helmet, Max yanked the Reaper up and into his arms. He stepped back from Darren, who was shaking his head, attempting to get up. Max supposed that Darren had hit his head somehow during the fall because his movements were slow.

Knowing where the Pyro and the Reaper were, Max scanned the ground for Darren's original weapon. He could feel the Reaper humming against his chest. A stream of curse words from Darren broke through the noise. Max felt light-headed. There was blood streaming from his glove, slowly dripping in dark drops down to the moon's surface.

[Run, Max!]

"You stupid kids!" Darren screamed, though it was muffled, like maybe his mouth was filled liquid. Blood, Max supposed. *"I'm going to kill you both!*

Max spotted Darren's weapon. Without thinking, he aimed and squeezed the trigger on the Reaper. There was a flash of pale blue light, and then the ground next to Darren exploded. Darren grunted, his body flung to the side, away from the satellite. The Reaper hadn't kicked, hadn't moved, as if being used for such an inconsequential task wasn't worthy of a reaction. There were areas of the ground that had been transformed from dirt to blackish puddles of magma.

[What did you—]

But Max cut her off, not letting her overtake his thoughts. He backed away from the satellite, putting more distance between himself and Darren at the same time. He didn't see any trace of Darren's weapon. So, unless Darren had another weapon he hadn't revealed, Max had the upper hand.

Max pointed the Reaper at Darren, who was attempting to get up again—the blood-splattered shard of metal protruding from his leg. There were thin streams of blood leaking down the ankle of his suit. As Darren stood, he grabbed the shard of metal and pulled it from his leg. The shard glinted red and silver as Darren tossed it aside. He reached into a pocket at his thigh and extracted something—a roll of tape. He peeled some off the roll and patched the hole in his spacesuit.

Max had a similar patch kit in one of his pockets as well, but he didn't think he could use it on his hand and still cover Darren with the Reaper.

"Don't make me use this," Max said, though the waver in his voice didn't lend much credibility to his threat. "Just stay there and let me and my sister go." Max risked a look over his shoulder. Holiday was over halfway back to the escape pod. Good. She was going to make it. Now, if he could just join her before he ran out of oxygen or bled to death. He did his best to press his hand against the Reaper. Maybe that would slow the outflow of blood a little.

Darren laughed. *"You don't have the guts to use that on me. Now, if it were your sister, I could believe it. She's a little spitfire, she is, and she's not afraid to pull a trigger when a trigger needs pulled. If she were a little older, I'd ask her to join up with—"*

"Shut up!" Max said. "You're going to stay right there while I leave. You're not going to follow me, or I'm…I'm going to have to do something I don't want to."

Darren turned his back to Max. *"You just don't get it, Max. I don't care about you or your sister. You were just tools that I needed to use. Now that I'm done with you, now that your sister got me what I needed, you're useless to me. So, go ahead and leave. Go find your parents, if they're still alive that is."* Darren moved toward the satellite. He was limping from what Max had just done to him, but also from the hole Holiday had put in his foot. Max was glad. He hoped Darren would limp forever for what he'd done. Actually, a limp was the least of the punishments he'd wish on Captain Darren Meaney.

"They're alive."

"Sure they are, kid. Go on, get out of here. If I see you again, I'll kill you."

Thoughts of aiming and firing, watching the Reaper perform its designed function flittered darkly through Max's mind.

[Max, I made it! Had a whole two minutes of oxygen left! Wait, what are you doing? Get back here!]

Max knew he should be running for the escape pod, but he was stuck backing up slowly, watching Darren, unable to let the man out of his sight. Darren was desperately searching for the Crux. Max saw it first, partially obscured by the shards of a shattered solar panel. It was resting against the main body of the satellite, and it wasn't as white as it had been before. Now, the shiny surface was polluted with lifeless, gray dirt.

[Hurry, Max! Get to the escape pod before he comes after you! He might have some other weapon!]

Darren spotted the Crux, bending down to grab it.

Max didn't know where the urge came from, but something almost made him reverse direction and head back towards the satellite, back towards Darren. So that he could…what? Stop Darren from taking something from a wrecked satellite? Maybe it was the simple fact that the Crux was important to Darren. And if it was important or worth something to a scum sucker like Darren, then just maybe it was important enough to try to prevent him from getting away with it. Max wasn't sure, and that's why he kept moving backwards, vaguely aware that he was shivering.

[Max, please hurry back! There's something…feels like…strange…] Her thoughts trailed off.

Darren spun around, holding up the Crux triumphantly. Though, something wasn't quite right. His body swayed, his legs unsteady. Max wondered if Darren had a concussion. Darren reached out to steady himself, his hand against the rust-covered skin of the satellite.

Max was feeling a little light-headed himself, his chest muscles tight. Thankfully, the searing pain in his hand was allowing him to maintain a degree of clarity. His mind registered that he was standing still, no longer moving toward the safety of the escape pod.

"What are you still doing here, kid?" Darren spat, holding the Crux close to his helmet.

Max didn't know how to answer that. He knew he'd sensed something wrong, and whatever it was, he couldn't leave till he knew what it was.

"You need to leave before I change my mind about not killing you." Darren stepped away from the satellite, his gloved hand coming away covered in reddish-brown dust.

"Is the Crux worth all you've done?" Max found himself asking.

Darren let the Crux lower to his side. *"You can't even imagine. It's priceless."*

"What does it do?"

"That's the beauty of it. I don't even know. And you know what? I don't care what it does. I just know how important it is to others. That means they'll pay, and they'll pay big."

"Money? That's all? You did all of this just for money?" This was stupid. He should've already been back in the escape pod instead of standing here talking to the monster who had beat his mother unconscious.

"Don't act so surprised. You're not a naïve little girl like your sister. You know how the world works."

Max shook his head, swirling with anger and disappointment.

Then.

Then he saw it.

Darren's arm was covered in the reddish-brown dirt that had previously only been on his hand. Max watched in horror as the dirt *moved*.

It was really accelerating now, flowing up Darren's arm and onto his shoulder.

Max opened his mouth to warn Darren, but nothing came out except a pathetic, unmanly squeak.

[Max, I can see you on the monitor. Is there someone else there? I can feel...is it Riven? I can't see her. And the computer says your spacesuit has a hole, and your blood pressure is dropping. Are you hurt? Why aren't you running back here?]

Darren dropped the Crux when he noticed the infection spreading across the surface of his spacesuit. He brushed at the dirt that wasn't dirt, managing to get some of it off, only to have it spread to his other hand. Max realized that the dirt wasn't moving.

It was *growing*.

Darren issued a wet, bubbly curse, frantically beating at his body in an attempt to dislodge the infection.

Max could only stand and watch. He saw the Crux, resting where it had landed, a little over a meter away from where Darren struggled, and decided to go for it. He was moving forward quickly, aware that every time he took a step, his hand throbbed like it was going to fall off. Should it really hurt that much? Seriously, had he damaged it that much? He could still move his fingers. How badly could he be hurt if he was still able to move his fingers?

By the time he reached the Crux, Darren had stumbled back and tripped, half-standing, half-sitting against the core of the satellite. He was grunting with his efforts to brush the infection away.

Not dirt, thought Max. *Something…else. Something…*

Alien.

Darren's scream pierced the atmosphere of Max's helmet when the infection reached the tape he'd placed over the hole in his spacesuit. Max was close enough to see the tape come loose, the infection pouring inside through the tear. Darren grabbed at his leg just above the knee in an attempt to intercept the spread.

Max snagged the Crux with his free hand, though it was awkward to wield the Reaper with only one hand. He jumped back when he saw a finger of reddish-brown color reach toward his boot. The gray of the moon's surface was quickly changing to rust. He was completely cut off from Darren, a wide patch of the infection between the two of them.

[Do you see that? Run!]

Max turned to run, only then seeing that Holiday hadn't been referring to the alien infection, but to the ghostly spaceship that was suddenly visible above them. It was a small shuttle, with a narrow, angled body. Max could see a single primary thruster at the rear of the shuttle, with several maneuvering thrusters around the fuselage. The surface was black, still shimmering as it became more and more solid. It was descending slowly.

Darren stood, one arm raised toward his ship, though his body was thrashing.

Clutching the Crux and the Reaper tightly, Max turned and ran.

"Help me," Darren pleaded.

Max slowed, hesitated, then turned.

Only to see Darren pulling his flight helmet off.

The infection quickly crawled up his neck and over his face. He was screaming, but Max couldn't hear him anymore.

Darren Meaney crumpled to the ground and went still.

[Oh, Max, RUN!]

The shuttle, perhaps following Darren's last, confused command, was no longer descending slowly. Instead, its thrusters were blazing, accelerating it moonward.

Max ran, the numbers flashing in his HUD alarmingly low. He found the numbers hard to comprehend. Black spots began to pop into his vision. Also, breathing was a real challenge now, which was strange, since he wasn't feeling panicked. His sister's thoughts should have been loud in his mind, but they were distant and muffled, as if she were yelling while covering her mouth.

He never saw the shuttle's impact, the way it punctured the satellite, its nose crumpling like paper. He never saw the explosion that followed. But the shockwave took him down, sending him tumbling, the Crux and the Reaper lost.

The stars, he thought, when he had come to a stop on his back, *they're so close. Nika would love them up close like this.*

Then the stars, one by one, winked out.

[Chapter Twenty-Four]

What Happened After Maximillion Woke Up

Max came awake, calmly enough, to his sister's cheery face. She was smiling, but she stared at him for several seconds, those almost-black eyes of hers searching his, a million questions behind them. She looked quickly over her shoulder at something Max couldn't see.

"What's wrong?" Max asked. His throat felt dry, but he realized that the rest of him felt fine; he wasn't in any pain.

Holiday turned back, her voice low. "Nothing. I just want to make sure that Mom and Dad weren't standing in the doorway. They've been doing that all day. But it's okay now, they're resting in their room."

Max looked around. It looked like a hotel room. He was on the bed, cool covers up to his chest. The floral print on the bedcover was hideous. The walls were white, bland with some generic wall decorations. Pale yellow light came from a row of tubes in the ceiling. "Mom and Dad are okay?" he asked.

Holiday nodded. "They're good. Obviously, they made it back safe. Dad found a way to make their escape pod land close to Luna One. He's a really good pilot. And mom's fine. Mr. Meaney hurt her, but the doctors here fixed her."

Max was beyond relieved.

Holiday looked at the door again, then lowered her voice some more. "Max, I know you want to see Mom and Dad, but we need to talk first. I have something I need to—"

"Wait. First, tell me what happened."

She sighed. "Okay, well the shuttle—it sort of looked like it was from the *Venge* didn't it?—anyway, it crashed, and it exploded. It knocked you down, and I was really afraid that you'd been hurt. But the escape pod computer was still able to communicate with your spacesuit, and it said you were fine. When I got to you, you were unconscious. I pulled you into the escape pod, and then drove it here."

"To Luna One?"

"Of course, silly," Holiday said. "Where else could we be? We're still on the moon."

"Oh good," Max exhaled. A rather large part of him had wished he'd awakened back on Earth. "So, you put me into the escape pod?"

"Yeah, and it wasn't easy. First I had to resupply my suit with oxygen. I couldn't undo the computer hack Mr. Meaney did, so I just used a patch kit and covered the port so I wouldn't lose any more air. Then I had to drag you inside the pod. You're pretty heavy. So anyway, I did that all by myself."

"Holiday," Max said. "Thank you. You saved my life."

Holiday hugged him, smiling. "You're my only brother. It's not like I was going to leave you there."

Max examined his hurt hand. It was heavy with a bandage that wrapped his entire palm, restricting his ability to move his fingers. "I would have died out there without you, Holi."

Holiday touched his shoulder. "Really, it wasn't as bad as you might've thought. You lost some blood, but you weren't in danger of bleeding to death or anything, at least not with me there. You had at least fifteen minutes of oxygen left. And as far as you being unconscious, at first I thought the explosion knocked you out, but the doctors here said you had no signs of head trauma. I think you just fainted."

"I didn't faint," Max said.

"Okay, well I guess you were probably in shock then."

Yeah, shock sounded much better. Tons less unmanly.

Holiday grabbed his good hand and squeezed. "Really, shock is understandable, with what happened to you and to…Mr. Meaney."

The image of Darren falling to the ground, his skin consumed by infection would never be banished from Max's mind. He was trying not to think about it.

"Max, the stuff that was on Mr. Meaney," Holiday said, "what do you think it was?"

She would just read his thoughts if he said anything other than what he was thinking. "It wasn't rust."

"So the satellite wasn't old like we thought."

"Doesn't really seem like it, does it?" Max let silence fall between them for a minute. He couldn't look his sister in the eye. "It doesn't really matter how old it is though. It was obviously from Earth, but the question we need to be asking ourselves is more about where exactly it's been."

"You mean where did it go that it could have brought back some alien life form?" There, she'd said it.

"Yes," Max croaked, his throat suddenly tight. First, telepathy. Now, aliens. Wonderful. He really hated that science fiction was turning out to be more fact than fiction. "You'd think if a satellite found alien life somewhere we would have heard something about it."

"Maybe. But if that satellite has been outside our solar system, maybe farther than anything's ever been, then it's possible that alien stuff hitched a ride back?"

"But how could the satellite travel that far? We don't have faster-than-light travel yet."

"Maybe it went through a wormhole or something."

"A wormhole?"

"Yeah, you know, a shortcut between two points in space. Everybody believes they're theoretical, but what if they're real? If this satellite went through a wormhole, it could have gone anywhere."

"And then it came back."

"Yeah."

"Somehow."

"Yeah, somehow."

"Do you think that alien stuff is still there?" Holiday asked. She looked concerned.

Max had been afraid she was going to ask that. "I guess anything's possible, but I don't see how. The satellite was completely destroyed. Nothing could have lived through that." Max's head was beginning to hurt. "And really, does it matter to us? I'm just glad we're all alive and safe. We'll let the adults handle the rest. Just tell the truth to Mom and Dad. Really though, it's over. Darren's dead. That alien stuff and the Crux got obliterated. We're done with this."

Holiday nodded, hesitated, then said, "Uh, Max, about that. You know that thing I needed to talk you about—"

"Max!" came the shout from the doorway.

Sabatha Storm rushed across the room and slammed Max into the tightest, most lung-crushing hug she'd ever given him. He hugged her back, tears springing into life at the corners of his eyes. She kissed his neck, and he could feel her tears on his cheek. Behind her, Max saw his dad. Sabatha drew Rian and Holiday in, turning it into a family hug. Max's dad almost always cried if his mom did, and this was no exception. Holiday usually only cried if she absolutely couldn't get her way, but seeing her whole family reunited was too overwhelming.

Questions and answers, almost too many of each to count, would certainly follow, but right then, Max was happy. He was safe. His family was safe. The bad guys were gone, and the plague-like alien life—if that's what it was—had been eradicated by the exploding shuttle.

For the first time on the Storm family space vacation, Max was truly happy.

CHAPTER TWENTY-FIVE

WHAT HAPPENED AT THE LOW-G GYMNASTICS EXHIBITION SPONSORED BY ENERGISTIX

Max wasn't really into gymnastics—he was mostly preoccupied with figuring out how to sneak in a call to Nika without his parents finding out—but he had to admit that somebody doing twenty somersaults in a single vault was pretty impressive.

Holiday was literally jumping up and down with excitement. And in the low gravity of the moon, that meant that Rian and Sabatha kept having to reach out and keep her from leaping ten feet in the air.

The exhibition was being held in an open-air area. High above, the clear dome of Luna One afforded everybody a dazzling view of Earth and the stars surrounding it. Max got dizzy if he looked up for too long, so he mainly kept his focus closer to the ground.

It was the last night of the exhibition and despite all that had happened, nobody was going to tell Holiday that she wasn't going to be able to go.

There were a lot of logistics involved when the spaceship you left Earth with didn't make it all the way to Luna. Rian had let the whole family know that there would be questions, more questions, and still more questions after that. There would be long interview sessions. Oh, and lots of paperwork. Max didn't know how his dad had managed it, but he'd received permission for the family to attend the exhibition. It was a brief stay of execution, but it was enough for the family to experience a small piece of the *vacation* part of their space vacation.

"Did you see that?" Holiday exclaimed. "That was so cosmic! I'm going to be able to do that some day!"

"Of course you will, honey," Sabatha said, adjusting her new glasses. The frames were thick and purple.

At times, Max couldn't stop thinking of how close he'd come to losing them. Though, in hindsight, he shouldn't have worried much. Rian was an expert pilot, and his history in the Space Command had trained him for a variety of emergency scenarios. Once they arrived at Luna One, Sabatha had received immediate medical attention. Amazingly, she didn't have a concussion. Neither of them had suffered any permanent damage.

Even with Rian's contacts, there had been little he could do except sit with his wife and wait for word about their children.

Max let his mind wander. His parents hadn't left him alone with Holiday since they'd found him awake in their hotel. He knew Holiday wanted to talk with him about something. There just hadn't been time. It was probably nothing. Just the next *Quantum Girl!!* episode he supposed.

"I'll be right back," Max said, standing. There had to be a holo station in the arena somewhere. Now was as good a time as any to talk to Nika. Assuming she'd take a call from him.

"Where are you going?" Rian asked.

"Restroom." There was immediate guilt about lying to his dad, but he justified it by telling himself that he would visit the facilities. Then it wouldn't be a lie. Not *exactly* a lie. Just misdirection.

Max made his way to the end of the row of seats, then up a line of steps, till he found the tunnel that led to the open ring around the stadium. There were numerous shops to his left and right. The ring was filled with endless ways for visitors to spend their money. Max wasn't interested, so he didn't give most of the shops more than a passing glance.

Despite the open air nature of the place, Max felt a touch of claustrophobia. He had the sudden urge to go back to the hotel room. But no, he needed to contact Nika. He needed to see her face and hear her sweet voice. Then he'd feel better. Even if she was still angry with him, he'd feel better just seeing her. It would give him hope.

He came to a stop in front of a store called *Moonbeams*. Through transparent doors, he could see a line of sleek, ovoid cubicles with video screens.

Cosmic.

His hand was on the door handle when a shiver ran down his spine. There was pressure in his side, the smell of something minty mixed with strawberries in his nose, and a familiar voice at his ear.

"What're you doing here, Max? Calling your girlfriend? Oh, good idea, but Miss Pretty Pants will have to wait. That pressure in your side is an injection capsule for a very potent, very quick poison. Come with me. We need to talk."

Though he would have had every right to freeze up, to let panic have its way with him, Max found that he was entirely calm as he turned and faced her.

And he even managed to smile as he let Riven Meaney lead him away.

[CHAPTER TWENTY-SIX]

WHAT HAPPENED TO RIVEN MEANEY

Given their surroundings—the women's restroom of a nearly-vacant restaurant that served only soups—Riven had no right to look as beautiful as she did. And yet, there she was, hair all over the place, falling around her clean, radiant face as if sculpted by a professional hairstylist, though Max suspected she never ran a comb through it. She probably didn't take but a fraction of the time to get ready as Nika did.

She was wearing a tight leather jacket over a shirt with detailed stitching. Her waist was set with a silver belt. She wore jeans and silver boots with thick, rugged soles. Max imagined her kicking him, her foot going all the way through his body. She'd jammed the door with something she'd pulled from one of her front pockets. Then she'd pushed him up against the counter and taken a step back, regarding him with an expression that Max was entirely unable to fathom. He supposed she hated him. What else could she possibly be feeling?

Max had two questions for her. He asked the one he really wanted to know. "How did you survive?"

Riven laughed. "I like you, Max, you know that, right? Here we are. I've kidnapped you and all you want to know is how I survived when the *Starburst* exploded."

"I thought you and your dad were dead."

Riven grunted. "He's not my dad. But you already knew that. Okay, I'll tell you. It's simple really. The *Venge* was never really disabled, and it wasn't out of fuel. We programmed it to rendezvous with us. We had already docked the shuttle to the *Starburst*. When you took the last pod, we escaped on the shuttle. I do have to tell you, we barely made it. You and your troublemaker of a sister didn't leave us much time. Darren took the shuttle to the satellite crash site and I took the *Venge* here. What? Why are you looking at me like that?"

"It's weird," Max said, finding that he was in an unusual state of mind. Maybe he was going crazy—one crisis too many leaving him unbalanced, willing and able to voice his feelings without fear. "I should be angry at you, scared perhaps, but all I'm really feeling is…I'm glad you're alive."

"Stop," Riven said, reaching for something on her belt that clearly wasn't there. It looked like she'd been reaching for a gun. "Don't say things like that. It's not going to be like that between us. You're going to give me what I want, and then we're never going to see each other again."

He was glad she was alive—had a strange urge to go over and hug her in spite of how life-threatening that was likely to be—but her callous rejection caused his anger to rise. Still, he found his voice calm when he responded. "Okay, so it's not enough that you ruined my family's vacation and almost got us all killed. Now you want something from me? I didn't have anything to begin with, and I don't have anything now. Seriously, what could I possibly have that you would want?"

"The object you took from the satellite. The Crux. Give it to me."

Max couldn't stop himself. He laughed, and he held her eyes when he did it.

"Stop laughing, Max. I mean it."

He stopped as best he could. "Sorry, but I don't have the Crux. It got vaporized when your shuttle crashed."

"You're lying."

"Look at me. I'm not. I had it, but when the shuttle crashed, the shockwave hit me hard. I couldn't hold onto it. I lost the Crux and the weapon I was holding. I blacked out shortly after that. When I woke up, I was here at Luna One. If the Crux wasn't destroyed, then it might still be out there, just waiting for you to get it. Go ahead, I'm not going to stop you, and I won't tell anybody. I promise."

Riven's face remained calm, but he could tell that she was seething inside. She looked like she was deciding between believing him and tearing off his arms. Maybe both. Her left hand, which still held the injection capsule, was shaking.

"You know, you drugged me before I could tell you the best story I've got," Max said.

"Better than the one we've created over the past couple of days?" Riven said bitterly. Still, she hadn't attacked him, so that was a positive.

Max considered that. "Ok, so now it's my second best story. Anyway, I had a part-time job at Galactic Taco. Worked mostly on the weekends. Being the new guy, I always got stuck with the late night shift. Since business was slow late at night, there were only three of us working that night. It was Emy, Tama, and me. Tama and I cooked while Emy took orders."

Riven was listening, and Max wasn't exactly sure why.

"One night, three men came in with guns. They jumped over the counter. One pushed Emy's head down on the counter and shoved his gun against her cheek. They made Tama sit on the floor. While they walked around, breaking things and taking whatever they wanted."

"What about you?" Riven asked.

"It was so stupid. They wanted me to cook for them."

"That's it?"

"That's it. They didn't even take any money. But it didn't matter. I was frozen, totally locked up. They could've put a gun to my head and I wouldn't have been able to cook for them. I was standing there, watching them put a gun to Emy's head, and all I could think of was how I was going to be next. My nose started bleeding, and I was just standing there paralyzed."

"Why are you telling me this?"

"Because I'm not afraid of you like you want me to be. Ever since that night, I've been unable to control my fear. I've let it consume me. My situations have been controlling me. Now, thanks to you and Darren, I've had to face down everything that was holding me back."

"Okay, that's great. Glad I could help."

"You should let me go," Max said.

Riven shook her head, all that beautiful hair waving. "I can't do that. I still need you."

Max took a couple of steps closer to her. She actually stepped back, raising the injection capsule. The green liquid inside it sloshed around. "You're better than this, Riven."

"No I'm not."

He took another step. The urge to hug her was almost overwhelming. He really didn't understand it. They were close in age, and here he was, attracted to her, sure, but also wanting to protect her, as if he were her older brother. "You *are* better than this. I don't have the Crux. How else can you use me? C'mon, Darren is dead. Whatever hold he had on you is gone. You don't have to be like him anymore." Max realized then that by bringing the *Venge* to Luna One instead of waiting for Darren, she'd already been planning on leaving her partner.

Max forced himself to hold her eyes—something he normally couldn't do with a girl as jaw-droppingly pretty as she was. She backed down first, her hand holding the injection capsule dropping to her side. Her shoulders slumped. Max turned his head. He didn't want her to think he'd seen the tear on her cheek.

"This is what I know," Riven said.

Max didn't dare touch her, though he was close enough to do just that. "People can change. They do it every day. I did, and so can you. I'll help if I can."

She sniffed, her eyes liquid. "You're such a saint," she said, then the next thing Max knew he was pressed up against the counter, Riven's body tight and close against his.

Oh, and she was kissing him.

This.

This was unexpected.

He was too surprised to do anything other than stand there passively, his hands braced on the counter. There was pain in his hurt hand, but with the warmth and wet of her lips on his he wouldn't have felt somebody amputating the whole limb.

When she pulled back, she said, breathing hard. "You're a terrible kisser, and don't think I'm not still mad at you for depressurizing the *Starburst,*" she said. Then, before Max could respond, she did it again.

Powerless to fight back, Max closed his eyes and luxuriated in the soft press of her mouth, kissing her back. This time when she pulled away, they were both trying to catch their breath. Riven wiped her mouth, pointing the injection capsule at him. "Ok, let's go. If you don't have the Crux, then maybe your sister does. Let's go talk to her."

"But what about—"

Riven showed him brilliant teeth set in a brilliant smile. "I really do like you, Max. You're the nicest boy I've ever met, but you're wrong about me. I have to do this, and I can't let my regard for you get in the way of what I have to do."

"It's not too late," he said.

Riven motioned toward the door. "You're sweet, really you are, but you're wrong about me."

"I'm sorry," Max said, shaking his head.

"Me too. You have no idea how much."

"You didn't get this way on your own. Who did this to you? What

263

happened to make you like this?"

Riven grabbed him by the shoulder, gently turned him, and prodded him toward the door. She removed a small device from the doorjamb and pulled the door inward for him.

Max looked out into the restaurant. He was a little shocked to find that there were more people than before. A lot more, but he managed not to react. "Don't you want to know how my Galactic Taco story ends?"

"Can you talk and walk at the same time?"

"No," Max said, stopping in the doorway, looking over his shoulder at Riven. "So get this. Tama's on the floor, Emy's on the counter with the gun on her cheek, and I'm standing there, locked up hard. They all get so preoccupied with trying to get a reaction out of me that they eventually leave Tama and Emy alone. They are so distracted that they don't notice when Tama and Emy sneak out. The weird thing is, they kept trying to get a reaction without touching me. They could've hit me, knocked me over, shot me, but instead they kept trying to *scare* me into a reaction."

"I get it," Riven says. "Drugs make people stupid. Thanks for the lesson."

Every eye in the restaurant was on Max now. They all looked at him expectantly. They were waiting for...*what?*

"That's not the end."

"Okay, fine, what happened in the end?"

"Well, they never hurt me. The police came, and these guys just gave themselves up."

Riven waited several seconds, waiting for Max to continue, but when he didn't, she said, "Max, I truly do like you, but that's the most anticlimactic ending to a story that I've ever heard."

"Oh, I don't know, I sort of like it," Max said.

And he stepped into the hallway, where he was immediately shoved to the ground by a Luna One security officer. Riven was left facing a room full of officers. All of them were pointing guns at her. There were a lot of them.

"Freeze or we'll ground you!" one of them shouted.

Riven scanned the room, but her eyes settled on Max. He saw such regret, that for a moment he was afraid she'd use the poison on herself, but she raised her hands, then slowly bent her knees and lowered herself to all-fours, never breaking eye contact with Max. "I'm sorry, Max. One day, maybe you can forgive me."

Before Max could respond, the security officers swarmed her.

Max was pulled to his feet and ushered outside where Holiday and his parents were waiting. There were lots of flashing blue and white lights from a wide array of official security vehicles. When Sabatha was done hugging him and checking him for any damage, Holiday playfully punched him on the arm. "I knew that girl would turn up sooner or later."

"And how exactly did you know that?" Max asked.

"Episode 78!" she exclaimed cheerfully.

"I'm going to have to watch this *Quantum Girl!!* show sometime aren't I?" Rian asked.

"Oh, Dad, you totally should! We can start at the beginning and watch it together!"

"It'll be fun," Rian said.

Sabatha sighed. "Oh, not you too."

"You're not hurt," Rian said to Max. "Holiday said you weren't."

"Riven wouldn't hurt me, Dad," Max said. "She's not all bad. She's just a little lost."

"You mean *a lot* lost," Holiday said.

There was a commotion at the entry to the restaurant, which as it turned out was named *The Soupy Way*. Riven had her hands secured behind her back and was being led toward one of the security vehicles.

Max moved toward her but was blocked by an officer.

"Riven!" Max shouted. "You're not like him. You're better than he ever was! Don't give up on yourself! Please don't let this be the end!" Then she was gone. But Max was happy enough. Just before she'd disappeared into the vehicle, she'd managed to turn her head and mouth a single word to him:

"Never."

[Chapter Twenty-Seven]

What Happened To Holiday Storm

Holiday sat cross-legged on her bed and stared at her Quantum Girl!! action figure. It stood in an exaggerated action pose on the small table in her room. This one, with its scandalously-tailored spacesuit, was her favorite.

She stared, and she concentrated. Tomorrow, the whole family was going to be tied up dealing with the aftermath of the *Starburst* explosion. It wasn't going to be fun. She already knew they were going to ask her a lot of questions about that, plus a whole lot of other questions she didn't want to answer, not to mention the ones she *didn't know how to answer.* Questions about her and Max's trip in the escape pod and everything they'd seen. They were probably going to ask about Darren Meaney. She didn't dare ask her parents what to say, because they would just instruct her to tell the truth.

Still, it would all be over eventually, and their actual vacation could continue. Hopefully. She was looking forward to that. The gymnastics exhibition had been utterly cosmic, and she hoped she could get some time in the arena. He parents said they were going to try, even though they couldn't guarantee her anything.

Quantum Girl!! stared back, her eyes twin accusers. Holiday felt guilty.

She'd lied to her parents a lot earlier, and it hadn't felt good. First, when she'd first sensed danger from Max, she'd lied and said she had to use the restroom. She'd used Max's random thoughts about his surroundings to track him to *The Soupy Way*, then she'd returned to her parents and told them she'd seen Riven take Max inside.

She'd told her parents some of what had happened to her and Max on the *Starburst* and the escape pod. She'd told them the basics of what Darren had done.

But it was what she hadn't told them that was pricking at her conscience. She hadn't told them she'd shot Darren in the foot. She hadn't told them that Darren had been attacked by some sort of alien infection, and she hadn't told them the exact details about the Crux.

Like, for example, that she still had it. Hidden, along with the Oculus.

She hadn't told Max that either, though she'd certainly tried. She didn't want to do it telepathically. No, that had to be done face-to-face. She'd do it soon. Maybe when they got back to Earth.

Some people out there thought the Crux was important. Holiday wondered why. She wondered where it came from and what it did. Had it been made on Earth? Had it always been a part of the satellite? Or had it been placed there by some alien race on the other side of the wormhole?

She wasn't quite sure why she'd taken the Crux and hadn't told anybody. Part of it was not so much about the Crux but that somebody had gone to the trouble of creating a device—the Oculus—specifically for locating the Crux. That was a big enough deal if everything had originated on Earth, but if the Crux had come from the other side of a wormhole…

Holiday shivered at the thought. That type of story was worthy of a multi-episode *Quantum Girl!!* story arc.

Still she didn't feel good about lying. And she'd lied to Max too, about one little thing.

Holiday stared again at Quantum Girl!! and wondered.

She wondered how tall she'd be when she grew up. And whether she'd be as pretty as her mother. She wondered if Max was going to marry Nika. She wondered where her dad had got those guns, and why he'd risked bringing them onboard the *Starburst*. She wondered how she was able to remember all those *Quantum Girl!!* episodes. She wondered how she was able to read other people's thoughts. What had caused that ability to manifest? She wondered what the future held. She closed her mind and thought of the lie she'd told her brother. She thought of him lying there, covered in the dust and dirt of the moon, and of her pulling and pulling, and how he was so heavy even on the moon, and there was no way she was going to be able to drag him into the escape pod. She'd pulled and pulled, crying, until she'd pulled with everything she had, knowing that it wasn't enough, continuing to imagine her brother's body safe within the escape pod, and then suddenly his body was light, oh so very light, and she'd been able to lift him like he'd weighed nothing, his body sailing forward though the hatch, dropping slowly onto one of the mattresses.

As Holiday remembered the moment of relief when the escape pod door had closed and she'd cradled her brother in her arms, quietly weeping against his chest, over on the table, her Quantum Girl!! action figure shivered once, then twice, then fell over.

[CHAPTER TWENTY-EIGHT]

WHAT HAPPENED TO RIAN AND SABATHA STORM

"You're in big trouble," Sabatha Storm said, her heart pounding loud in her chest as she closed the door to their bathroom and entered their bedroom. It was bigger than the kids' rooms combined. The bed was huge, taking up the entire far wall. The walls were rich with reds and gold, the bed with a shifting palette that changed based on body heat.

"What did I do now?" Rian said.

Sabatha crossed her arms, locked her knees and waited wordlessly.

"I'm sorry," he said reflexively.

Her unblinking gaze was his only response.

Rian grinned. "You're not trying to get me to confess to something by just staring at me and making me think that you already know what I've done are you?"

Sabatha didn't answer.

Rian backed up till he could sit on the bed. He kicked off his shoes and swung his feet up, reclining back against the pillows, bringing his hands behind his head. "You know that doesn't work on me, right?"

Sabatha advanced, climbing onto the bed, straddling Rian, taking both his hands in hers and raising them above his head. Her hair hung free, red and black around her face. She made sure her eyes were dangerous though. She was a little angry with him. Just a little.

"The guns, Rian," she said, forced to ignore her husband's commanding presence. This close to him, it was all-consuming. Even after all those years of marriage, she could still lose her train of thought looking into his eyes.

"The guns," he repeated. "I brought those for our protection."

"It's not the guns, it's why you knew you'd have to bring them."

"I—"

"Careful what you say here. I know you don't have some boring desk job for the city, or an occasional job working private security. I know you work for the government." She'd known for a long time.

Rian was smiling.

"Oh, get that smile off your face. You're so smug."

"I thought you'd be surprised. This is much better."

"Can you tell me why you brought the guns?"

"I'm not supposed to."

Sabatha knew he was going to say that.

"But I don't want there to be so many secrets between us. So, I got the call, get up to the moon and investigate a crashed satellite. It was supposed to be a one-man, fact-finding mission, quick and precise. I needed to get there before anybody else. And the guns...I don't go on assignment without them."

"So, you didn't know about Darren or Riven ahead of time."

"Absolutely not," Rian said, deadly serious. "I don't know how they found out about me, but I intend to investigate. I've already had communication with my boss about this. She's on it. I think she knows how I'm capable of handling any and all threats to my family."

"So she's going to look into this?"

"I feel really horrible that my job put us all in danger. I'll do anything to prevent this from ever happening again. We'll *both* be looking into it. Trust me, she knows how serious I am. I used all capital letters."

"Thank you." Sabatha kissed Rian's neck, which was scratchy since he hadn't shaved in several days. She released his hands.

Rian's strong arms came around her, crushing her down against his body. "I love you," he said, kissing the top of her head.

"Love you too."

"What's so important about the satellite?" Sabatha asked.

"Do you remember the *Journey X?*"

"It made it outside the solar system, didn't it?"

"Yeah, it did. Then they lost contact with it. Everybody assumed that some critical system had failed. Well, it's been what, ten years?"

"Sounds about right."

"Three days ago, it crashed into Luna."

Sabatha thought about that, but was too exhausted to let her mind stray too far from her family.

"So," Rian said after a minute or two, "now that we have my real employment status cleared up, it's your turn."

Uh oh. Sabatha pushed up and away. "What do you mean?"

"It's only fair, now that I've told you what I do, that you go ahead and come clean about what you really do all day. Fair is fair."

Sabatha rolled off her husband, lying down next to him. "Okay, fine, I work for the government too. But you obviously already knew that." She had been so sure that she'd never let anything slip. She had been so careful! "It's just a desk job though. I work from home. I play connect-the-dots with data."

"Yeah, I know that too."

"Guess we're not very good at keeping secrets from each other."

"Not very, and that's a good thing."

Sabatha rolled so she could throw an arm across her husband, smiling, comforted by his closeness, his warmth. "Yeah, so you know all my secrets now?"

"I'm pretty sure I do."

"Oh yeah?" she grunted, getting up from the bed and moving to the bathroom. Her hands were shaking, but not from fear. She retrieved the thin object from the counter, then walked back to the bed, tossing the object into the air. She knew she was beaming a stupid grin at him, but she didn't care.

Rian caught the small testing kit with one hand, but he didn't have to read what it said to know that the winds of change were altering the Storm family's course once again.

[CHAPTER TWENTY-NINE]

WHAT HAPPENED TO MAXIMILLION STORM

Max sat at a booth in *Moonbeams*, his hand hovering over the touch screen that was used to activate the call. He was having trouble focusing. His mind was skittering all over the place. From the *Starburst* to the escape pod, from Darren to Riven, to the satellite and the Crux and to the alien infection, and to his mom and dad, and the future.

Holiday's thoughts had hit him last night as he was creeping toward slumber: *[Mom's pregnant. I thought you might like to know. Try to act surprised when they tell us.]*

Another brother or sister, or who knew, maybe one of each. It was a lot to take in along with everything else. Still, he was excited. He liked Holiday tons. Another one or two couldn't hurt. It'd be good for his mother and father at least. He'd probably be leaving the house in a year or so to be on his own. They'd need something to help take their mind off him. A new kid might do the trick.

He wanted to talk to Nika. He *did,* but he wasn't sure if he was up to it. She made him half-crazy as it was. Through no fault of hers, he always felt inadequate around her. Would talking to her help him process everything he needed to work out internally?

Taking the decision from him, his hand landed on the touch screen, activating the call. It rang only once, the screen remained black though.

"Hello, Max," Nika said.

Max hadn't expected her voice to sound so real. "Hi! I can hear you, but I can't see you."

"Then turn around, sweetie."

Max turned in the direction of the voice, and there she was, in all her glory, with her swishy skirt and her too-tight tank top, her boots and her ankle-high socks, her hair sparkling with silver nano-ribbons, her fingernails cycling through the colors of her mood.

Max's capacity for speech had been stolen. He sat there with his mouth gaping.

"I hear you've been getting into trouble without me," she said. "That changes right now. Anyway, Wilderness Camp got triple wrecked by an earthquake, and I got bored." She took a step toward him, her hips swaying. "Good thing my parents are rich, right?"

She was real, and she was there on the moon with him.

She smiled, white through lips of glittery pink.

Max smiled back, ignoring all questions, and went to her. Their bodies collided. In the quiet rapture of his girlfriend's embrace, Max let the events of the past few days flee from his mind. There, with Nika whispering her breathless affections in his ear, her perfume an intoxicating scent, he was finally at peace.

Max's space vacation had only just begun.

THE END...

Thanks to...

...Megan, Lily, Jack, and Cora, who inspire me.

...Benjie, for the artwork.

...the Inklings, for helping me push through.

About the Author

Ethan A. Cooper was born and raised in southern California, cutting his teeth on a steady diet of sci-fi/horror movies, cartoons, and comic books. While not being haunted by nightmares of Darth Vader and invading space aliens, he was listening to radio dramas like *The War of the Worlds* and *X Minus One*.

In addition to writing novels and short stories, Ethan performs writing duties on the webcomic *Angel the Demoness*.

Ethan, his wife, and their three offspring reside in Texas where they can all be found fighting crime and solving mysteries.

What Happened On My Space Vacation is Ethan's first published novel.

Join Ethan on Facebook:
https://www.facebook.com/author.ethanacooper/

And find out what Ethan's working on next:
http://necrotictimes.blogspot.com

About the Illustrator

Once described by the actress Margot Kidder as "a renaissance man," Benjamin Cooper is a southern California native with a diverse love for experiencing and creating art and music. Growing up, these artistic inclinations often manifested themselves in the form of drawing or writing when he was supposed to be doing things like schoolwork or chores around the house. His creative creed is one of stylistic ambiguity, producing pieces in the style or medium which best serves the needs of the project. This is evident in the *What Happened On My Space Vacation* artwork, which was meant to give a stylistic nod to classic sci-fi and children's novels. The book cover was hand-painted with acrylic on canvas, while the inside illustrations were hand-drawn, then inked. The LT-6677 mission patch was created entirely in Adobe Photoshop. When Benjamin isn't drawing or making music, he enjoys cooking, using the Force and gaming with friends on Steam.

Made in the USA
Middletown, DE
20 February 2022

61566520R00168